EDEN

A novel by

Michelle Haley

This book is dedicated to Best. Without you, I wouldn't have even tried.

CHAPTERS

24. DECIDING

"There is a fountain of youth: it is your mind, your talents, the creativity you bring to your life and the lives of people you love. When you learn to tap this resource, you will truly have defeated age." - Sophia Loren

ARCHANGEL

I met him the day my parents were buried, and I've lived for him ever since. Two coffins stood side-by-side in the sticky southern heat. The humidity and rain mixed together were stifling. Grandma Millie could barely stand up from the grief that was eating its way into our hearts. Losing a son and a cherished daughter-in-law the same day was something she would never recover from. Uncle Doug had his arms wrapped around her, drowning her sobs, tears pouring down his weathered face as well. I was five years old.

My perpetually tangled hair stuck to my face in wet clumps. My little mind did not understand the things the man in black was saying for our comfort. I stared straight ahead, trying to be brave for Grandma Millie, but all I really wanted was to wake up the ones whose bodies lay in the shiny boxes before me.

The twisted metal of their car was beyond recognition. Had Millie not taken me grocery shopping with her the day they were killed, my tiny coffin would have stood alongside theirs. I would not know until I was much older the things which my parents had sacrificed for me. I could never have known then the secrets my parents had so carefully guarded would one day indefinitely alter and extend my life.

A malnourished looking blond-haired boy around my age came and stood next to me as the preacher droned on about life being a vapor. He stared at the ground and silently reached for my hand and threaded his dirty fingers through mine, his eyes never straying from the grass-like carpeting we stood on.

Bringing food to a family after they've suffered a loss is an honored tradition in the South. The house was full of strangers who came to pay their respects and spoke in hushed voices. I wasn't surprised to see the little boy arrive with his father at Millie's house she shared with Uncle Doug, my home too from then on.

The boy found me hiding in the corner of Millie's living room, beside her worn recliner and pulled my knees to my chest. He plopped down beside me. His light brown eyes were huge, almost too large for his face. "I lost my mama too," he shared. "My name is Gabriel. You don't have to talk if you don't wanna. I understand."

I eyed the intruder of my hiding spot curiously. "My name is Arianna. I'm really scared," I whispered.

He didn't say another word. He gently slipped his fingers around mine, just as he had done at the funeral. We sat there in silence the rest of the day until it was time for him to go home.

Gabriel showed up again and again after that. Every day for about a week, he would come over and sit with me until dark, neither of us speaking. I didn't know anything about him but his name and the devastating fact we had in common.

One day Gabriel came, and instead of holding my hand, he slipped something inside of it. It was a Christmas ornament once upon a time, a porcelain angel with the halo broken off.

"Thank you," I said, and meant it.

"It's just like our mamas. They're angels now." He grinned. It was the first time I had smiled since Uncle Doug sat me down in an itchy blue chair outside the ICU to tell me that my parents were in heaven. I knew at that moment that Gabriel was an angel too, one who was chosen to look after me.

It turned out his house was only two doors down from Millie's. We both lived in the poorer part of town. I didn't have everything I wanted, but I always had more than I needed. Millie was more than a grandmother to me. She and Uncle Doug treated me like a princess.

Millie lost touch for a while after the funeral. After my Paw-Paw passed (as I referred to the kind-eyed old man in all the portraits of my family, even though I never got to meet him) nine years before, seeing the coffin of her youngest son lowered into the grave was more than she could handle. Somehow though, Gabriel brought us all back to life.

Gabriel's dad worked long hours at the metal refinery with Uncle Doug, so he was at my house more than he was at his. I never went even a day without him coming over to see me. From the first time I met him he lived up to his name. Gabriel. My archangel. He had been with me through everything, and it wasn't long before playmates became best friends.

Now, thirteen years later, best friends were turning into…I wasn't exactly sure. The last few weeks marked the end of winter, and I couldn't seem to help myself from noticing how muscular his arms were in his short-sleeved shirts. Or how his dark blond hair curled perfectly around the tops of his ears. Or how those familiar brown eyes he finally grew into made my face hot when they met mine.

"Arianna?" Gabriel waved his hand in front of my glassy eyes, bringing me out of my reverie. "You have a customer."

Gabriel motioned to the Barbie clone and two of her friends about to walk up to the counter. Gabriel and I had gotten jobs at the local pizza place last year in the summer before we became Seniors at Kennedy High.

"Great," I grumbled. "It's Brittany and her crew. I think they want you to help them anyway."

I wasn't the only one who had noticed Gabriel's good looks, though I was probably the last. Brittany Roberts had been after Gabriel at least since we were Sophomores. She was the kind of girl in high school with nice handwriting and great skin and a sense of entitlement. Everyone loathed her, and yet she still somehow managed to get herself crowned prom queen, homecoming queen, and whatever other ridiculous royalty crap they held elections for.

Gabriel and I were exclusive best friends. I had never had or wanted any other friends in my entire life. By middle school, girls had given up trying to relate to me, and the boys were too afraid of Gabriel, who stood several inches over six foot.

"Gabriel," Brittany called in her singsong voice. Ugh. Gabriel stalked up to the front rolling his eyes and making a gagging face when he passed me.

"Hey, Brittany. What can I get you?" He absentmindedly tapped his pen on the cash drawer.

"Oh, we aren't eating. Not here anyway." She made a disgusted face. Of course she didn't eat pizza. Carbs making people fat and all. "We came to see if you wanted to come to my birthday party Friday night." Brittany beamed at him.

Gabriel ran his fingers through his hair. "Um, that's not really my kind of thing," he replied. Brittany's face fell.

I was lingering behind him to see what pathetic attempts Brittany would make to attract Gabriel's attention this time.

"See you tomorrow at school!" I said as I gave her my biggest, fakest smile.

With that, she shot me a look of pure hatred, turned around, and walked out of the door.

I crossed my arms with a smug grin. Point made. Territory marked.

"You didn't have to be so mean," Gabriel told me, frowning.

"What?" I answered innocently.

"You know I'm not going anywhere with her. Besides, we have plans Friday. I'm going to see if my dad or Uncle Doug will let me borrow their car." Gabriel had long ago adopted "Grandma Millie" and "Uncle Doug" instead of "Miss Millicent" and "Mr. Foster".

"I was thinking we could go catch a movie or something."

"Sure. Sounds great. I'll check with Millie when I get home. I need to get out of this town anyway."

We lived in Ellaville, Georgia, a slow, one-horse town with one stop light and two restaurants. It was a beautiful place to live, but if you blinked when you drove through, you'd miss it. Ellaville was a safe place; Gabriel and I usually walked to school and work together, unless it was raining, then Millie would drive us. It's hardly ever cold in the deep South, and even in the winter the temp gets up to seventy degrees sometimes. The weather was nice, and everyone knew each other, but you had to find other places to go for entertainment.

I was thrilled Gabriel and I would get to spend some time together alone without having to worry about running into people like Brittany batting their fake eyelashes at Gabriel, but I was hoping to go somewhere we could actually talk. The closest movie theater was twenty-five miles away, so at least we would have the car ride. I sighed.

"So what do you want to go see?" Gabriel asked.

"Comedy?" I offered.

"Yeah, there's this…" Gabriel took off on some spiel about this hilarious commercial for some new movie. I was having trouble paying attention to what he was saying, because I could only focus on his gorgeous body I had just begun to notice.

"Are you even listening Arianna? Wasn't that funny?" Gabriel asked, waving his hand once again in front of my eyes. I looked up at him blankly. He knew when he was being ignored. "Are you okay today? It isn't Millie is it?"

"Huh? Millie? Oh, no. Nothing like that. I'm sorry. I've just been feeling kinda sick." It was the first excuse I could think of. I had been using it for years in P.E.

He knit his eyebrows together in worry. "Why don't you go sit down in the back?   I can close up by myself. Ricky will be back from his delivery soon anyway."

"No. I'm okay. I don't want to leave you by yourself. I'm going to go ahead and sweep up."

Gabriel gave my hand his special squeeze and smiled. "Don't keep anything from me. If you're sick, tell me. I've been worried about Millie anyway," he scolded.

"Me too, but she insists she's fine. She goes to the doctor on the fifth of April. It's only a few weeks away. Just think, graduation is in less than three months," I reminded him, trying to change the subject.

Millie had been diagnosed with cancer a few years ago, but thanks to a new treatment, we had recently gotten the good news that she was in remission.

"Please go sit down in the back okay?" Gabriel urged. "For me?" His smile revealed a perfect set of even white teeth.

I almost melted. "No. I'll be fine," I said. "Let's clean up and go home."

Gabriel and I walked the mile home in silence. Gabriel was normally a quiet person, unless he was talking about something he was really interested in.

I brushed my teeth and got ready for bed thinking of how comfortable my life with him had become. I had recently begun to fantasize about how and when we would make the transition from best friends to *more*. It seemed natural, predictable, and safe to spend my life with Gabriel. I drifted into a deep, dreamless sleep.

The next morning, I showered and pulled on my black leggings and baggy gray dress. My Converse were covered in pizza dust, but I put them on anyway. I threw on a silver necklace and took off out the door. Gabriel was usually waiting in my living room for me to get ready, but I had been so excited about going to the movies with him that I woke up much earlier than usual for school. I crossed the street and walked three doors down. Gabriel met me halfway across his yard.

"Good morning early bird," he said brightly. "You look pretty today."

"Yeah, right," I laughed self-consciously. "Are you ready for our English test?" I asked him. It was a dumb question. Gabriel always aced every subject.

"Yeah, how 'bout you?"

"I didn't get much studying in, but I should do okay." English was my favorite subject, and the test was on *Pride and Prejudice*. I knew the book and movie by heart. "Did you ask your dad about borrowing his car?"

"He has a bowling tournament Friday. Maybe Uncle Doug will let me have his. I'd rather drive the truck instead of Dad's car anyway." Gabriel replied.

"We could always borrow Millie's van. It's out of the shop," I offered.

I heard the soft purr of an engine, and Brittany's car idled next to us.

"Hey Gabriel. Want a ride?" Brittany asked.

"No thanks. Not unless Arianna can come too," he answered, and threw his arm around my shoulders.

Brittany squealed tires past us.

"Wonder when she'll give it up?" he asked.

"What guy wouldn't want to date her? Her parents have tons of money, and I'm sure she could offer you more of a good time than fried chicken and pot roast and old movies with me and Millie on the weekends," I murmured dismally.

"The time I spend with you is a million times better than anything

Brittany or her rich parents have to offer." He smiled at me. "I want to talk to you about some stuff this weekend. I've been thinking about…you know, and I want to know how you feel about…everything." Gabriel ground the toe of his sneaker into the gravel.

"Um, okay, yeah. Stuff," I said.

When we finally arrived at the front doors to the school, my stomach was twisted into knots wondering what Gabriel meant by "everything", "stuff", and "you know".

As we passed Brittany's locker, she stopped the angry whispers she was sharing with her friends. She pretended not to see us, but embarrassment was written all over her flushed cheeks. She continued brushing her frizzy hair in her locker mirror.

Gabriel and I settled into our seats next to each other in our first period math class. I hated math. Like Gabriel, I aced most of my classes, but theorems and equations were not my strong points. I opened my notebook and took notes, furiously scribbling, trying to keep up.

Just before the end of the period, Mr. Keller, our teacher asked for our homework answers to be passed to the front. Just as I was about to panic, a folded piece of notebook paper plopped on top of my notes. I furrowed my brow in confusion and opened the paper.

In handwriting that did, in fact, look much like mine, was the homework assignment. I looked around, and Gabriel winked at me. I passed my paper forward and hurried out of the classroom.

"Gabriel, you could have gotten yourself in trouble! How did you even know I forgot about it?" I demanded.

Gabriel chuckled. "I asked if you had any problems with it last night at work right before I noticed you had completely spaced out."

"Well, *I've* never cheated in my life," I said.

"It wasn't cheating. You just forgot. You would have gotten all the answers right if you had remembered anyway." Gabriel pressed my fingers into his palm. "See you at lunch."

I headed to the bathroom wondering when and if Gabriel would stop rescuing me. I was so lucky to have him all to myself. I caught Brittany's cold reflection in the bathroom mirror.

At least for now, I thought somberly to myself.

Millie always made my lunch as well as Gabriel's. We sat at a quiet spot on the lawn, and ate our sandwiches. The teachers didn't like the students to eat outside, but Gabriel was every teacher's pet.

"The movie starts at 6:40 or 7:20. What time do you want to go?" Gabriel asked.

"It doesn't matter. I just can't wait to get away for a few hours," I replied.

Gabriel stretched out his long legs and patted a place between them. "Come listen to this song."

He flipped through his MP3 player and selected a song. I sat down with my back to him between his legs. He handed me one of his ear buds, and put the other in his ear.

"If you like this band, we should go see them sometime. They play a few hours from here every couple of months," Gabriel told me.

Gabriel silently mouthed the lyrics and began to twist the tip of a piece of my waist length brown hair. I had heard some of the band's songs, most were loud yelling rock (which I loved), but this one was slow and pretty. The words were so sad and real, they almost made me cry.

"Promise me you'll never cut your hair," Gabriel said seriously.

"Why?"

"Just promise."

"Okay, I promise," I agreed.

Gabriel deejayed the rest of lunch hour. We laughed at some of the songs and sang loudly to others. We trotted off to our last three classes still laughing from the fact that he had one of our old favorite kids' songs on his MP3. Gabriel was the only person I could be myself with one hundred percent.

We rounded the corner to my locker. The only class we shared was first period math. "See you after gym," I called.

*****

We met at my locker for the walk home. Gabriel picked up my book bag and slung it over his shoulder. "I'm not completely helpless," I told him.

"I know," he replied, "I like doing things for you."

I would never in a million years come close to anything that approached a good enough girl for Gabriel.

We walked home talking about the oral English assignment Gabriel had to give that morning before the test. David Wells, the class clown had recited a love poem about Principal McAfee. Juvenile? Yes. Funny? Yes.

We walked up to the front steps to my house and heard muffled arguing inside. I had never ever, in my eighteen years, heard Millie and Doug fight about anything.

"We *cannot* let her know about this!" Doug yelled.

"I don't know what else to do besides to tell her. She has the right to know!" Millie yelled back.

I opened the unlocked door. Gabriel followed a ways behind me, unaware of the quarrel within.

"Hey, Uncle D," Gabriel called inside, "can I borrow the truck this weekend? I wanted to take Arianna…" He stopped abruptly, Grandma Millie's red cheeks giving him indication that something serious was going on.

"Gabriel, you need to go on home," Uncle Doug told him.

"What's going on? Grandma Millie? What's wrong?" I demanded.

Gabriel was always welcome at our house. No one had ever asked him to leave. He stood frozen at the front door.

"I'm so sorry. I'm-um-I'll-see you," Gabriel stammered, and headed out of the door.

"Arianna, you need to sit down." Uncle Doug said. "Millie will be taking you to school and picking you up from now on. You need to give notice, because you won't be working anymore after the end of this week. After school, you will not be going anywhere unless we give you permission. And no more Gabriel."

"Uncle Doug! This is totally unfair! What did I do wrong?" I pleaded.

My mind was reeling. I had never done anything bad enough to get in trouble. I always tried so hard to please Grandma Millie and Uncle Doug. Tears slid down my cheeks.

"You are grounded from now on. Not another word, Arianna," Uncle Doug commanded.

"Grounded? For what? Millie? *What is going on*?"

"For arguing with me!" he roared. "Go to your room!"

"Doug! Don't you ever raise your voice to my grandbaby that way again." Millie came and wrapped her warm, mothering arms around me. "Your Uncle Doug is right. You need to stick close to home for now. It's for the best, baby. I know you don't understand, but try to trust us okay?"

I hadn't seen Millie this upset since my parents died. I was terrified.

I lifted my head and walked down the creaky hall to my room. I fell next to my bed crying in broken sobs, not because I was in trouble, but terrified at the thought of not seeing Gabriel. I did trust Millie, but I couldn't live without my angel.

ETHEREAL

I stayed in my room freaking out for most of the evening. Millie came in with a plate of food sometime after it got dark outside. She gently tucked my hair behind my ears over and over.

"I know we haven't explained ourselves to you, but we can't right now. We just need you to be careful the next few days," Millie said.

"Are we in some kind of danger?" I asked.

"No honey, I would never let anything happen to you. That's why I need you to trust me right now. I've never let you down before, have I? You know how protective Doug is. He's trying to look out for you, baby. He just went about it the wrong way."

"That's an understatement," I said, and Millie smirked. "What about Gabriel, Grandma Millie? Why can't I see him anymore?"

"Of course you can! He's my grandbaby too!" Millie cried. "We just wanted to talk to you alone, but I guess Doug ruined that. He was always the hotheaded one. My Thomas was the calmest, most gentle child I ever met." Millie's eyes misted over. "Until I met you, that is. Doug was a rough and tumble little boy. Always whoopin' and hollerin'. Your daddy was a cakewalk after I had Doug, but I always wanted a little girl.

"When Thomas brought your mama home, I thought I was in heaven. I had never seen a more beautiful girl, and she had a heart of gold. She and your daddy worshiped each other. Then, you came along, and I realized I had no idea what heaven was until I held you." Millie hugged me tight to her warm chest.

"Enough of my chattering now. Girl, you have school tomorrow. Go call Gabriel, and tell him not to be scared to come over in the morning. I'll talk to him when he gets here. If he doesn't mind riding to school in your grandma's van every day, you two will be as inseparable as you ever were."

I threw my arms around her. "I'll always trust you Millie," I assured her.

I did trust her, but I was angry at the fact that neither she nor Doug trusted *me* enough to tell me what was going on.

"You need to eat your supper," she said.

"I'm not hungry, but will you tuck me in?"

Millie wrapped the warm covers around me and kissed the top of my head. She hummed an ancient, familiar tune, and I nodded off.

Sometime later, the creaking of the hardwood floors woke me up. A tall and lanky male silhouette stood in my doorway, bumping my CD's off the dresser as he clumsily stomped into my room. I sat up quickly holding my covers close to my chest.

"Arie?" I breathed a sigh of relief at the recognition of Uncle Doug's favorite nickname for me.

"Yeah?" I answered.

"Ow!" He quickly muted a yelp of pain as he bumped my bedside table covered with a myriad of teen paraphernalia. My nametag from work, and a bottle of black nail polish fell to the floor. "Are you awake?"

"Um, now I am," I answered him.

"I just wanted to tell you that I didn't mean to upset you today." He scratched his head as if it would stimulate the magical words to make his niece forgive his erratic behavior of the evening. He lowered his eyes. "I promised your dad once that I would take care of you if anything ever happened to him, and I guess I let him down tonight, huh?"

I sighed. "Uncle Doug, since I was five years old you *have* been my daddy, and you are the best one I could have asked for. I just wish you guys would clue me in as to why I have to be chauffeured and quit my job."

I had forgotten that small detail in his rant until then. I really liked my job. Gabriel and I were saving for nice cars, instead of getting something cheap just because we could. Millie had offered to give me the van and get something else, but I knew she couldn't afford it.

"I guess I went a little overboard. You can keep working, but Mama will be driving you to and picking you up from work. I know she talked to you already, but we need you to trust us. I love you Arie, and I will always do what's best for you. I'm just not good at these things." He chuckled lightly. "I don't think we've ever had to punish you for anything. You're a good girl. Just like your mama."

"Thanks Uncle Doug." I yawned.

"Get some sleep, and I'm really sorry I upset you." He caught me up in an awkward hug. "Night," he called and walked back down the hall.

"Night," I called back. I felt a lot better, but not completely relieved. I had tried so hard to make Millie and Uncle Doug proud. I guess I felt like that was my way of earning my keep. I knew they loved me, but I wasn't their child, wasn't their responsibility. They would probably die if they could read my mind; they never made me feel like I was unwanted.

Still, I wondered what was going on. The most exciting thing to happen around my house was a new season of one of my favorite shows. I rolled over, dreaming about being chased by the police, and asking them what I did wrong. My alarm clock buzzed far too early, and I swore to never take a college class before 10 am. I heard rain beating down on the roof, and I smirked. Millie would have had to drive us today, anyway. I hadn't called Gabriel because I was too mortified, so I was surprised to see him lounging on my couch talking to Millie when I got out of the shower.

"Good morning, sleepyhead." Gabriel grinned.

"Since I tucked you in last night, I went ahead and called Gabriel, but Doug had beaten me to the punch. He called and apologized to Gabriel himself," Millie said as she walked into the kitchen. She brought me a hot plate of bacon and a side of biscuits dripping with butter and grape jelly.

I took a bite and glanced out the front window watching the rain.

"It's cool out today; probably the last cold snap," Millie told us. "Make

sure to take your jackets to school."

I ate the rest of my breakfast listening to the generic weather conversation between Millie and Gabriel. Millie was a short in stature and looked like a sweet old grandma, but her head full of bright red hair told otherwise. I loved to listen to her and Gabriel talk. The sound of their voices combined was the most soothing sound in the world to me, even when they lovingly argued about inappropriate things like politics and religion. Leave it to Gabriel to be up on every current event and denomination known to man.

We piled up in Millie's van and headed to school. She dropped us off in front of the double doors, and I heard one of Brittany's friends snicker and whisper something about riding to school with my grandma. Gabriel frowned.

"You don't have to ride with me you know," I said loudly.

I had never been rude to Gabriel a day in my life, but I was so disgusted with my current situation I lashed out at him. Why couldn't my family have money, and why did he have to be so understanding? I knew I wasn't good enough for him. He could have any girl in this school, and probably most girls at any other, so why did he have to take it all in stride for dirt poor me? I was confused and mad and having one heck of a pity party.

I arrived at my locker and quickly spun the dial. I grabbed my books and turned to him. His eyes were so hurt, but it just made the situation worse.

"Leave me alone, Gabriel. You know, sometimes I get so tired of you following me around like a dog," I said loudly, slamming the door to my locker.

"Arianna, what is going on?" Gabriel grabbed my arm gently. "What in the world is wrong with you? You don't mean that." He tried to sound convincing, but he was only trying to convince himself.

"Yes I do! Just go." I started to cry. "Please," I whispered. A crowd had stopped in the hallway to get front row seats to our very first fight. A fight that I started. Gabriel punched my locker so hard it flew open. He looked me dead in my eyes for what seemed like a hundred years. He pushed through the crowd suddenly and stalked to class alone.

I lifted my head and walked slowly to class, fighting tears. I sat in the front row, as far from Gabriel as I could get. My ears were ringing, and I thought I was going to pass out. A flurry of voices was all around, and I caught snippets of conversations including my name and Gabriel's. Until that moment, I would have bet anything in the world that no one in my school even knew my name. I sat up straighter in my desk. I didn't dare look at Gabriel, because I was terrified of what I might see.

The next few periods flew by, and I was surprised at how many people came to ask if I was okay. Several guys (including Brian Ames, the football jock) stopped to talk. He walked me to lunch and I held my head high. My eyes scanned the cafeteria for Gabriel, but I figured he was outside in our usual spot. My stomach dropped when I saw him sitting with Brittany.

Isn't that what you wanted? Isn't that what he deserves? a voice in my head asked.

I glanced his way, but I already knew he was staring at me. I could almost feel his burning gaze as his eyes bore into me.

I quickly grabbed a tray of food and sat down next to Brian. He pulled out my chair and started talking to the rest of the people at the table as soon as I sat down. I would never have been able to recall any of the people who sat at that table or anything that was said. I walked out of lunch by myself feeling more alone than ever, even though I made more new friends in one day than I ever had in all the years in Ellaville's public school system combined.

I didn't see Gabriel for the rest of the day at school. I went out of my way to keep from bumping into him. Millie's van pulled right up front as it had that morning, and I scrambled in so fast I almost fell on my face. The door to the van wasn't even shut before I burst into tears.

"Please take me home. I had a terrible fight with Gabriel, and it's all my fault. I-I-I..." I couldn't find words to convey my despair, so I buried my face deep into Millie's chest. I didn't care if the whole school saw.

"What happened, baby?" Millie asked as she quickly drove away.

I couldn't exactly tell Millie I was embarrassed to be seen riding with her, or that I was jealous of another girl in town having rich parents. I sobbed harder. I saw Gabriel standing next to Brittany's car when we passed the school parking lot, and I blacked out. I don't remember the ride home. I don't remember any of Millie's questions. I don't remember falling into my bed. All of those things must have happened though, because in my bed is where I found myself the next morning.

Gabriel wasn't in my living room, and he wasn't waiting outside to ride with Millie and I. The repercussions of my actions began to sink in. It was over. Together, I knew I could take on the world with him, but now I couldn't even stomach first period math. I almost chickened out and called Millie to turn around and come get me as soon as I found myself alone outside the school doors.

I hurried to class, and sat down in the front seat just I had done yesterday. I didn't turn to see if Gabriel was present, but I knew he was. I looked out the window and saw a brand new black car in the front parking lot of the school. I knew nothing about cars, but I knew enough to know that no one in town, not even Brittany's rich father, had a car quite so nice. I twirled my hair wondering if the school board had come down to inspect the plot being cleared for our new gym.

Ring! Ring!

I jumped out of my seat at the urgent ringing of the fire alarm.

"Alright everyone. Single file," our teacher said. "Out to the front lawn."

Great, I thought, *now I can't help but see Gabriel and his new girlfriend.*

I gathered my books and walked out to the front lawn. I made sure to stand back from all the other students, especially Gabriel. Normally a fire drill was a fun way to take a break from class and talk to Gabriel. I quickly scanned the throng for him. I didn't see him immediately, which surprised me. I could always pick Gabriel out of a crowd.

I walked to the far edge of the lawn, and I noticed the black car again. I was about fifteen feet away, and the pitch black tinted window of the driver's side began to roll down.

My mouth dropped open. There were two girls in the car. They were both blond. The passenger had short, shoulder length ringlets, and the driver had a stacked bob. They were both dressed in solid white. The thing that stunned me most wasn't their hair, and it wasn't the pricey car. These were the two most beautiful people I had ever seen. It almost hurt to stare, but it was impossible to tear my gaze from them. Silence fell over the members of Kennedy High when the occupants of the car came into view. If a pin was dropped, everyone outside would have heard it.

David Wells walked over to the car, followed by Brian Ames. So much for loyalty. "Hey, is there anything I can help you with?" David asked, giving the girls his goofiest grin.

The driver said something to him, but it was so quiet, if I hadn't seen her lips moving I would have sworn she hadn't said anything at all. She stuck a wad of money out of the window, and placed it in David's hand.

He looked at the money as if it were a deadly snake, and slowly scanned the crowd. His eyes moved back and forth, and came to a quick stop. He pointed directly at me.

The driver clasped her hand over her mouth with a sharp cry. The passenger drew in a harsh breath. They just sat there, staring at me with expressions so shocked, it terrified me.

Principal McAfee bounded outside. "Everyone back to your classes *now*," he barked. "I had better not see anyone outside again until school is out." He began walking toward the black car, but before he could reach it, it spun out of sight.

I stood frozen in my place, unable to register anything but fear. The driver's piercing gaze scared me to death. I knew in my heart that my being grounded and this visit were related. I had never met those women in my life, I was sure of it. They weren't people anyone could just forget. Neither one looked a day over twenty-five, but their faces held a look of maturity. There was something supernatural about them. They were old and young at the same time and so very, very, beautiful. Not quite human. They were fairy-like creatures.

The first word that popped into my head was ethereal. These women were angelic. I couldn't get their haunting faces out of my mind. They were almost too beautiful. I knew in my heart I wasn't supposed to meet them. They were what Millie and Doug were keeping from me. I was forbidden to leave my house alone because of them.

Everyone had begun to return inside except me. Principal McAfee trotted my way, and I gulped.

"Do you know those women, Miss Foster?"

I wondered if he was asking out of curiosity about the women or for my safety. Probably the former.

"No, she's never met them," came a voice from behind me. Principal McAfee grunted and retreated. I looked up at Gabriel, and he pulled my hand to follow him. As soon as our principal was out of earshot, Gabriel threw down my arm and spoke. "You need to watch out. You know we aren't allowed to have visitors at school. Who were those people anyway? Apparently you made some new friends," Gabriel spat.

I was so angry at myself. I finally succeeded in alienating the only person I would die for. Not even that kept me from lashing out.

"Speaking of new, maybe if you weren't so busy with your girlfriend you might have noticed I have an improved concept of who I deem important enough to spend time with."

He looked crestfallen for a moment, but it soon turned to anger. "You are unbelievable Arianna. You know what? I'm going to give you exactly what you want and leave you alone from now on." He stormed off ahead of me.

What was wrong with me? I knew I should run and beg his forgiveness, but I didn't. I finished out the day in the girl's bathroom, speaking to no one. Millie sensed how upset I was when she picked me up. She must have been too afraid to upset me, because she didn't try to make any small talk on the ride home, at dinner, or at bed time.

I called the restaurant where I worked at closing time, and told my boss I was giving my two weeks' notice. It would have been unbearable to be working so closely with Gabriel, even though Uncle Doug told me he wasn't forcing me to quit. The manager told me a notice wasn't necessary unless I needed the extra money. Business had been slow the last few weeks. I was only on the schedule for two nights the next week anyway. I took the offer of not going back, and I was assured I always had a position there if I wanted one.

I went to bed around eleven, and expected another wasted, angry day tomorrow. Sometime during the night I found myself dreaming in a dark room with stone walls and floor-to-ceiling windows. On one side, dead leaves covered the black and white marble floor. The room was empty except for lavender silk damask curtains that hung to the floor drowning out all of the light from all the windows, except one that was open. I was clothed in the same tank top and pair of pajama pants that I had fallen asleep wearing. A figure was posed next to the open window in the shadows, and I walked slowly toward it.

"You are Arianna?" His voice startled me, and he sounded surprised himself.

The figure stepped into the moonlight, and touched my shoulder. A more beautiful man could not have been found on the entire planet. Ever. He was even more beautiful than Gabriel. His eyes were the lightest blue I had ever seen. Almost white. Eyes that startle you when you pass someone with eyes like his. The blue of his eyes was fringed with long, jet black lashes. He was tall and thin, with longish, dark hair that fell into his eyes. Although he wasn't as muscular as Gabriel, he looked *way* more threatening. His jaw line was made of sharp, beautiful angles. His prominent cheekbones shifted as he ground his teeth together concentrating on my reaction to him. He reached forward and traced the outline of my face.

The strangest thing was that I recognized him in my dream, though I had never seen him before. I was no stranger to vivid dreams- I had them almost every night. This was different, though. I could smell, taste, touch, *feel*. It was completely lucid. I had control of what I said and did.

He guided me through the open door to where he was standing when I appeared. He led me out through the tall window onto a small balcony with a wrought-iron banister that overlooked the sea. No sound could be heard besides the crashing of the turbulent ocean waves. I looked out at the stars and the inky black sky.

"I have waited a lifetime for you. Now that I've found you, everything is going to be okay," he whispered in my ear, and I instantly believed him.

"How do I know you?" I asked.

He kissed my shoulder, and I gasped. He lowered his face toward mine, and I leaned in, wholeheartedly accepting of anything he wanted. I could not have torn away my gaze for anything. He had the profile of an Adonis. Like the women at my school, he was so perfect it hurt to look at him. He smiled.

His teeth gleamed white as snow in the dark of the night, but I was not afraid.

"What is your name?" I asked him.

"It isn't important. You will know me soon."

"Why won't you tell me your name? I feel like I know you, but I would remember if I had met you before."

"Shhh," he quieted me. "Just be with me right now. I need you as much as you need me." He put his hand in the small of my back, and I stopped my futile attempts to talk. Just being next to him should have unnerved me, but his presence was strangely calming.

We stood on the balcony until the sun crept up, turning the endless black waves a burning, lava red.

"It's time for you to go home," he told me.

"When will I see you again?" I asked him. I wasn't ready to leave. I *needed* to be next to him.

He guided me to the door of the room. On the other side of it was my room in Ellaville, exactly how I left it. He leaned in and kissed my forehead, and closed the door behind him.

I laid down in my bed, and my eyes closed and opened in a fraction of a second, nothing more than a blink. Had I dreamed it? My alarm clock went off.

CONSPIRACY

Friday morning arrived. The day I had so anxiously awaited. The day Gabriel and I were going to "talk" about where we stood. I should have been upset about missing my chance, but I wasn't.

The man I had watched the sun rise with that morning penetrated my every thought. Who was he? Was he real? He seemed very real at the time. I could still feel his warm breath on my shoulder as he kissed it. I shivered. His light blue eyes were the only thing I could see when I closed mine. I carried his assurance that everything would be okay as my personal mantra as I got ready and made my way into the school.

"Hey Arianna. Was that girl your sister? If she is, tell her to come visit again anytime," David yelled as I walked past him to my locker.

The whole school was buzzing with the disbelief that poor, quiet Arianna Foster could know people so beautiful and important looking. Brittany eyed me suspiciously all morning, but I found consolation in the fact that Gabriel had not been seen with her. Actually, he hadn't been seen with anyone. He wasn't in first period or lunch. He had never missed a day of school, unless he was playing hooky while I was sick. He finally appeared in the hall beside my English class as I was on my way to last period P.E.

He walked by me as if I did not exist. I went on to P.E. and suffered my way through badminton. I waited by the front doors for Millie, but she never showed. School let out at 3:15, so by 3:45 I was worried. I began walking home by myself, turning down a ride from Brian. Gabriel was walking a few yards ahead of me, but I didn't call out to him. I cut through my neighbor's yard so he wouldn't see me if he turned around. As soon as my house came in sight, so did the black car from yesterday.

I immediately knew something big was happening inside. As angry as my family had been when they grounded me, nothing good could be happening that involved the inhabitants of black car. I flew up the front steps to my house and stopped to eavesdrop when I heard yelling.

"Absolutely not!" Uncle Doug bellowed.

"She is eighteen years old, who's going to stop her?" an unfamiliar female voice railed back.

"I don't know what you're into, but she will not end up like my brother and Rose. She is not going and that's final." I winced at the sound of my mother's name so raw on Uncle Doug's voice.

"What do you have to offer her *Doug*?" She spit out his name as if it were a filthy word. "With all due respect Millicent," she continued, "let her decide. I can give her the life she deserves. I can take her places she will only dream of seeing in this town."

"No!" Uncle Doug screamed at the top of his lungs. "God knows where she will end up with a guardian like you. All I know is, when Thomas and Rose returned home, you were never seen or mentioned again. My brother shows up here after being gone for three years with a pregnant and distraught wife. If I'm correct, you never would have known they passed if Millie hadn't let you know."

"*You*," she bit off. "You know nothing of my mistakes, or my relationship with my sister."

Sister? Wait. That would mean she was my...aunt.

"Doug," Millie said calmly, "she's right. If Arianna wants to go we are going to let her."

"*What!?*" they cried in unison.

Go where? With whom? I couldn't take it anymore. I had to know what was going on. I burst through the door.

"Go to your room. Now," Uncle Doug ordered.

The woman stepped between a livid Uncle Doug and I.

Her beautiful face scanned mine. She tried to speak several times, but her voice kept quavering. She finally gathered the strength to address me. "It's so nice to meet you Arianna. You are so beautiful. You look just like your mother."

The woman was the driver of the black car, but this time she had apparently come alone. The passenger was not in my house, and I was pretty sure she wasn't in the car.

She placed her hand on one of my shoulders. "I'm Ava. Your aunt."

I was instantly confused. My aunt? This woman couldn't have been more than a toddler or a small child when my mother died. This woman was no more than twenty-five, if that. She looked more like what I'd call a girl, not a woman.

Seven years older than me, maybe. Probably not even that much of a stretch between our ages. How could she have had a falling out with my mother at seven years old? Somehow I doubted that was the case. I didn't know I had an aunt at all; no one had ever spoken of my mama's family. I thought the reason Millie and Doug didn't want to talk about my parents was because of the grief it caused even after all these years. I assumed my mama's family had passed. I would never have guessed that they were estranged.

Ava took a step closer to me. "I would be honored if you would come stay with me this summer, after you graduate. Please, I know you don't know me, but I would love to know you."

It was hard to look at her straight in the eye; calling her pretty didn't do her justice. She wore a thin, yellow and black patterned slip dress. It hugged all of her curves that I would have killed for.

"Arie, no. Please, baby girl, these people aren't right," Uncle Doug pleaded.

I ignored him, intrigued by the situation. I had no college prospects, and Gabriel and I weren't speaking. Without Gabriel, nothing was keeping me here. Besides, it was only for the summer. I could come back home anytime I wanted.

"Where do you live?" I asked her.

"At the beach," she answered vaguely. "We will have so much fun. At least think about it."

I took a deep breath. Why not?

Uncle Doug kept trying to cut in, but Millie kept shushing him. "Actually, I think I'd like to go. I graduate in a few months, and I would love to spend the summer at the beach with you."

"Really?" she asked excitedly.

I nodded. "Do we have any other relatives?"

"No, I'm the only family your mother ever had, besides your dad and what you see here."

My mind was about to burst with everything I wanted to know. I began spouting off questions. "Are you married? What do I need to bring? How much money will I need? I just quit my job. I have a little saved, but-"

"Money?" She laughed uncontrollably until Millie shot her a warning glance. "Oh, I have a feeling everything will be taken care of, and no, I'm not married."

I thought for a moment I saw a smug grin pass over Uncle Doug's face.

We quickly discussed the situation and my graduation date. We decided to play it by ear as to when she would pick me up, even though I would have left that very minute.

"It's time for you to leave, Ava." Uncle Doug hurried her out the door.

"I do have to go now, but I'll get everything ready in time." She gave me a quick hug. "I'll be back soon. Take care of yourself."

Right before she turned to go, she hugged me again, and whispered in my ear a cryptic clue. "Memento Mori." With that, she disappeared from our house as quickly, and with the same air of secrecy with which she had arrived at my school the previous afternoon.

Millie walked to her bedroom, as though nothing strange had occurred. Uncle Doug was extremely late for work the second time in a row, so he left shortly after Ava without speaking to me. He had to go in at 2:30 on the weekdays, sometimes earlier. I wondered how long Ava was at my house before I got home.

I didn't dare tell Millie she was at my school the day before. I retreated to my room relieved no one followed me. I picked up a book and concentrated on it, trying to block out the depression from my separation from Gabriel, and the excitement and fear I faced surrounding my commitment to Ava.

Friday night blurred into Saturday night. For the first time in my life, I went a whole day without seeing Gabriel. My nerves were in knots, and I caught myself more than once gazing out the window on the off chance I might see him in his yard. Where was he? Was he going out with Brittany, and I missed the news? Did he go to her party and slow dance with her in front of everyone? I didn't think Gabriel would be caught dead dancing, but my mind was running away with me. My stomach had butterflies constantly, even though they felt more like bats.

I went to bed early, trying to concentrate on the man who had visited two nights before, but the only images I conjured up in my dreams were of Gabriel dancing on the beach with Ava.

I watched a classic TV show marathon Sunday morning, and my mood had not brightened one bit. The only thing that kept me going was the prospect of spending time with my mysterious Aunt Ava. Millie spent Saturday with her friends, so by the time she came home, I had already eaten a microwave dinner and turned in for the night. Uncle Doug was fishing all weekend with Gabriel's dad, but he refused to speak to me anyway. I asked him to catch some big fish for us, but he just grunted and slammed the door behind him.

I was lounging on the couch around ten in the morning on Sunday, a time when I was usually fast asleep for another hour on the weekends. As the wooden clock on the wall clicked the seconds off, I felt as if I'd jump out of my skin. I searched the window, constantly slipping the threadbare curtains open a fraction of an inch to see if Gabriel was outside. I killed time by absorbing myself in a crime show more appropriate for someone Millie's age, when I heard the loud engine of a truck and a knock at our door.

Millie had finished showering, and she shuffled to the door in her slippers and wet hair. She opened it with a yawn. "Can I help you?"

"I'm looking for an Arianna Foster." I peeked around the corner to see a middle-aged man with a pot belly wearing a beige shirt with holes in it. He held a clipboard.

"I'm Arianna." I hopped up bravely and met him at the door.

"Well, you sure are a lucky little lady. I have a delivery for you."

I peered around his wide frame and let out a delighted squeal when I saw what he had brought me. "*That* is for *me*?" I pushed past the man, and bounded toward the flatbed truck he had backed into my driveway.

There, on the platform of the bed, was a brand new black car, identical to the one Ava drove. The windows were blacked out, and the only difference was this one still had the price tag taped to the passenger window. I jumped up and down.

"Can I keep it? Can I keep it?" I asked Millie excitedly

She walked out, still in her bedroom slippers, wearing a cautious smile. "Baby, it isn't mine to give back. If you want it, it's all yours."

I screamed so loud, several of the neighbors peeked out to see what the commotion was. Gabriel and I had gotten our driver's licenses on our respective birthdays when we turned sixteen, so I knew how to drive. I took Millie's van to the corner store often enough.

"Ma'am," the truck driver called. "I need you to sign this paper so I can unload this pretty piece of metal." I snatched the clipboard and signed my name, hands shaking.

I clapped my hands as he unloaded it into my yard. The poor thing looked really out of place. He handed me the keys.

"Take good care of her now." I wondered if he was referring to Millie or the car. He tipped his hat to Millie, jumped into his truck, and went barreling out of the neighborhood.

I could barely contain myself. "Oh Grandma Millie, I can't wait to show it to…"

It struck me. I had no one to share my good news with. What point was a new car if you had to ride in it alone? The past few days came crashing down on my conscience. Gabriel might never forgive me, but I was at least going to try to explain myself.

"I guess I'm gonna go talk to Gabriel," I said in a low voice.

"I was wondering when you two were going to work things out. I'm going inside. Lunch will be ready if you need it, but I have a feeling you'll be too busy keeping the roads hot."

"Thanks Grandma Millie."

I walked across the street and into Gabriel's yard. Since his dad wasn't home, I twisted the doorknob and let myself in. I figured he'd be up watching TV, but the den was empty. "Gabriel," I called.

I heard the fan humming in his bedroom. That was strange. Gabriel never slept this late, ever. I crept down his hallway and took a deep breath when I arrived at his room. I had never been alone in a house with Gabriel in either of our bedrooms. Millie was strict about those things. His fan whirred louder as I stepped closer; I knew he always slept with one running. I opened his door, and he stirred.

Gabriel had the cleanest room of anyone's I had ever seen. Since he was a child, he took care of each of his belongings as though it were his only possession. From books to video games, everything was neatly organized.

"Hey," I whispered. He twisted his bare torso toward me. My cheeks flamed when I realized he was only wearing boxers.

"Hey back." He ran his fingers through his hair, and a piece fell over his forehead. He sat up and adjusted the covers around his waist, exposing his lean, muscular chest. He shifted back so I would have room to sit down. His eyes were swollen and red. I could tell he had slept little the last several nights.

"I came to talk to you." I cracked my knuckles nervously. "So, I'm leaving after graduation. Do you remember the car in the parking lot Friday?"

Of course he remembered. What guy could forget the two hottest women they had ever seen, with a black sports car to boot? I spilled the events that led to my soon departure, when I noticed him smiling. "What?" I demanded.

"I already know. Uncle Doug called and tried to get me to talk you out of it."

"Well, what do you think?" I asked, trying to feel him out.

"I think that I have nothing more to offer you than this town. Go, see the world. You'll be back after summer, right?"

"Of course. Will you miss me?"

"Just because you're acting like a lunatic lately doesn't mean I'm looking forward to losing you."

"Gabriel, you will never lose me. Oh and hey, maybe you can come visit! Aunt Ava lives at the beach. And guess what?" I was suddenly giddy. "She bought me a car."

"When? I gotta see this." He moved to get out of bed.

"Wait!" I shrieked, unwilling to see him half naked. I would probably have proposed marriage then and there.

"What's wrong?"

I tried to think of an excuse for him not to get up, and I thought of the perfect one. "Why did you eat lunch with Brittany? Did you ride home with her?"

"Hmmm…let me think, jealous girl. I was not about to let you sit in the cafeteria with all those boys, and me not be around to threaten their lives if they said anything out of the way to you. And no, I did not ride home with her. I left school walking through the parking lot since I didn't have a ride home, and she cornered me when I passed her car. Any more questions, or did I satisfy your sudden jealous streak?"

I growled and playfully punched him in the arm. He pushed me off the bed, breaking my fall with his ready arms. I looked up at him and closed my eyes. I tipped up my chin toward his head. I waited and waited and waited. He cleared his throat and stood up, offering me his hand. "Let's go see this car."

I walked out of his room so he could get dressed. He hurried off to the bathroom, but he was still taking too long. I bounced from one foot to the other, barely able to keep from screaming in excitement. He came out of the bathroom wearing a fresh pair of perfectly ripped jeans and a band tee. He held open his front door for me, and I dashed through, unable to contain myself.

As we rounded the corner, my car came into view. Gabriel let out a low whistle. "BMW, eh?"

"Really? Is that what kind it is?" I squeaked.

Gabriel rolled his eyes. "You get my dream car as a gift, and you don't even know what kind it is."

I hadn't gotten a good look at it before, and up close it was better than I imagined. Sunroof, leather, fully loaded…a teenage girl's dream. I glanced at the price sticker and balked.

"Whoa, this is worth more than our house," I said, half joking.

Gabriel came in for a look. "Better make that both our houses together," he laughed.

I tossed him the keys. "Do you want to do the honors?" I asked him.

"Uh-uh. I'm scared I might scratch it. You first." Gabriel clicked the locks open with the keyless entry. We climbed in the black leather seats, and I stuck the key in. The engine purred softly.

"Here goes nothing."

We spun around the neighborhood a few times, and then we turned home. I was still barefooted and in my pajamas, so I wanted to change clothes before we rode into town. I heard Millie on the phone as we walked in my house.

"Yes, of course she loves it. She just walked in, hold on." She handed the phone to me.

"Hello?"

"What did you think? Did you love it?" Ava asked.

"Oh my gosh, Aunt Ava! Of course I love it, but there's no way I can pay you back for this."

"Pay for it?" She laughed. "You know better. It's a gift. Now listen, I have to go out of town soon, but I'm sending some things for you in the mail. You should be getting a package tomorrow. It needs to be our little secret, okay?"

I listened, nervous and intent. I felt an instant connection to Ava. There was no way I would break her trust. "Okay, I promise, but the car was more than enough…"

She cut me off. "I have to go Arianna. I love you. Be careful. Memento

Mori." The line went dead with her final cryptic message.

I handed Millie the phone. "I'm going to change. Give me just a minute," I told Gabriel.   I went into my room and turned on my stone age computer. I threw on some jeans, a tank top, and some flip flops. I logged on to the internet, and typed in Ava's words. Memento Mori. The definition popped up immediately. "Remember you are mortal." What the heck was that supposed to mean?

Gabriel and I spent all day Sunday and a tank of gas driving as far as we could and still make it back by dark. We ate at a popular drive-in fast food restaurant, and left the waitress on skates a huge tip to make us feel as important as we looked in my fancy car.

I finally convinced Gabriel to take a turn at the wheel, and he nearly scared me to death. There was no one else I would have trusted with my car, but Gabriel drove like a maniac. I only let him have his thrill for a few minutes before I told him I wanted to drive again. We turned the radio up and rolled the windows down. On our way back home he cut the radio off suddenly.

"Why did you leave me?" Gabriel asked seriously.

I slowed the car onto the shoulder of the road and put it in park. "Gabriel, there's something I want to say to you, and then I never want to bring this up again," I took his hand. "First of all I'm so sorry. I will always be here for you, but sometimes I feel like I hold you back. I know I'm your little friend from the neighborhood, but you deserve more than that. I'm not pretty and I'm not rich. Before Ava came along Friday, I would probably never have seen anything outside of Ellaville, and that was okay with me. But I know there's something better for you out there."

"There's nothing out there for me at all without you, Arianna. You're right though. You aren't pretty." My heart dropped. "You are beautiful." He cupped my face in his hands and kissed my eyelids. It was the most tender, gentle touch I had ever felt.

Gabriel clicked the radio back on and stared straight ahead. I knew the conversation was over, but I felt as though a weight was lifted off me. He didn't let go of my hand. He held it tight until we reached home and got out of the car.

"So, you want a ride to school tomorrow?"

"Nah," he joked. "I think I'll walk."

I stuck my tongue out at him, and he made a face back at me. I floated inside, and finally settled into bed after a shower and kiss on the cheek from Millie.

I felt guilty, but I so badly wanted to dream of the blue-eyed stranger again and thank him for his reassurance. I knew it sounded silly, but in some weird way, I just knew he was responsible for all that had happened.

GLOATING

I dressed carefully Monday morning. I slid on my favorite jeans and a low cut white top, channeling my inner Ava. I took time to apply makeup and straighten my hair. I put on my silver ring and bracelet Gabriel had given me the November before for my birthday. I went into the living room, and of course Gabriel was waiting there for me. He had just finished his cereal.

"Ready to go show off, or are you eating breakfast first?" Gabriel asked.

"Not today. I'm not hungry. Where's Millie?"

"She went to the store. Don't worry, she won't be force-feeding you this morning," he said as he rinsed his bowl out and put it in the sink.

I laughed. I hated eating breakfast, but Millie would not let me out most mornings without having consumed a plate of food that would feed a small army.

We left the house, and I pulled slowly out onto the street. It was too short a distance from school to satisfy my road lust, but as I pulled up, everyone gaped. The windows were impossibly dark, so everyone got close to see who was inside.

"They're probably expecting Ava," I laughed. "What a disappointment."

"Oh, I have a feeling they'll all be satisfied," Gabriel said.

Gabriel and I opened the doors simultaneously.

"Arianna? Whoa, where'd you get the car?" Brian asked.

"Her *aunt* bought her this to match the one she brought to school last week," Gabriel answered with a sly wink at me. He knew I was nervous getting all this attention.

"That chick was your aunt?" David asked, unbelieving.

My attention turned elsewhere as Brittany pulled into the lot. When she got out of her car her face flashed from confusion to irritation to fury. I gave her a bright smile and a wave.

"So can I get a look inside or what?" David asked.

I tossed Gabriel the keys. "He'll do the honors. He knows more about it than I do."

My only wish was that Gabriel had gotten a similar gift. It didn't feel right that he shouldn't share my glory. He demonstrated the GPS navigation, the sunroof, and the sound system before the parking lot began to clear.

"We're going to be late," I warned him and the group of guys kneeling beside the open driver's side door.

We made it to class just in time. We definitely got celebrity treatment at school all day, something foreign to both of us. One of the teachers even stopped to compliment my new ride. We ate lunch outside alone though, making up for the time we missed last week because of my selfish tirade.

I raced to the mailbox after school, but Millie had gotten there first, as usual.

"Millie, did I get anything today?" I panted.

"Priority overnight, shipped from Chicago." She handed me a bubble-wrapped package. "Wonder what she sent?"

Gabriel and I went into my room, and I closed the door for privacy. It was a good thing Millie wasn't sensitive. She was used to Gabriel and I living in our own world.

I promised Ava I wouldn't show anyone the package, but she must have meant Millie and Doug. Surely she wouldn't mind me including Gabriel in our secret. Who would he tell? Besides I promised not to keep anything from him anymore. Not even my feelings. The only thing I didn't share was the freak encounter with the man literally in my dreams.

I tore the package impatiently. I didn't immediately see a note, just a paper with four numbers. At the bottom of the envelope was a debit card with my name written on plastic, embossed letters. I flipped the card over.

A post it note was attached to the back that read, "For anything else you need. Love, Ava. Memento Mori."

"How much do you think it's for?" Gabriel asked, staring at the card with wide eyes.

"Let's go find out." I grinned.

We scrambled into the living room. "Hey, Grandma Millie, we're going to the store."

"Alright. See you at supper. It'll be ready around 7:00."

I drove as fast as I could to the only bank in town. I inserted the card and punched in the four digit code.

"There's a $2.00 fee since I'm not at the bank the card is from. Think it'll be okay?"

"Just do it. She gave you the card, I bet she won't mind," Gabriel assured me.

I accepted the charge and pressed the keys for a balance inquiry. The screen didn't display a number, but a paper printed out. I tore it off, but I was afraid to look.

"What if there's a thousand dollars in there?" I asked Gabriel jokingly.

"Just look! It's killing me."

I peeked at the paper. I stared at it, until I thought I would cry.

"What is it? Come on!" I handed him the paper. "Oh my God," he breathed.

The total amount in the bank account was about three times as much as the car cost.

"It has to be a mistake, Gabriel. No way would she give me that much money. I'm only eighteen years old for crying out loud!"

"I don't know. She doesn't look much older than us, but where would she get that kind of money anyway?" He spoke in a low voice, even though no one could hear us inside the car. His expression was wary. I was a little worried myself.

"I can't spend it. Millie would freak out if she knew I had access to this kind of cash. Let's go home. I'll hide the card somewhere, and only use it for gas."

"You'd better hide it well. There's no telling what would happen if anyone knew about this. The car draws enough attention as it is," Gabriel warned.

"It does, doesn't it?" I said thoughtfully. I laughed, but there was a nervous edge to it. "Let's go home, we have school tomorrow."

*****

Over the next few weeks, Ava sent gifts every other day. The first gift after the bankcard was a silver necklace with a charm of an angel's wing covered in black sparkly gems. Although Gabriel and I suspected they were real stones, I threw caution to the wind and wore the necklace every day.

Ava sent expensive clothes, designer shoes, priceless handbags, and every cool thing I could imagine. One of my favorite things was an MP3 player like Gabriel's, which he promptly loaded with all my favorite songs. The prices on the attached tags never ceased to blow my mind. Whatever it was Ava did, she was making a killing doing it. All of the clothing she sent had a funky, bohemian feel to it; it all matched my style as if it had been hand-picked by me.

By May, graduation was creeping up on us, and prom was a week away. Gabriel and I decided to skip the big event, but Ava sent a dress so perfect, we decided to make it a date. The bandeaux top was red satin covered in black lace. The form fitting skirt fell straight to my ankles, in the same black lace overlay. The set exposed my entire stomach, something that would normally mortify me, but the glazed look in Gabriel's eyes when I tried it on as a joke made me take the plunge. I wore my angel wing necklace, and topped the ensemble off with bloodred strappy heels Ava sent a month before.

Gabriel came over an hour or so before prom to placate Millie by taking pictures with me. Millie alerted me to his arrival by squealing delightedly over how handsome he looked all dressed up.

I stepped into the hallway, my heels clicking loudly on the wood floors. I nervously rounded the corner to my living room, and Millie shrieked. I was fully prepared for her shock over my daring gown, but instead of trying to cover up my bare waist, she hugged me tightly and told me how pretty I looked.

I glanced at Gabriel. He was wearing a crisp white dress shirt with a pair of black tuxedo pants and a thin red tie. No cheesy shiny shoes or tacky cufflinks, he looked young and fresh. His baby face appeared more grown up than it had before.

Uncle Doug wiped his eyes. He stood up to twirl me. "My girl's grown. I wish your daddy was able to see you. I'm so proud of you Arie."

"You look beautiful," Gabriel told me. He took my hand, and instead of holding it, he brushed a kiss across my palm. I must have blushed a deep enough red enough to match my dress. He produced a single red rose tied with a black ribbon. I wasn't surprised how accurate to my taste it was. He knew me better than I knew myself. Death and doom to corsages everywhere.

Millie grabbed her camera. "Okay, stand over by the wall." She shooed us to her chosen spot for photo torture.

I begged off at just the right time; another five minutes and we would have been late. Gabriel drove us to the school gym where prom was taking place. We walked through the crepe paper entrance, and I couldn't believe what a great job prom committee did with the drab, gray room.

"Hey Gabe, Arianna." He nodded to each of us. "Want to sit with us?" Brian slapped Gabriel on the back, and I tried not to wince at the nickname Brian gave him.

Gabriel looked to get my approval, and I gave a slight nod of my head. "Sure, we'll sit with you."

We sat down at a table trussed up in a dark purple cloth covered with silver candles and confetti. I recognized most of the people at our table as the popular crowd, none of whom I had said a word to in my life, save Brian. I was happy to see Gabriel making some new friends. All the guys seemed to find a comradeship in him. A few weeks before, I even let him take my car out around the block with the guys.

"We're going to go dance," Brian told us. "Come on," he urged.

Gabriel stuck out his hand, and I balked. "We didn't get all done up for nothing. Besides, I want to show you off."

The song was fast, and I wasn't much of a dancer, but Gabriel twirled and spun me at just the right times. I had to admit, he wasn't bad at this, and I didn't think we looked too terrible out there on the dance floor. We laughed and danced to the fast songs, and he held me just close enough on the slow ones. I started to feel winded, so we sat down to cool off and eat a plate of chicken parmesan.

"Having fun?" Gabriel yelled above the noise.

"Yes. I really am. Are you?" I was surprised. I *was* having a great time.
 He nodded.

"Hey Arianna, I love your dress." A few girls from my science class walked over to our table to chat. The one that spoke was Brittany's friend.

"Thanks!" I tried to think of something to say to fill the awkward silence. "The gym looks great, huh?" I remarked.

"Oh, yeah." She blew off my attempt at small talk and leaned in closer. "Are you and Gabriel like, *together*?"

"Um, not like that." I scrunched my nose, trying to avoid her question.

That must have pacified her because she asked, "Do you want to dance with us? I *love* this song."

The song playing was an overplayed bubblegum pop tune that I hated from the instant I heard it. "Not right now, maybe in a minute." I motioned to Gabriel.

"Sure, we'll talk later, k?"

"See ya." I waved. They skipped off happily, and I leaned toward Gabriel. "Weird."

He laughed. Brittany walked past in a foamy pink nightmare with neon orange sparkles. She stared ahead ignoring us completely, and Gabriel grabbed his chest in mock heartbreak. We got up and danced a few more songs, and the time came to announce the king and queen.

"Let's go home. Unless you want to see the coronation ceremony," I added sarcastically.

"Nah, I'll pass." Gabriel and I left the prom, politely stopping to say our goodbyes to the others at our table. "That wasn't so bad," Gabriel said as we pulled out of the parking lot.

"No, I had a great time."

We went straight home, and he walked me to my door. My heart raced. He squeezed my hand. "See you tomorrow. You were the prettiest girl there tonight." He turned toward his house and walked away.

I stared after him, and when he was out of sight I sat down on my porch steps and propped my elbows on my knees. I squished my cheeks in my hands and pouted. What was it going to take to get him to see me as a girlfriend instead of the little girl he used to catch tadpoles with?

I thought about Gabriel, about Ava, about the money. I thought about everything for the first time. I let my mind ask all the questions I didn't want the answers to as I sat on my porch that night. I finally went inside, and found Millie sleeping upright in the recliner. I kissed her on the cheek, and went to bed feeling lighter than I had in a long time, except one thing. I tried to remove the anger I felt toward all my rebuffed attempts at romancing Gabriel, but they were futile. I was frustrated.

I woke up in the marble-floored room facing the sea. The strange man beckoned me to come to him on the balcony. I reached him, and he kissed my cheek.

"Hello again, Arianna." I felt dizzy looking into his ice-blue eyes.

"Please tell me, what is your name?" I begged.

"Shhh. It's not important. Tonight could be the last time we see each other." He laughed lightly. "In our dreams, that is."

"Why?" I asked.

 He laughed again, and turned to the sea.

"Where are we?"

"I am at my home, and you are at yours."

"No. I'm not. I'm here. With you." We stood in silence for a long time. "Thank you," I said finally. Emotion flooded through me, and I felt the need to tell him what I was thinking. "The last time I saw you, you promised everything would be okay, and it was. The next day my life completely changed. It has only gotten better since. How do you know me? Are you real?" The questions rolled off my tongue as fast as they crossed my mind. I would normally have been embarrassed, but I wasn't. I felt as if I could ask him anything.

"I am as real as you. I am just another soul who needs comfort. We are brought together in dreams. I cannot explain why, but I do know our time is short." He brushed his hand over my hair. "Don't forget me, Arianna."

"How do you know my name? Please, tell me."

"I have to go now. Don't forget tonight."

The man pressed a cool hard object in my hands.

Instead of him leading me to the door this time, I was pulled back in a vacuum. My body thudded hard on my mattress, and I blinked. There was no waking, no groggy feeling. It was as if it all really happened, but I knew it didn't. It couldn't have.

I opened my palm to reveal a key. I hid the key deep into my pillowcase. I couldn't go back to sleep that night no matter how hard I tried.

Gabriel came over the next morning to help me wash my car. I jammed the key into my pocket before I got out of bed. Uncle Doug gave us a mop bucket and sponge he used to wash his old beater car. I reached across the top and spilled soapy water all down the side, soaking an unsuspecting Gabriel who was leaning down detailing one of the tires.

He jumped up, brandishing the water hose like a sword.

"Don't you dare!" I squealed. He twisted the nozzle and put the hose on full spray. "No!" I ran around the back of the car.

"Revenge is best served..." Gabriel soaked me in the icy water from the hose.

I ran toward him, and tried to wrestle the hose away. The attempt was futile; I was dripping wet, and Gabriel was practically bone dry except for the water I accidentally spilled from the bucket. Gabriel sat on my legs and pulled the hose toward him.

"Gabriel Bennett! Remove yourself from my granddaughter right now!" Millie yelled.

Gabriel glanced at Millie, and I read his unspoken words.

"Run Millie!"

I was too late. Gabriel turned the hose on Millie. Her perfectly styled flaming red helmet hair fell flat as soon as the water hit it. She looked like a drenched red poodle.

"You just wait," Millie threatened. She went inside for a moment, and returned with her hands behind her back. "How is revenge best served Gabriel?" Millie threw a pitcher of water and ice from the freezer on him.

"I surrender," Gabriel laughed with a shiver. He tossed his golden hair and his brown eyes flashed. He grinned, and I made up my mind. There was no way I was leaving Ellaville, because that would mean leaving Gabriel, something I would never do for any amount of money. I was no longer torn. I would stay.

Prom was the big topic of conversation Monday morning at school.

"Hey, did you guys hear? Amy Lyons and Peter Mathis won prom king and queen," David said as he walked with us to first period. I was really happy Brittany and Brian didn't win, which was expected. Brian was nice enough, but the people who won deserved it.

Amy was a quiet, bookish girl who had turned into a knockout last summer. She began dating Peter a few months ago. He held the lowest notch on the popularity totem pole until last semester, probably because he was one of the poorest kids at school. Everyone constantly tormented him until Amy asked him out, and suddenly he was "in". I knew Brittany wouldn't be as thrilled with the underdog story as we were.

*****

The days droned on. My initial excitement over the car had waned. Graduation loomed, making the dwindling days seem even longer. It was warm, and the promise of freedom left every Senior with a feeling of unrest during the school days. Gabriel and I were closer than we had ever been. I always drove him to work, sometimes staying his entire shift.

In my mind, prom was a blur of shimmering dresses and stage lighting. The night the Juniors and Seniors anticipated for so long was now just a faint memory, The only reminder was a champagne glass with "A Night to

Remember" written on the frosty glass.

As the days melted in to a whirlwind of cramming for finals for everyone else at Kennedy High, I was a girl on a mission. I wanted so badly to have some sort of commitment from Gabriel. Secretly, I knew I wasn't going anywhere. Ava's home was a pipe dream. I didn't tell him my plan to stay in Ellaville; maybe the promise of my leaving would jump start his interest in me aside from being my best friend. I exempted all of my finals except math. Gabriel kept an A average in all his classes, so he exempted all of his. I was only three points from exempting the math final too, but our teacher was relentless about not grading on the curve.

I trudged into school alone. The final would only take around an hour, but I was bummed I didn't get to share the last official day of high school with Gabriel. Forty-five minutes into the exam I dropped my pencil on the paper, finished. I knew I got an A. I took a deep breath, and handed in the last test I would take as a high school Senior.

My step was lighter, and freedom was within reach. The only thing to wait for was a ceremony to make it legitimate. I was all grown up. I left the class feeling lonely and a little bit afraid. No one would hold my hand and walk me through things I didn't understand. It was my job to figure life out all by myself now. I never put too much stock in high school. I always had a "good riddance" attitude about graduating before, but now, I felt a little bit sad. It was probably more of my lack of direction than anything.

I wasn't planning on going to college immediately, mostly due to lack of funds. I qualified for a small scholarship, but with no colleges nearby, room and board posed quite a problem. I had been avoiding Millie and Doug's questions about college plans. They wanted so badly for me to attend, but they made enough sacrifices for me over the years without having to go into debt to help me pay for my classes. Aside from no plans for college, I had no idea what type of profession would suit me. Nursing was out of the question; I was as squeamish as they came. Teaching, or anything else that involved speaking in front of people was not an option. I had terrible stage fright. I was a little artistic, but pursuing painting for a living didn't seem like the best choice. I wasn't *that* great.

I was absolutely sure, though, I did not want to be a bum who sponged off Millie and Doug for the rest of my life.

I went to clear out my locker, and when I opened it, a red rose was tucked inside. I looked around and saw Gabriel leaning against one of the lockers, wearing his aviator sunglasses and a white tee.

"Congratulations. You're done." He grinned his blinding white smile.

"Not until Saturday night," I reminded him.

We walked through the doors for the last time and out to my car. The parking lot was almost empty.

"How are you?" he asked seriously, ducking into the car.

"Fine. Scared. Terrified."

"Terrified? You have the whole summer to lay out on some beach and figure out what to do with your life."

"Gabriel, I'm not *really* going with Ava."

"What are you talking about? Of course you are."

"I can't leave you and Millie and Doug. Besides, I barely know her. You are my family, and Ellaville is my home. I'll send back all the presents after graduation, and tell her I changed my mind. Even the car. Sure, a summer of freedom would be nice, but you don't really expect-"

"You *are* going," he broke in. "There is nothing here for you. She's obviously loaded. Loaded, as in money. Something no one we know has. Think about what she can give you. You *won't* pass this opportunity up. It may be the only one you get."

"I'm not arguing this with you. I'm not going." I crossed my arms like a small child and pouted.

"Oh, yes. You. Are." I laughed at the anger written on his face. He was literally grinding his teeth together as we pulled into my driveway. "I'm not laughing. If you ruin this chance Arianna, I swear on anything, you will *never* see me again."

My jaw dropped. "What!?"

"Don't pretend you have forgotten the same reversed argument we had a few months ago. You pulled the same crap with me, but I'm not budging. Like you said to me, I have absolutely nothing to offer you, and I won't let you ruin your life by staying here in this town just to make me happy."

"What if it makes me happy?"

"Don't try to be funny. This conversation is over," he said.

"Fine!" I slammed my car door.

"Fine!" Gabriel slammed his door.

"Arianna," Millie called from inside, "you have a package from Ava."

I stuck my tongue out at Gabriel. "We might as well go see what it is if you're forcing me to stay with her."

He grinned.

"Wonder what it could be," Millie said.

"Probably the deed to a small country," Uncle Doug called from the kitchen.

"Ha ha," I said sarcastically. "Good to see you're home early."

Uncle Doug walked into the living room, smiling. "I'm just messin' with you, Arie." He raised his eyebrows, and motioned to the package in my hands. "Well, come on. Let's see what it is."

I ripped the bubble wrap, and pulled out a card. It had a sparkly graduation cap and tassel on the front. I quickly read Ava's hand scrawled note telling me congratulations and she couldn't wait to see me soon.

At the bottom of the envelope was a small, black velvet drawstring bag. I opened it carefully, and pulled out an intricately woven silver chain with a heavy charm. I held it high and saw that the charm was a small glass vial, hanging onto the necklace by an elaborately patterned twist of wires. The wires stemmed from a silver lid engraved with a picture of a tree and a river. The liquid in the vial was at the same time transparent and opaque. It swirled like some sort of sparkly oil poured into water, never quite mixing but moving constantly. I recognized the necklace immediately.

"I haven't seen one of those in years," Millie gasped. "Not since…"

"My parents."

My mother had worn one exactly like it in the only picture I had of her. My father carried one in his pocket, and he would let me try to shake it up to keep me pacified as a child. Ava wore one too, now that I thought about it. It wasn't feminine, but it wasn't masculine, either. They were all beautiful and each one was unique. My mother had been buried with hers around her neck, and I suspected my father's met with the same fate.

"I wonder what it is." Uncle Doug took it gently out of my hands. "Probably something to do with that cult," he muttered.

"It is no such thing," Millie assured me, snatching the vial it from Doug. She glared at him. "Don't you forget, when you make comments like that, it insults my son and daughter. Thomas was your brother. How could you say something like that?" She turned to me. "Your parents were *not* in a cult."

"Sorry, Arie," Uncle Doug said sheepishly. "It's just that Ava waltzes in here, trying to take over-"

"Not another word." Millie glared at him.

"Come on. Let's go to my room," I said to Gabriel, laughing.

We sat on my bed, and I shook the bottle over and over. The liquid spun like threads, in constant movement. The silvery fluid never mixed with the clear, watery liquid inside. The silver part shone like a million microscopic diamonds with countless facets cut into them. The bright light the water exuded glinted off the glass vial and blinded me for a moment. Gabriel shook the vial, and turned it upside down.

"Is it some sort of perfume?" he wondered aloud.

"I don't have a clue. My mama and daddy each had one like it. Ava wears one around her neck."

"If it's perfume, it ought to smell really wonderful to count as your graduation present. You got a BMW for the heck of it."

"Only one way to find out." I tried to unscrew the lid. It was on super tight. The sharp metal lip on the top cut my hand wide open when I twisted. "Ouch!" I flapped my hand. It was bleeding pretty bad.

"You alright? I'll go get you a towel," Gabriel offered.

"No, it's fine. You got me all worked up about it. Now I have to know what's in it." We were being ridiculous.

"Careful," Gabriel warned as I successfully dislodged the lid.

A cork was stuck inside. I wiggled and wiggled, and just as I got it out, the liquid spilled all over my hands.

"Dang it." Just as I was about to wipe it off, I noticed that a smoky mist was coming off my hands in the places the liquid had touched. "Whoa." I

stared, mesmerized.

"Arianna," Gabriel whispered. "Your cut is gone."

DEPARTURE

I slowly flipped my hand front to back. Gabriel was right, the cut was gone. More amazingly, so was the pain. I had a bad habit of biting my cuticles, so they were normally ripped up, but my nails were perfect. A manicurist could not have done a better job. My hands were beautiful. The vapor hung in the air around the spots of my hand it touched.

"What is in that bottle?" Gabriel stared at me.

"I don't know any better than you. Super powerful hydrocortisone?" I joked.

"Arianna. This is not funny. Is your aunt some sort of...witch?"

"Of course not! Mama was very spiritual. She wasn't a member of the occult! Why would you say that? You've been paying too much attention to Doug." I frowned.

"Well, what else could explain this? I don't mean to suggest that your mama was a-" he cleared his throat. "Anyway, this is insane. Give me that bottle."

Suddenly I became very protective of my bauble. "No. I'm going to put it away. You just don't worry about it." I plugged the cork in and screwed the cap back on.

"Something isn't right with any of this. How old is Ava, Arianna? She couldn't even pass for twenty in my book. The car, the debit card, everything. It doesn't make sense to me." He shook his head violently. "To top it off, you have some kind of …I don't know…potion," he spat out, "that could be the greatest medical advancement in the history of mankind. And you tell me not to worry about it. Does it even hurt?" He grabbed my hand to inspect it.

I snatched away. "Stop it. My mama and daddy would not have associated with bad people. What are you saying? Even if we are all…witches, my family is none of your business." He was starting to hurt my feelings.

He softened. "I'm not saying that. Have you even asked Millie about her? Millie didn't even let you leave the house alone until Ava came over and saw you for herself. The whole situation ended after that. Why hasn't she met you before now? How did she not know her only living relative had passed away, or better yet, had a baby? Where does she live? The beach? That's not an answer."

"Millie wouldn't let me leave with anyone who would hurt me or get me into trouble. And besides, maybe I didn't cut myself that bad." I tried to sound convincing, but he saw through my unsure voice.

"There was blood. There *is* blood." He gestured to a tiny crimson stain on my shirt.

"Drop it. I'll ask her whatever I need to know when I go visit her. You were the one who insisted I go."

I was irritated with Gabriel's questions, but only because he was right.

None of it made sense, and when I saw what the water was capable of, it scared me even more. I wished I could have asked Millie, but she would never tell me anything, even if she knew the answers herself.

"Yeah. I'm just concerned now." He hesitated for a moment, but his eyes held nothing but concern when they met mine. "Fine. You're probably right. I trust Millie, and Doug has a slight tendency to go overboard."

"Slight. And don't you dare say anything to anyone about this."

"Alright, alright."

"Are you staying for lunch?" I asked.

"I guess so. Dad's working. I'll be home alone as usual," he grumbled.

"Can you, uh, go in the living room?"

"For what?"

"I need a shower, and I don't want to prowl through my underwear drawer for a clean pair with you sitting here."

"I don't mind." He leaned back on the bed and crossed his arms behind his head. I threw a pillow at him. "Okay, white flag." He waved an invisible flag to ease my irritation. He rolled off the bed with a grin, but I saw something smoldering beneath his gaze.

Millie offered to take us out to lunch, and we happily accepted. Uncle Doug joined us, and the graduation mood inspired everyone to take turns discussing their future plans. Gabriel missed being salutatorian by a fraction of a point, but he had several scholarships pending. Uncle Doug wanted to buy some land and raise horses on the side as soon as he was promoted. Grandma Millie wanted to live near water in a house close to her great-grandchildren. I listened quietly, until Millie embarrassed me by "slipping up" and mentioning something about my children having Gabriel's eyes.

"What?" Gabriel and I exclaimed in unison.

Millie changed the subject with an innocent smile. "What do you want to do with your life, baby?"

Everyone looked at me anxiously.

"I want to be close to my family always."

"Well, that sounds like a plan to me." Millie slid closer in the circular booth and put her arm around me.

I spent the next couple of days lying around the house until Thursday, when Ava called. "Two more days 'till graduation! Are you excited?" Ava asked.

"I'm just ready to get it over with. Are you going to be able to make it?"

"Oh, no honey. I'm sorry. I'm still out of town. When do you want me to come get you? You haven't changed your mind have you?"

"Nope."

"What day is good for you?" I was surprised by her consideration. I had no plans in Ellaville. Ever.

"I can be there Monday. Is that too soon?" she asked.

"Not at all. What should I pack?"

"Everything you need will be here waiting for you, but feel free to bring whatever you would like from home. Have you used the card? It's always hot here, and the house is on the beach. We have a pool, too," Ava informed me.

"That's awesome! And no. I haven't used the card," I admitted sheepishly.

"Why not? There's enough money in there for anything you could possible want. I gave it to you to use."

I gulped, praying Millie hadn't heard the exchange and would question me later about my secret bank account. "I have some money left from before I quit my job. So do you live alone?" I asked, switching topics.

"Not exactly." Ava paused. "Well, you *have* to go shopping. That's the whole point of the card," she chided, laughing. "I can't believe you didn't use it."

"I guess I do need a swimsuit. I don't have one. By the way, who lives with you?"

"Justafewfriendslloveyousweetielhavetogo." Her reply was so fast, it sounded like one word. She talked so quickly when I questioned her living arrangements, I knew Gabriel must be right. She was hiding something. "Good luck Saturday night. See you Monday, and be careful. Memento Mori."

"You too, Aunt Ava," I replied, but she had already hung up.

I dialed Gabriel's house. "Hello?"

"It's me. Want to go shopping tomorrow?"

*****

The next day Gabriel drove us in my car to the closet town with a decent mall. It was an hour-and-a-half drive, so we filled up with gas and hit the road. We listened to the radio and opened the sunroof. Millie told us her friend had said there was a new mall in the town, so we decided to let the GPS take us there. Gabriel had to get a shirt and tie for graduation the next day, so it worked out perfectly that he was able to get off work and come along.

The first store I wanted to visit had swimsuits. We visited the creek every once in a while during the summer, but I usually wore a tank top and cut-offs. The last swimsuit I owned was purchased when I was four. My parents took me to Savannah on a weekend trip, and we went to Tybee Island.

"You sure you don't want to go to a different store while I'm looking?" I asked Gabriel.

"Nah, I'd rather stay with you. What about this one?" Gabriel held up a hot pink bikini with a barely existent bottom.

"In your dreams. I like this one." I chose a black string bikini with crystal skulls on the chest. I flipped the tag over. "Never mind."

Gabriel raised his eyebrows. "Sticker shock?" he asked and snickered. "How much money is in that bank account again?" he whispered quietly.

We both knew the answer to that question. There was enough to buy the contents of the store and then some.

"You know I don't feel right about spending Ava's money." He took the swimsuit out of my hands and marched to the counter. "What are you doing?"

"Buying you a graduation gift." He smiled and handed the cashier several twenties.

"Thanks. Have a *great* weekend." The cashier winked at him. I pulled his arm and dragged him out of the shop.

"I can't take you anywhere," I muttered.

"Me? The guy at the gas station was falling over himself when you paid him."

"He was, like, I don't know, sixty years old?"

"What about the guys at school?"

"Brian? Please, Gabriel he was just being nice."

Gabriel spun me around. "What about me?"

"What about you?" I demanded.

"Am *I* just being nice?"

Gabriel leaned forward and kissed me. His mouth was soft and warm. He placed his hand in the small of my back and pulled me closer. It felt so natural to kiss Gabriel. He touched his fingers on my cheekbone, and deepened the kiss. I moaned softly, but when I ground my chest into his, he jerked away.

"I'm sorry. That was a mistake." Gabriel wiped his mouth on his sleeve and began walking toward a department store. I stood there for a moment, crestfallen, waiting for him to come back and explain what I did wrong.

My first kiss. A "mistake". Wow. Every girl's dream.

I made my way to a bench and flopped down. If he didn't want me, fine. I was sure to meet plenty of guys at Ava's house. Maybe he was right, who cared about Ellaville anyway?

I did. But maybe being gone would make him miss me and realize I was what he wanted.

As much as I'd long awaited leaving Ellaville from the time I was a kid, now that I had the chance, I couldn't bear to go. Still, maybe leaving was the best thing to do. He'd come to his senses, and realize he had feelings for me. I trotted off to find him. He met me halfway down a sidewalk, and pretended nothing unnatural happened at all.

"What's for lunch? There's a Chinese restaurant around the corner. The food smells so good, it's making my stomach hurt."

I could play his game too. Determination overtook frustration. I flashed Gabriel my most brilliant smile. "Sure. Sesame chicken sounds delicious."

Gabriel ended up finding a shirt and tie on sale, and I broke down and spent some of Ava's money. I bought some shorts and a few shirts to take to the beach. To top it off, I found the perfect graduation dress. I was planning on wearing something I already owned, but it was casual enough to wear anytime. All in all, I had a great day shopping with Gabriel. The kiss, if you could call it that after everything was said and done, was the only thing that ruined it all.

Saturday dawned sunny and bright, full of promise for the occasion. I messed with the cap until I said the heck with it. My hair looked completely flat, and I felt like a blimp in the billowing blue fabric. I despised the way the cap and gown looked on me, but I was proud to wear it, nonetheless.

My graduating class of only 187 students filed in the school gym. The metal building felt as if it would burst with all the friends and families gathered to wish us the best.

Gabriel Bennett was around forty names ahead of Arianna Foster, so I sat a few rows behind Gabriel. When they called out his name, my eyes brimmed with tears and I cheered with all my might. My turn came, and I was terrified I was going to trip over all the wires duct taped to the floor for the microphones and the onstage lighting. I looked out into the audience and saw Millie with her video camera, and I heard Uncle Doug yelling "Woo-hoo!" above all the noise. I nervously took my diploma from Mr. McAfee, and quickly returned to my seat without a hitch. High school was officially over.

After the ceremony, I met up with Millie and Doug outside the gym. It was sweltering inside, so we decided before the fact that we would meet by my car to avoid getting lost in the crowd. Gabriel and his dad walked up behind us.

"We did it!" Gabriel said excitedly.

"Ha! No more math," I told everyone.

"At least until college," Uncle Doug warned, and I swallowed what felt like a golf ball. I still hadn't told them I wasn't planning on going right away.

"What are the plans for tonight? Don't you two have some party to go to or something?" Mr. Bennett asked us.

"I'm actually pretty tired. I thought we could order pizza or something. Is that okay Millie? Gabriel, I can go to Peter's party later on if you want to," I offered.

"Nah. Pizza sounds perfect." Gabriel grinned.

Everyone agreed that pizza at Millie's house for the evening plans would be a great way to end the day. I still had to pack before Monday morning, and I wanted to get some extra sleep before my trip. Who knew what was in store for me?

Uncle Doug and Mr. Bennett played cards at the kitchen table, while Millie, Gabriel, and I sat and talked in the living room. Millie shared stories about my childhood, some about my parents even I had never heard. We all went to bed late, and I got up extra early (and extra tired) Sunday to begin packing.

Gabriel was in my living room when I woke up, and he followed me into my room to give me a hand. "So you're really going." It was a statement, not a question.

"I guess so," I muttered. I grabbed a duffel bag Millie bought me for my fifteenth birthday that I had never used. I shoved in a few pair of flip flops, my sneakers, and all the fancy shoes Ava sent.

"I'm going to be lonely without having you to talk to. Millie will have some big shoes to fill," he joked. He began folding a stack of shirts. "Are you ready?"

"Well, since I'm being forced against my will…No, I'm looking forward to getting to know my aunt better. I don't know anything about Mama's family, and I'd like the chance to find out all the things I never got a chance to ask her."

"I wish I had a chance like that, but I have Dad. He talks about my mama sometimes, and he answers whatever questions I have. It would be hard not to have at least one parent. I'm so sorry Arianna." Gabriel squeezed my hand.

"It's okay. I have parents, just not ones like anyone else. Maybe Ava will become like a new part of my family," I said hopefully.

"Are you going to ask her?" he asked in a low voice.

"About what?" I knew what.

"The necklace," Gabriel said.

"I'm going to let her tell me whatever she wants me to know. I want to make this work with her. When she trusts me enough, she'll explain." I prayed that was true. In fact, I was dying to discover the secrets of the vial, but I didn't want Gabriel to know that I was worrying about it.

"I have to work tonight," Gabriel said as we packed the last of my belongings.

"I want to see you before I leave." I sat on Millie's suitcase I was borrowing, trying to cram everything inside. Gabriel shook his head and reopened the suitcase to reorganize it to accommodate everything I was bringing along.

"I don't want to see you tomorrow," he said.

"Why not?" I was flabbergasted. He wasn't kidding.

"I'm not going to see you for three months. I don't want Millie to be crying, and Uncle Doug cursing Ava under his breath when I say goodbye to you. I'm selfish. I want my own goodbye." He held both my hands tight, and brought them up to his face. He kissed my knuckles. "I'm going to miss you so much. Don't forget me when you're on some warm, sunny beach."

"Oh Gabriel! I could never forget you." I hugged him tightly.

"I almost forgot." He pulled a wrinkled card out of his pocket.

"What's this?" I started to open it slowly.

"Not yet," he said, stopping my hands. "It's just a graduation card. Open it when you miss me."

"Then I'll open it as soon as you leave."

"I have to get going. I don't want to be late for work," Gabriel said. He tucked the card into my bag for good measure.

"Okay."

He hugged me one last time. "Arianna?"

"Yeah?" My heart was thudding. This had to be it. He would sweep me up and beg me to stay and…

"See you later." He pulled away, and left my room for the last time.

I didn't cry, but my heart shattered inside. If I would have begun to cry, I wouldn't have been able to stop. I stared at my reflection in my dresser mirror. I was amazed I could be so broken on the inside, and outside I could appear normal and happy. My world was more black than it had ever been. When I attempted to separate myself from Gabriel before, I still had the comfort of knowing he was only a short distance away from me. Now we would be separated by who knew how many miles? I curled up in the fetal position, never moving. I spent the day in my abnormally bare room, sleeping on my bed Gabriel made up for me while I was packing. Even the prospect of the beach with Ava couldn't bring me out of my despair. I wanted to go visit Gabriel at work for the last time, but I decided against it. We had already said our farewells, and I knew I wouldn't be able to hold it together a second time.

I woke up Monday morning, watching the dust sparkle in the ray of light creeping through my curtains. The alarm clock read 10:15, and I wondered when Ava would arrive. I hurried to the bathroom, brushed my teeth, and took a shower. As I was towel drying my hair, I heard Ava's muffled voice through the bathroom door. I applied eyeliner and lipgloss and threw on a pair of comfy shorts I selected for travel. I peeked out the window and saw Ava's sleek BMW parked next to mine. I could immediately tell the difference because hers was much cleaner, probably because she got it professionally detailed. I assumed we were driving to her house in separate cars. I came out of the bathroom to greet her.

"Ready?" she asked brightly.

"Yep. Am I following you?" I smiled, trying to hide the fact that I felt like a zombie, and my heart was surely bleeding it hurt so badly.

"I really want to get to know you before you meet everyone. One of my friends will come to pick up your car this weekend if it's okay with you. I knew you'd want to have it with you. Can you go without it until then?"

"Of course. I'm glad. I wanted to ride with you," I answered truthfully.

"All packed?"

"I sure am. Let's get going."

Gabriel's prophecy came true immediately after I went to get my suitcase. Uncle Doug was up, ready to see me off. He insisted on helping me carry my things to Ava's car, but not without muttering curses to Ava all the way out the door. Millie cried hysterically and demanded that I call her every thirty minutes until I safely reached my destination. Uncle Doug threatened Ava's life one last time should she let anything happen to me, and with a rude gesture from Ava to him out the window, we were off.

EDEN

"How far are we driving?" I asked Ava.

"About three hours. We can stop as often as you'd like, and anywhere you want along the way. Hungry?"

"I'm not much of a breakfast person, but I would like something to eat. We can get on the road a while if you want. I can wait a while. There's not much to choose from in Ellaville."

Ava laughed. "I remember. We'll stop at the first place you see that sounds good."

"Okay, Aunt Ava."

"Please just call me Ava. I feel old enough as it is." She gave a hysterical little laugh, but quickly regained her composure.

I frowned. She really didn't look any much older than me, and the early morning sunlight was unforgiving. *She'll be really upset when she actually starts to look her age*, I thought.

"So you were Mama's younger sister?" The answer should have been obvious, my mother would have been around thirty-seven years old.

"No, I'm the older one."

I stifled a gasp. "I'm sorry. You just look really, really young. When did you find out you had a niece?" I asked, steering clear of anything leading to a discussion about what was really going on. In truth, I didn't want to know.

"Not until I visited you at school. I had a falling out with your mother before she passed. I hadn't spoken to her in a long time, so I didn't know she was pregnant. Millie found a forwarding address in Rose's things to contact me about the tragedy, but I was too ashamed to attend her funeral. Millie and I kept in touch, but her letters suddenly stopped. When I couldn't reach her, I became concerned. I went to your house, and Millie explained about having to go out of town for several months for her chemotherapy. There were pictures of you everywhere, and I knew immediately. She told me they were pictures of a close friend's granddaughter, but you looked so much like Rose..." Ava trailed off and wiped her teary eyes. "I'm so sorry. If I would have known, everything would have been different. I would have been there for you. I would have been there for Rose. It's all my fault. I never meant to let that stupid argument go on so long..."

She trailed off for a moment, and her expression was at the same time pained and wistful. She patted my hand. "I came back of course, and when I pushed Millie to tell me the truth about you, she actually caved a little. Then Doug came in. Needless to say he was ballistic."

"What did Mama and you have a fight about? I'm sure it wasn't all either of your faults."

"Do you know how your parents met?" I shook my head. She took a deep breath. "Rose and I went out of town to do some shopping. I wanted to take the back roads and sightsee. We stopped at a tune-up shop in Ellaville, and the man that pumped our gas asked your mama out. She was so taken with him she said yes. All three of us, along with Doug, ended up staying out all night talking. The man at the gas station was your daddy.

"Your mother and I went back home a few days later, but we returned every weekend for four or five months. Rose invited Thomas to come live with us, and he did for a long time. I was very jealous of the relationship between your mom and dad. I never had anyone else, and I was terrified of losing your mama. In the end, I pushed her so far from me I lost her anyway. She told me that they were leaving, and I was furious. I refused to speak to her, and I returned all of her letters. I had no idea she was pregnant when she left."

"Why did she leave you in the first place?" I asked. My heart was racing from what Ava told me. I learned more about my parents in the thirty minutes we had spent in the car than the entire time I lived with Millie and Doug.

"I put a strain on Thomas and Rose's relationship. We fought constantly. I found out later, the reason she wanted to leave was the circumstances in which we lived. Back then especially, Eden was a constant party, and I'll admit it was not a conducive environment to raise a child."

"Eden?"

"That's the nickname for Julian's house," she told me.

"Who is Julian?"

"My boss. I live with him and the other people that work for him. There's Sebastien, his… ah…girlfriend Savannah, and Sebastien's twin brother Ethan. Then there's Walker and Jade. You might recognize Savannah as the one in the car with me the day we went to your school.

"Sorry about that, by the way. It was my idea to pull the fire alarm. I had to know for sure. Anyway, we all work for Julian. It's calmed down a ton since your parents left. We have all grown up a lot since then."

Not literally, it seemed to me.

"Do all the same people live there now that lived there with Mama and Daddy?"

"The only newcomer is Savannah. Everyone else knew your mother for years," Ava told me.

"What do you do? I mean as far as work goes."

"We deliver…things. We take turns, so most of the time we shop, eat, travel, whatever we want. We simply enjoy our lives. We are going to have so much fun together," she assured me.

We drove for a while and stopped for a quick lunch. I called Millie from Ava's cell phone to let her know I was fine. I didn't have a clue where we were going, until I saw a sign that read "Welcome to Florida" in bright orange letters.

"You live in Florida?" I asked. I guess if I'd thought about it, it should have been clear. She said she lived at the beach, and the mirror in her car had the same little box on it as mine that read like a compass. It had a constant S that indicated we were going south the whole way.

"On the panhandle in the Gulf. The water should be clear this week. The seaweed has been there for a month, I swear."

"What city?"

"It's actually a small town called Panacea not too far outside Naples. Panacea is just a small fishing town. Let's see, we have a boat, but we never take it out. Everyone has their own jet ski too, and we race them all the time. We're all pretty good, but Julian always wins. He is absolutely fearless on those things. The races are some of the only times Julian ventures off of the grounds. Julian makes sure we have all the toys, even ones that are rarely used."

"So, you said you have a pool?"

"Yep. The pool has columns all around it and a waterfall. It's really beautiful. Julian spent a lot of time designing it. It has a slide, too."

I absolutely loved to swim, so I was starting to get a little excited. We definitely couldn't afford a pool in Ellaville; the only place I could swim was the creek. Thinking of the creek, I realized Gabriel had not crossed my mind once during the trip until now, well over two hours in. Even two hours was the longest amount of waking time I ever went without thinking of him. I would have to call him when I arrived.

"Great." Ava slowed her car to the shoulder of the road, and I saw blue lights reflected on the side mirror.

"Oh, no. How fast were we going?" I asked. I went on blind faith that we were maintaining a normal speed since Ava was an adult, but I did feel a little like we were flying the entire way. She grinned sheepishly and shrugged her shoulders. The gesture made her look younger than ever. She rolled the window down, and the police officer's jaw dropped.

"Is there a problem?" Ava asked the officer, examining her nails.

"No ma'am. I just noticed you were speeding just a bit back there."

"Maybe I was. I didn't notice." She stared directly into his eyes. "Just so we understand each other, I'm not going to be getting a ticket today," she told him firmly. I waited for him to ask her to step out of the car into a pair of shiny handcuffs, or at the very least sign a hefty ticket, but he did neither.

"Oh, no ma'am. I just wanted to tell you to be careful. We don't want anything to happen to two lovely ladies like you."

She smiled her dazzling smile. "If that's all, we really need to be going."

"Sorry to hold you up. Have a nice day."

Ava rolled the window up, and spun tires off the side of the road back onto the interstate. The policeman stood in a cloud of our dust, scratching his head.

"How did you just get away with that?" I asked, still shocked at the shameless way she got out of a ticket, not to mention made the officer apologize for wasting her time.

"People skills, I guess." She glanced at my stunned expression. "Just kidding." She adjusted her mirror. "We will be there soon."

I sat up straighter in my seat. "What is everyone like?"

"Well, Walker is loud and funny. He loves a good time, and everyone likes him no matter where we go. Ethan is very quiet, but very wise. He gives great advice. Savannah is our little angel. She's beautiful, and has a heart of gold. Sebastien is outspoken, and isn't afraid of anything. Sebastien is a very strong person, but Savannah is his ultimate weakness. He is absolutely smitten with her. Jade is…an asset. I need to warn you though, she's not my favorite person, and I'm not hers. She is valuable to Julian, and it ends there." She hesitated for a long time before she continued.

"Lastly, Julian is…well, you'll just have to meet Julian."

"So, you don't get along with him?"

"Oh, no, we get along fine. He's hard to describe. Julian's the biggest daredevil of our group. He's pensive, brooding." Ava laughed. "Julian is unlike anyone you will meet as long as you live."

I was terrified. What if I said something wrong to him? He was Ava's boss. What if he hated me? Ava must have sensed my fear, because she touched my shoulder to reassure me.

"Julian loved your mother, and he will love you. He knows all about you. He's the one who suggested the car. I was really surprised, actually, by how well he responded to my bringing you here. The money in the account was all put there by him."

Ava's words calmed my fears, but not for long. I smelled the salty air, and I knew we were getting close. We turned on a long winding road that seemed to lead nowhere. There were trees covered in Spanish moss on both sides, and I saw a sign that told me we would be arriving in Panacea in three miles.

"I'm nervous," I confessed to Ava. My palms were beginning to sweat.

"There's nothing to be nervous about. Everyone is thrilled to finally meet you."

We went a few miles further before we turned onto a long driveway. Ava swiped a plastic key card along a post and caused a huge black gate to swing open slowly. "Welcome to Eden," she said as the house came into view.

I knew she had money, but for some reason, I still half-expected a cramped beachfront apartment with a community pool.

I gasped. Eden was a peach-colored stone mansion with four columns towering over the entrance. Ava later informed me that the columned entrance was called a portico. Ivy grew up the sides, and I could see the beach just behind the house. A stone fountain the same color of the house sat in the center of the circular cobblestone driveway. A fleet of black cars identical to mine were parked in a row on the edge of the house, and Ava told me Julian was having an upgraded garage built on one side to house the cars. Several smaller peach colored buildings stood on both sides of the house.

Ava parked right out front, and stepped out. I felt dwarfed by the looming palatial residence that would serve as my home for the next few months.

A man strutted out of the house. His skin was the color of cocoa, and he had green eyes someone could see from a mile off. His hair was dark and curly, and he had huge, muscular arms with tattoos all the way up one of them. He was as beautiful as Ava and Savannah.

"What's up Ava. Where's my new roommate?" I stepped out shyly into view. "Arianna. You *do* look like Rose. I'm Walker. Don't believe anything Ava tells you about me."

I liked him instantly. He was great-looking and definitely someone who would make me laugh. "Hi. It's nice to meet you."

"Come on in. I'll get your things. Savannah and Jade are out of town, but Ethan and Sebastien are dying to get a look at you."

As I walked through the double doors to the house, my breath was taken right out of my chest. My entire home in Ellaville would have fit in the foyer. The floors were black marble, and thick curtains were drawn to block out the afternoon sun. There were gilded framed pictures on every wall, and intricately woven rugs were scattered about the floor. Beautiful crown moulding traced the outline of the ceiling, and broke the center of the room in a chair rail.

The house was huge, even bigger than it appeared from outside.

Black winding wrought iron was the décor of choice, from the winding staircases, to the outside gate, to the enormous chandeliers; the largest one by far hung above the entrance. Chaise lounges and lush chairs were scattered about the marble floors, along with huge pots dripping with beautiful, exotic-looking plants.

Two men impossible to tell apart approached me. "I'm Sebastien, and this is Ethan. We're so glad to have you stay." The man who was identified as Ethan took my hand, but dropped it just as quickly as if it were poker hot.

They both had dark, cropped hair and caramel eyes. Their skin was tanned, as was Ava's, and it wasn't hard to see what Savannah saw in Sebastien.

Everyone was gorgeous, young, and sophisticated. Almost uncomfortably so.

"Hello." I looked down at the ground, afraid to make eye contact.

"Ava, Why don't you show Arianna to her room?" Ethan suggested, and practically ran away from us.

I said a silent prayer that the next time I saw either of them, they'd be wearing the same clothes. There was no way I'd be able to tell them apart if they changed. *Red shirt, Ethan. Brown stripes, Sebastien*, I memorized silently.

"Come on sweetie. I'm sure you're ready to get settled." Ava gestured for me to follow her up one of the staircases off the left side of the room in which we stood.

"Nice to meet you guys," I called.

Walker gave me a 100 watt smile, and Sebastien nodded. Ethan was still out of sight.

Ava led me down a long hallway with open windows overlooking the ocean. I walked slowly behind her, mesmerized by the view. I tried to keep up and memorize the path, but gave up halfway. I knew I'd never be able to find my room again without help. The home seemed to grow larger the deeper we ventured into it. Hallways twisted and turned into more hallways, each leading to rows of huge, dark wooden doors with intricate patterns carved into them.

"Your room is the same one your parents lived in. I hope that's okay. We redecorated it for you, and I guessed on the size of your clothes. Savannah and I took the liberty of stocking your closet and bathroom."

We came to a shiny wooden door, unlike any of the others, shaped like an A. I could barely contain my excitement. Ava turned the knob, and opened the door. I stood outside the room, stunned.

I had been here before. The man, he was here.

In this room with the balcony overlooking the sea, we watched the sun come up. Twice. The damask curtains, the patterned marble floor, I recognized it all.

The furniture was the only thing that hadn't been here before. A four-poster bed stood in the center of the room. Filmy lavender cloth hung over the posts of the bed, creating a canopy. Beautiful, embroidered throw pillows took up half of my bed. A wardrobe, a table, and what appeared to be an entertainment center were tucked into corners of the room. All the furniture was a pale colored wood with lavender and darker purple and gold accents. The room reeked of priceless things, thing that were a fairy tale in Ellaville.

"Do you like it?" Ava wrung her hands nervously. "We worked really hard to get it ready, but don't be shy if you want to change it."

"It's bigger than my whole house! Are you kidding? It's perfect!" I assured her. I walked into my new room and threw myself backward on the bed. If I had not been so shocked by the fact that I dreamed of this place already, I probably would have run circles around the room squealing in happiness.

"I'm so glad you like it here. Do you want to take a walk around, or do you want me to let you rest?" Ava asked.

"Rest? Ha! No way am I tired."

"Awesome. Change into your suit, and we'll go down to the pool or the beach. If you need me, my room is four doors past yours."

"My swimsuit's in the car. I'll walk down and get it," I offered.

"That's okay, there are several in the closet," Ava said.

I looked around. Closet? There were no visible doors. The only door I knew of was obscured from view by one of the heavy curtains and existed on the opposite end of the room. It led to the balcony.

Our balcony, I thought.

"Sorry, here you go."

Ava slid back one of the wall panels, and revealed another room. Through the door was a bathroom that I was sure rivaled any four star hotel accommodations. The bathroom was bright white. It had a shower with jets coming out all over and a claw-footed tub to one side. The sink was as long as the entire hallway leading to my bedroom at Millie's.

To the left was a mirrored door, which Ava pulled to one side revealing a huge white closet. There were racks of clothes and shelves of shoes, all neatly tucked into the walls and the small island in the center. Drawers lined one wall. Mirrors in frames hung anywhere there was space. There were stores at the mall that offered fewer things. Ava opened one of the drawers, revealing twenty or so swimsuits.

"See if there's one you like, and I'll meet you back here in five minutes," Ava told me.

I picked through the drawer, and pulled out a cobalt blue bikini. I choked when I flipped the still attached price tag toward me. The more I was around Ava, the less it seemed that I would ever have to worry about money again. It would have taken me, like six years working at the pizza place to afford the top to the swimsuit. Everything in the closet was brand new, and it all still had the mind boggling price tags attached.

I flipped through the shelves, running my hands over the fabrics. I loved every piece. Articles of clothing I had no idea how to put on, along with stunning pieces I would have killed for before hung in front of me, begging to be worn.

I realized that I was taking practically an eternity to don a simple swimsuit, so I dressed hurriedly and tried not to keep Ava waiting. I was uneasy about stripping down in such an unfamiliar place, but I hopped into my suit, and checked myself out in one of the mirrors.

I began to laugh, wondering how in the heck I found myself in such a place. I was the weird hippie girl back home with tangled hair. No parents. No money. I was going to be living like a freaking princess here. Definitely the ugly duckling of the bunch, but still, a princess.

I walked back out into the main space, and touched the trinkets on the table in my room. There was a stand that held hanging beaded candle holders. A mosaic vase and a bright, corrugated glass-paned lantern stood on the table.

A picture of my parents sat in the corner. A black and white print showed a happy couple laughing on the beach. My mother and father were just as beautiful as the people they had lived with, but I never really noticed until that moment. I loved them and missed them so much when I looked at their pictures, I never noticed how extraordinary their looks were. A resemblance between my mother and I was nonexistent. I knew that all of the people who told me I looked like her were just trying to be nice or have something polite to say.

"Ready?" Ava knocked softly, but opened the door without waiting for my reply. Her yellow swimsuit showed off her golden skin.

I literally paled in comparison.

We went downstairs and passed through a glass-enclosed room overlooking the back of the house. Just as Ava said, there was a monstrosity of a pool. The pool was surrounded by columns the same warm, peachy color as the house. At one end, a marble sculpture of a beautiful tree stood, and water spewed out of a waterfall and into the pool. The statue was identical to the picture on my vial. A slide hovered at one end, if you could call it that. It was more like a tall piece of artwork that was an alternate, albeit more fun route to the pool.

We walked past the pool and made our way to the beach. A huge boat floated along with a large number of jet skis. They were all anchored to a fifty foot dock, stretching far into the sea.

"Our beach is private. It's a secluded half-mile each way."

Perfectly-tended gardens completely blocked the view of the house and the grounds surrounding it as far as I could see. We passed part of the gardens, walking side-by-side, through another iron gate onto the powdered sugar beach sand that makes Florida beaches so famous. The air smelled of flowers from the garden mixed with the tangy scent of sea salt.

"This is unbelievable. I can't possibly be here. I mean, nothing like this ever happens to me," I told Ava.

"I'm only sorry we couldn't have spent every summer together, and every holiday, too," Ava said.

"Where is the other guy? Your boss? Is he working?"

"I'll introduce you to Julian later. I wanted to show you around first."

The beach was foreign to me. For someone who had seen the sea only once, and that being fifteen years ago, I was bursting with excitement. Ava walked into the surf. The water was turquoise, no seaweed in sight. She dove bravely into the waves, and burst through the surface of the water far from where I stood on the beach. I was right behind her into the water, and I laid back and let the waves carry me. I closed my eyes, and felt the sun baking my skin. I sat for the longest time on the beach with my legs stretched out where the tide met the sand. The water submerged my legs when the tide rolled in, and made little rivulets when I pulled my legs out and the tide ebbed.

Ava and I talked about a hundred things on the beach that day. She told me that my mama's favorite food was lasagna, and my daddy's fashion staple was always a pair of loafers with no socks. I laughed with her, and confided that I slept with my teddy bear until I was thirteen. I told her I wanted to visit my parent's graves, and she promised she would take me there. I hadn't been to the cemetery since they passed, and I was always too afraid to ask Millie about visiting their final resting place. The more we talked, the more I relaxed. I felt a tremendous weight lifted off of me when I was done talking to

Ava.

We stayed on the beach several hours, and when dusk began to fall, I remembered to call Millie. We returned to the house, and Ava directed me to the phone in the downstairs hall. For all the money, this was the only phone I had seen in the entire house. I called Millie and apologized for not calling sooner.

"I was worried sick! You didn't even call me once you got there," Millie reprimanded me.

Ava impatiently tapped her nails on the table next to the phone I was using.

"I promise I'll call once a day. I love you, Millie. Tell Uncle Doug too. I have to go." I hung up the phone as fast as I could, embarrassed by Millie's undying affection for her only grandchild.

"I'm going to shower. Ethan's cooking for us tonight. He's amazing," she droned. "You won't believe his culinary skills until you experience them firsthand."

My stomach growled at the prospect of real food. I was half-crazed with starvation, but I was too embarrassed to ask for something to fulfill my hunger.

"Can you help me find my room?" I asked Ava shyly.

She laughed. "Yes, and after we get the sand off I'll teach you an easy way to find your way around."

She swept me away to my door, but I was more lost than ever. I finished cleaning myself off in the shower, and donned a long halter dress I discovered in my closet. I snacked on fresh fruit I found on a silver platter in my room. Ava must have known I'd be starving. As I brushed out my hair, I noticed my cheeks were red from being out so long in the sun. I made a mental note to ask for sunscreen if we visited a store. Ava knocked on my door and began the tour.

She took me slowly through the house, stopping to show me where each person's room was located. I wasn't surprised to find a music room, a state-of-the-art kitchen, pool tables, and a huge den equipped with every movie and video game console known to man. Ava led me to one door that when opened, revealed a room that instantly became my favorite place in the house.

The room was dark, like something out of an English manor in a mystery movie. Scores of books on numerous shelves lay before me. A great walnut desk sat against one wall, and cozy chairs sat before a fireplace large enough for several men to stand in. I clapped my hands. Volumes upon volumes of unread works hid among the shelves, and I couldn't wait to get my hands on them.

"This is Julian's private office, but it also serves as our library. You are free to take anything you'd like. All of the new bestsellers arrive on a weekly basis, and the classics are all here, too. Julian is an avid reader, and he loves to discuss recent releases."

I was speechless. Everything in the house was right up my alley, as if I dreamed it all up.

We got to the second floor, and I was sure I had seen every room but two. She skipped one room on the first floor with a complicated looking lock on the outside, and one down a long hallway on the second floor.

"What's in that room?" I asked Ava, pointing to the door she avoided on the second floor.

She took a deep breath. "Arianna, I think it's time for you to meet Julian.

JULIAN

Ava knocked three times on the door. "Julian?"

"Come in," a smooth voice called from inside. Ava turned the knob, and I had no idea what I was going to see. The room was the largest and most decadent of the house so far. A small anteroom led to the main chambers, and the anteroom itself dwarfed my bedroom at Millie's. The room was painted dark gray, and a huge bed was the focal point. The rug on the floor was red, and it matched the comforter and the scarlet drapes. A tapestry of Gustav Klimt's "Tree of Life" painting hung behind the bed. I remembered the painting from a project in my tenth-grade art class. A hulking stone fireplace took over one wall, almost as large as the one in the library. A dark figure posed next to the bed, leaning on one of the posts. His icy-blue eyes were vivid even in the darkness of his room.

"*You*. I know you," I blurted out.

"You must be mistaken. I'm Julian, and I am so glad you have come to stay with us," he said. "Ava, could you leave us alone for a moment?" It was a command.

"O-okay. Arianna, I'll be in the den."   She eyed us suspiciously, knitting her eyebrows together with worry. She reluctantly left the room, and closed the door behind her with a soft click.

"Yes, I *have* met you. You are the man I met in my dreams. I know you. I knew it was you all along." I withdrew the key from a pocket-like fold in my dress.

I always carried the key. I didn't know what lock it would unclasp, but it gave me strength in knowing it was a final piece of the puzzle I was trying so desperately to solve in my mind.

Julian stepped forward. He took my face in his hands. "Arianna. I've been waiting for you. I thought I would go crazy waiting for you to come to me."

"How did you do it? How did you make me dream of you, of this place?" I demanded. "It wasn't a dream at all. The key, you, it was all real," I spilled out in disbelief. I grasped the cold, hard key in my hand tightly, ensuring myself I wasn't nuts.

"I cannot explain what happened, but I know it's because you were meant to come here. It is your destiny. You are my destiny."

I found myself trembling. *Was* I nuts? His eyes, his eyes. I knew them. I felt them every moment since I saw them last.

"Are you disappointed? Is everything to your liking?" he asked.

"Your house, I've never seen anything that compares to it. It's beautiful."

"Everything I have is yours. From now on you answer to no one. You have free reign of anything that is mine."

I wondered if he was this hospitable to all of his guests, but deep down

I knew he wasn't.

"Thank you, but you and Ava have already given me more than I could need."

"You won't be denied anything. You're home now." He leaned in and whispered in my ear, "With me."

I shivered. I was frozen to the spot where I stood, and I lost all feeling in my legs. Sheer terror alone kept my knees from buckling. I opened my mouth, but nothing came out. I finally regained enough composure to speak.

"Ethan's cooking dinner," I said lamely.

Julian laughed, and I noticed something I had missed before. He had dimples so deep, I lost the last of my heart then and there. I don't know how I had overlooked them before.

"Are you hungry?" he asked and I nodded. "Let's go down and get you something to eat." He took my hand and led me through all the twists and turns of his sprawling home.

We walked into a dining room with a table right out of a castle. Candles were the lighting of choice, and there were enough seats for at least twenty people. Huge portraits hung on the walls. Bouquets of live roses and love-lies-bleeding spilled out of their vases in the center of the table, spaced evenly between every few chairs. Black crystal goblets and black china set the places for the guests, and the place settings added to the decadence of the room.

Walker sat at one end of the table next to Ava, and Ethan and Sebastien sat across from them. When we entered the dimly lit room, everyone became instantly silent.

"Walker move down. Arianna will be sitting beside me." Walker jumped at Julian's commanding presence, and took the seat on Ava's other side. Julian pulled out the chair for me. After I sat down, he seated himself at the head of the table. "What will we be having for dinner Ethan?" he asked smoothly.

Ava scanned my face, searching for signs of anything untoward. I gave her a big smile and turned my attention to Ethan.

"Butternut squash soup for the first course, followed by filet medallions topped with lobster, and bread pudding for dessert." Ethan lumbered into the kitchen, returning with several bowls. He served my soup first, then Ava's.

The soup was so good, I couldn't wait for the entrée. Everyone complimented Ethan's culinary skills, and took turns drilling me with questions.

"What school did you attend?" Sebastien asked.

"Kennedy High School."

"Any hot teachers?" Walker joked.

"Not really, it's a really small school," I replied.

"Did you have a boyfriend?" Ethan asked.

"Don't answer that Arianna." Ava shot Ethan a warning look. "That's enough, Ethan. Arianna's dating history is her business and none of yours."

My face reddened. "It's okay. I never dated," I said.

Walker winked at me, and Ethan went to get the main course. Everyone laughed and talked through dinner, but Julian remained pensive. He was everything Ava said about him- dark, brooding, and tormented. He didn't take his eyes off me once during the meal, and he never spoke a word. It was hard not to openly ogle him. Averting my eyes was a difficult feat.

Walker patted his rock hard abs. "Ethan, Ethan. That was the best meal I've had in a long time."

It was the best meal I'd ever had, period.

"Let's go finish our game. I'm going to smoke you tonight," Walker teased, pointing at Ethan and Sebastien.

"I'm going to bed," Ava said. "I'm beat after that drive."

"I'm right behind you," I said wearily. "Thank you for dinner. It was perfect." Ethan beamed at my compliment. "See you all tomorrow." I followed Ava out of the dining room and up the stairs.

When we arrived in my room she planted a kiss on my head. "I love you, Arianna."

She turned to leave my room, but she paused at the door. She hesitated for a few moments. "Did Julian..."

I knew what she was asking, and there was no way I was letting on. "Everything was fine. He just wanted to get to know me better," I broke in.

She furrowed her brows. "If you need me I'll be right down the hall."

"Goodnight Ava."

"Goodnight Arianna."

I brushed my teeth, put on my pajamas, and crawled into bed. I expected to fall asleep immediately, but I tossed and turned for a long time. My mind was still spinning from being over-stimulated, and I suddenly had an idea. I fumbled for the light in the bathroom, and went into the closet. I saw that my suitcases were empty and belongings had been put away. My skull bikini Gabriel purchased was in the drawer with the swimsuits Ava bought for me.

Gabriel. I had forgotten to call. Surely Millie told him I arrived safely. I wanted to hear his voice, but I knew it was late. He would already be in bed. I resolved to call him the next day; unquestionably he would understand.

I donned my black swimsuit and tiptoed to the pool. I slipped past the den, listening to Sebastien rub his video game victory in Ethan's face. I thought it a little strange that Walker was absent; all he talked about after dinner was wanting to play and beat Sebastien in a game. I didn't want them to feel as though I had to be constantly entertained, and I was glad for the solitary repose. Ethan glanced up at me from the couch where he was sitting next to his brother. His face was stricken, but he said nothing as I moved outside.

The night air chilled my skin, and the ocean breezes hissed through the palm trees flanking the pool area. I sat on the concrete and stuck my feet in the pool.

"What are you doing up?" A voice jarred me, and I was startled to realize I wasn't alone. Julian ran his hand through his dark hair, and shook the water off. He swam to the edge of the pool to where I was sitting. He looked so thin and lithe in his long green swimming trunks. He didn't look old enough to be anyone's boss, let alone own a mansion of these proportions.

"I needed some air, and I couldn't sleep," I told him. "I didn't mean to disturb you. I didn't think anyone would be out here." I gathered my towel, ready to go back inside.

"Please, don't go. I want you here with me," he said. I sat back down. "Come in. The pool heater's on. It should be warm enough for you."

I noticed the water was remarkably tepid when I stuck my feet in before. I hopped in the water and dunked my head under. I felt childish enough compared to Ava, but Julian made me feel downright infantile. I emerged from the water and squeezed out the excess moisture from my hair while trying to simultaneously adjust my top.

"How old are you, Julian?" I challenged bravely. My curiosity was absolutely killing me.

"How old do you think I am?"

"You didn't answer my question, but I'll answer yours. You look twenty, tops, but you would have to be around forty or so. You lived here with my parents."

"If I appear to the entire world as someone in his mid-twenties, then what does it matter how old I am? Take you for example. You seem much older to me than you actually are. People listen when you talk. People only acquire that skill when they become famous or reach middle-age. The way I see it, age is relative."

"In this case, it isn't."

"How so?"

"Why won't you answer me? I'm not the kind of girl to go out in the middle of the night with a forty-year-old man. I don't believe you're forty, but I don't believe you are twenty, either."

"There you go. I already asked how old you thought I was, and *you* wouldn't answer *me*."

I refused to let him confuse me. "How long have you lived here? A decade?" We both knew that couldn't be true. He had lived here far before then; my parents lived here almost twice that long ago.

"Much longer than a decade, Arianna. Be serious."

"Forty years?"

"Perhaps."

"A century?"

"Arianna, you know that is impossible."

"Do I?" Anything was possible in Eden.

Julian swam under the waterfall. "Come here," he beckoned. I paddled over to him. He pulled me under the waterfall, and pulled my back to his chest.

He made little circles on my bare shoulders with his thumbs. I spun to face him.

"What is this place? I dreamed of you, someone I had never met over two hundred miles away from where I was at the time. You are well over twice my age, and you look only a few years older than me. You pull me so deep into your existence here, after only a day, I can barely remember my other life."

Julian pulled me closer. "This is your life now." He stared into my eyes. His eyes were fathomless blue depths.

I shivered. "I think I want to go to bed," I told him. I wasn't uncomfortable, *unsure* was a better word.

"Then let's get you upstairs."

He must have sensed my retraction from him. My initial fear of him waned into undying curiosity. I was a little afraid though, of my lack of self-control when I was with him. We went upstairs, and he led me to my doorway. He opened his mouth to speak, but a few doors down the hall, Ava appeared bleary-eyed, coming out of her room. Julian put his hand over my mouth and twisted the knob to my door. The move propelled the two of us into my pitch black room. We were still dripping wet from the pool.

I broke free of his grasp and asked the obvious. "What are you doing?" I hissed.

"Ava would not approve of our late night tryst, no matter how innocent it was. I don't imagine she wants to find her niece in her swimsuit with a half-naked man. And the fact that I'm her boss matters about as much to her as it matters to me that you are her niece. Ava is very protective of you. She has already threatened every man's life in this house if we so much as stare at you for more than a moment."

I felt a huge thrill at having him in my bedroom hiding from my aunt. "How are you faring with her threats?" I asked.

"Doomed," he told me in his husky voice.

I remembered an old adage Uncle Doug had used a few times. It described him perfectly. Hard as a brick, smooth as velvet.

He smiled, lowering his head into a kiss that left my body screaming for more. At first, he was gentle. He slipped his warm tongue in and out of my mouth. He bit my lower lip softly, and pressed his wet, muscular chest to mine. The sensation of heat from our bodies and the cool water still beading on our skin became too much to handle. Julian pushed my body into the wall, and I felt him on every inch of me.

I couldn't help but make comparisons. I would surely go to hell for doing so.

Gabriel was warm, comforting, and familiar. Julian was hot, sinful, and foreign. He set me on fire. I *had* to make myself stop. I knew Gabriel eighteen years, and it had taken us that long to kiss for the first time. I hadn't even known Julian eighteen hours. Unless, of course, I counted the two nights I saw him in my dreams...

"Julian," I murmured, my mind finally taking over my hormones and forcing me to recoil from him. We had somehow made our way just a few steps away from my bed. "Please stop."

He snatched his body away immediately. "Oh, God. I don't understand what you do to me. Arianna, I never meant..."

"I know. I just need to get some sleep." I knew he didn't mean to take advantage of the situation. The feeling, it was so bizarre. Almost like a magnet pulled us to each other.

Julian pressed his hands on the wall and hung his head. "Give me a second." When his labored breathing finally slowed, he stood up. He brushed away a stray lock of his dark hair. "I apologize. This will not happen again." He stared at me for a long moment before he left. His blue eyes seared themselves into my brain.

He was gone in a flash of desire and electricity. What kind of power did he hold? I knew him *one day*, and Gabriel's face became a clouded memory.

What was I feeling for Julian? I mean, he came to me in my dreams. My *dreams*. My deepest subconscious thoughts. I felt connected to him in a different way than Gabriel. No matter what claim Julian staked in my life, I told myself, he would never hold the place in my heart Gabriel held.

I went to bed, and slept until noon the next day. I padded downstairs after a shower in my luxe bathroom, and somehow found my way into the kitchen. I was embarrassed to find that everyone else had been up for hours. Julian leaned lazily on one of the counters in a long-sleeved ocean blue shirt unbuttoned to his waist. His perfectly tailored black pants complimented his lean body. His feet were bare, and I noted how pretty his long tanned toes looked in contrast to the pale floors. He was beautiful even in places I found disgusting on most people.

"Hey. Did you sleep well?" Ava asked me. She handed me a glass of orange juice. "You went to bed so early. The sun always saps my energy, too. You poor thing, you must have been extra tired from swimming."

I choked on the sip of juice I had just taken. Julian's gaze bore into me. He looked almost smug. Ava patted me lightly on the back, and I held up one hand to let her know I was fine.

"What do you want to do today? We can do anything or go anywhere you want. No limits."

"I think I'd just like to go down to the beach again," I said. I was overwhelmed at the concept of "No limits".

"I never get tired of the beach." Ava smiled at me. "Meet you outside in ten."

I ran upstairs and changed. Ava and Walker were waiting at the bottom of the staircase.

"Do you mind if I tag along?" Walker's green eyes lit up. "Ethan and Sebastien want to come, too. Sebastien is going crazy with boredom without Savannah here."

"Sure. I mean, you don't have to ask my permission. It's your house.

Of course you can come. I love you guys already," I gushed.

Walker shot me a big smile and we went down to the beach. Ethan and Sebastien were right behind us. I sat in the sand and talked to Ava while the boys began a volleyball game.

Sebastien joined us after a while, and Walker and Ethan followed suit when they had exhausted themselves playing in the hot sun. Ethan sat pretty far away from us, and I felt self-conscious. He kept peering over to us, but never said a word. *He must have the same feeling the same thing I do,* I thought. I wasn't good enough to be around these people. I tried to ignore him, and listened to the others' conversation, trying to concentrate.

"Where do you plan to attend college?" Sebastien asked me.

"I don't really have any plans yet," I confessed.

"Oh. I'm sorry. I didn't mean to imply that you needed to go to college or anything," he mumbled, looking embarrassed.

"No, it's okay. I just haven't decided yet. I think I'm going to take a semester or two off. Did you go to college?" I hedged his question.

Sebastien smiled. "Yes. I hold a Masters in English literature, a Doctorate in law, philosophy, and engineering. Oh, and Savannah and I both attained a Masters in art history together." How was it that he could seem so humble telling me he was a genius?

"I go to college," Walker interrupted.

"Yeah, just for the girls," Ava swiped. We all laughed. "No, really,

Walker is almost done with *his* Doctorate in psychology." I gasped. "Arianna, calm down. The boys just like to show off. I knew I had it coming from Walker, so I toned him down." She stuck her tongue out at him.

He grabbed his chest in mock heart attack that she would make such a claim. Ethan smirked then, but remained silent the rest of the time. It hurt me that he seemed so repulsed by me, but I tried to not let his feelings become a damper on the great time I was having.

When the sun became too sweltering to endure on the scorching sand, we trudged our way deep into the sea. I swam in big circles, my body crashing in and out of the waves.

I suddenly felt an iron-hot sting under my foot. I spun around, looking for the culprit of the pain. A huge chunk of sea glass was lodged deep into my heel. I saw the water around my left leg turn pink, and I felt instantly dizzy. The blood made me swoon.

"Ava," I yelled over the sound of the waves. "Ow! Can you help me?" I hopped on one foot, trying not to pass out.

Ava snatched me out of the water, and blood poured from my foot. Great big red drops fell onto the snowy sand. She helped me sit down gently on the beach, and Ethan, Sebastien, and Walker flocked to us.

"What wrong?" Sebastien asked.

"It's really not a big deal. I cut my foot…" I tried to sound nonchalant, but most of my foot was covered in blood, and I was beginning to see spots.

"Let's get you inside," Ava said.

I felt a pair of strong arms lift me into the air and cradle me. Julian must have heard the fuss, because he appeared out of nowhere to personally carry me into the house.

"I can walk," I told him, putting on my pitiful excuse for a brave face.

He didn't seem to hear. He carried me into the kitchen and set me on the counter wearing his thundercloud expression. The granite countertop was smeared in red where my foot touched it. I glanced down and saw that the raw meat of my heel was exposed. I swooned at the sight and smell of the blood.

"I just need to lie down," I said in a garbled voice. My ears rang and my head suddenly felt very heavy and hard to support.

Julian pulled a tangle of keys out of his pocket, and fumbled with one that looked very old. The skeleton key. My key. It was identical to the one he gave me.

Ava and the guys ran into the kitchen just behind Julian and I. Ava looked at the key and stopped Julian's hand with hers. She spoke to him through an unreadable expression, and finally gave a slight nod. Julian left for a moment, and quickly returned with a large glass basin filled with the sparkly, magical water that my vial contained.

Ethan, Sebastien, and Walker watched in silence, covering their mouths with their hands. Julian poured the water on my legs, and they began to glow with the same gossamer haze as the day I cut my hand on the lid of the vial. The blood and the pain were instantly gone. The room silently awaited my inevitable response.

"Ava? What is in that water?"

KEEPERS

Julian lifted me from the counter and stood me upright. He handed Ava the skeleton key. Julian's gift to me was the key to a room, I correctly guessed. I remained silent, and Julian gave his head a little shake. She took the key and placed her hands on my shoulders.

"Arianna, I think it's time you knew what is really going on here. Come with me."

I followed her to the only room in the house I hadn't yet seen. She took a deep breath and unlocked the complicated bolt.

The room was beautiful. The marble patterns on the other floors in the house were not even comparable to this one. A heavy haze filled the room.

The walls were unpainted rose-colored stone. The ceiling was domed, and thousands upon thousands of tiny pieces of colored glass made it the most beautiful piece of architecture I had ever seen, pictures or otherwise.

The room was completely empty except for a tall, gilded fountain in the center of the room. The room was unlit and windowless, the only light radiated from the fountain and the rainbow of glass pouring in from the dome. Ava sat down at the fountain's edge, and I followed suit. There was a ledge that ran around the perimeter of the large fountain, and the water swirled around us. The haze grew thicker the closer we came, and when we sat down, I could barely make out Ava's face through the mist.

"Well, this is it. The answers to all the questions you have about us, about your parents, about my life."

I looked around. I definitely didn't see any answers. I gave her a quizzical look she may or may not have been able to discern through the mist.

"We are the Keepers of the Fountain of Youth."

Keepers? I envisioned hooded figures chanting around a bonfire. "Excuse me? What? Say that one more time!?"

I suddenly got chills on my arms even thought I felt like I was burning up, and tried hard to keep my teeth from chattering. I felt lightheaded. My body was freaking out as much as my mind. I knew there was something big going on here, but this? She could have told me Julian was the leader of a drug cartel and wouldn't have garnered such a response. In hindsight, that was kind of what I expected, even after seeing the effects of the water back home and in the kitchen earlier. I really *had* thought they were doing something illegal here. I mean, why the secrecy? The water had scared me to death before, but I chalked it up to some top secret medical advancement. I rationalized everything in my mind to make sense, but there wasn't anything rational in what she was telling me now.

Ava patted my knee. "Everything you see is real. I have waited a long time to bring you to this place and share this with you. You are my only living blood relative, and it is only fitting that you partake of what I can offer you.

There is so much I want to tell you. Do you want to hear the story?"

I nodded. I wanted to laugh, but the situation was far from humorous. I felt as if I was dreaming a very long drawn out dream. I would wake up soon and laugh and laugh and keep my craziness to myself. I was surely dreaming of the Fountain and of a man that was so far out of my league it wasn't even the same sport. Ancient legends hidden within a century-old mansion that I called home? *Ding! Ding! Ding!* I was officially nuts.

Ava's voice broke into my thoughts. "I guess I'll start with Julian's story. He *is* the reason that we, and no one else, are sitting here today. Julian was the son of a wealthy land prospector who was forcing him to marry one of his friend's daughters against his will. He and four of his friends came to Florida for one huge bachelor party, but not before doing his father a favor and looking at some property his father's company was interested in developing.

"This area is known for its healing waters and mineral springs. Julian's father wanted to build a resort around the springs. Julian wanted to please his father at any cost, so he was happy to look at the land. Ultimately he came here searching for an escape from his life before his forced marriage, and what he found would change it forever.

"While checking out the property, Julian noticed smoke coming off of a gush of water rising from the ground on the land. He dipped his finger in the water, and his friends went crazy when they saw the effect the water created. Julian noticed a scar he wore from childhood had disappeared from the contact with the water.

"Julian and his friends took turns applying the water to different scars, cuts, pockmarks, bruises. It never failed to erase any sign of pain or ugliness. Julian and his friends kept quiet about their findings, and the rest is history. Are you following me?"

"I think so. So, his friends are the people that live here? Ethan, Sebastien, and Walker, right?" I asked, unbelieving.

"Not exactly," she broke in. "The original four are Henry, Silas, Vincent, and Edgar. They all swore to secrecy. The Fountain only produces so much of its legendary water. They pooled their money together and bought the land from underneath Julian's father. Julian stayed here to protect the property while his friends left to go get materials to build here. They stayed gone for a long time, and when his friend Silas returned, he brought word Julian's father had passed.

"Julian locked himself into the house they collectively built, and eventually everyone but him grew tired of being confined here. All of them except Julian left and went elsewhere to lead their own lives."

"So they never came back?" I asked in disbelief. Who in the world would just walk away?

"They have no reason to return, but they do very seldom. All but Henry. We work for them. We deliver vials of the water to his friends, the original four, all around the world, and in turn, they pay us enormous amounts of money from their investments for our time."

"How long ago did Julian find this place?"

"Please don't flip out when I tell you this, okay?"

I wasn't making any promises.

"1880."

Neither of us spoke for a few moments. I guess she was giving me the chance to let me absorb some of the story she was telling me.

"Bach then, much of Florida was still unsettled, and his father correctly guessed that one day, the state would become a gold mine in tourism to the sunny beaches. He wanted a foot in the door before anyone else. Julian was nineteen."

My head swam as I tried to calculate his age. My brain twisted, and I knew there was another piece of the tale I was curious about . "So what happened with the girl? The one he was supposed to marry," I asked. Not that I cared that much or anything...

"She married one of his four friends that discovered the land with him, Edgar. Her name is Emily, and she comes to visit from time to time. Julian won't speak about his past. We only came to know Emily through Edgar, and the other parts we pieced together from his Vincent."

"How did you and Mama find Julian?"

"Julian became very lonely here. His very best friend, Henry, worried about him staying here alone. He decided to choose several special people to keep Julian company, not to mention to do his bidding so he didn't ever have to return here so often to drink from the Fountain.

"Henry is a primarily selfish person. He felt too tied down having to constantly return. He had some very large companies, and still does, around the globe, and he needs to maintain them at all times. As much as he hated sharing his water, he hated having to come back and forth all the time, so he handpicked us to go back and forth for him. Henry chose us based on three things: beauty, strength, and intelligence. We were tested and trained extensively before they told us anything and even more before Julian allowed us make a delivery. Things rarely go badly, but once or twice, we have almost all been exposed.

"Ethan and Sebastien arrived here as barely more than children at the turn of the century. Julian is more like their father than anything. Henry found your mother and I at a New Orleans orphanage in 1937. He brought us here to evoke a love interest from Julian. Obviously, it did not work the way it was supposed to."

She answered my next question before I could ask it. "I was sixteen, and Rose was fifteen."

I wanted to puke all of a sudden. But I didn't. I kept asking questions.

"So does Henry visit often?" It seemed to me that his very best friend would have just come back to stay with him instead of finding people to fill in. I felt sorry for Julian. For everything I'd heard so far, everyone in his early life

had deserted him.

"Henry only visits once every decade or so, but believe me, he keeps a very close tab on all the comings and goings of Eden. He wanted to live his own life, and he felt like Julian tied him down just as much as the Fountain. Julian was never the same after his father's death. Henry resents Julian because he knows what he does to him is wrong, but he truly does want the best for him."

"If everyone has to keep this a secret, what do the others tell their families as an excuse to skip out on their regular lives?" I interrupted. I couldn't imagine what explanation I would give to Millie and Doug as to why I looked eighteen when I was supposed to be forty or so. No wonder they didn't want me having anything to do with Ava. Seeing how young she appeared, and then finding out she was my aunt threw me *way* off guard. Millie probably made herself sick trying to come up with explanations.

Ava laughed. "Your father was the first to have a family, and we would all agree, it did not go well when he lived here."

"Did Henry choose my father too? You said before, you met him in Ellaville with my mother." My heart was racing so fast at the mention of my daddy, I thought it would beat out of my chest.

"The people that live here are all hand-picked by Henry, with the exception of your father, Jade, and Savannah. Walker is the one who found Jade. She is whip-smart, and as pretty as they come, but watch your back when it comes to being her friend.

"Each of the original people Henry chose is allowed to choose one person to stay here indefinitely with them. Sebastien chose Savannah. One catch. The only problem with our 'system' you might call it is the one that made your mother return to Ellaville permanently. It isn't the only reason she left, but it is the reason she never came back."

I sat on the very edge of the rim of the Fountain's basin, listening intently for the reason why my mother would leave such a magical place.

"We are forbidden to procreate. Period. As I said before, there is only so much water produced at a time. If one of us had a child, their children would have children, and so on. There would be nothing left."

"So you chose me?" I asked. Ava had foregone the chance of finding love because she had brought me here. I was her chosen one. I felt a surge of love for her.

"I chose you." Ava smoothed my hair.

"Where did the Fountain come from? How did it become forgotten?"

"We have our theories. A mass inquiry would draw unnecessary attention. Julian's theory leans toward the biblical, hence the embossing on the vial I gave you and the Fountain itself."

"Biblical? Julian doesn't strike me as the religious type," I said.

"You may be surprised. He could easily gain the title of 'The Most Powerful Man in the World.' There is not one dignitary or royal family that would fail to give their entire fortune for a drop of the fountain's offering. Julian never leaves for any reason, and he is more or less celibate."

I squirmed uncomfortably, but was relieved by the thought that he didn't share his midnight rendezvous with anyone else.

"So, what is his theory based on?"

"We've done a lot of our own research, and the only thing we can come up that we even come close to agreeing on is in the Garden of Eden. Genesis 2 talks about Eden, and it mentions a river flowing through the garden that separated into four headwaters. We think the water may have somehow become tainted by the tree that grew beside the Tree of Life. In Genesis 10, it also says that in the days of Peleg, the earth was divided. The Garden of Eden was in Mesopotamia, somewhere in the Middle East, but if the earth was once just one continent, maybe the Gulf was once part of Europe."

"So, you believe this is where the Garden of Eden was?" I asked Ava.

"Like I said, we all have theories, that is simply one of them. Some people believe the continents separated from one central piece of land, but who knows?" Ava smiled.

"So what exactly does the water do?"

"We drink every few days or months or years, depending on the person, to stay young. We do let ourselves age a bit from time to time, mostly because no one takes us seriously if we look sixteen. The water heals all sickness, and makes you invincible to the greatest enemy of human life. Time.

Every disease is cured by the water, and when you drink from the Fountain, you gain strength. Nothing phenomenal, but you are much stronger than the average person. Everything is dependant upon how much you drink. Julian only allows us a vial at a time, even if it has been years since we drank. The Fountain re-circulates the water, so there's no need to store it, but if it ever runs dry, that's it. We will age and die like any normal person.

"We also know the Fountain restores beauty, as I told you before. The ugliest person in the world would become one of the most beautiful with one sip. Beautiful people become spectacular. Savannah made all of our eyes pop out when she finally drank, but we weren't surprised, she was a knockout before. Our sweet little china doll transformed into a sexy siren." She grinned wickedly.

I laughed. Savannah looked every bit the china doll at my school, but Ava wasn't kidding about the siren part. She would make any man want to sell their soul just to get a good glimpse of her.

"The last side effect is one we don't discuss too often. We are able to slightly control people's minds. I couldn't, for instance, make someone sell me their mother, but the police officer that pulled us over would have probably thrown me in jail because I was driving so fast, no matter what I looked like."

Fat chance, I thought. Ava must have had no idea how beautiful she was. My mind immediately went to the beautiful Julian and the nights he appeared in my dreams. Was he controlling my mind, too? Is that why I was so drawn to him in my room the night before? I doubted it. He could have taken advantage of the situation; I was so taken with him, I probably wouldn't have stopped if pressed.

"Can you control each others' minds?"

"The water makes us immune from each other, but only to a certain extent. Julian and Sebastien experimented by ingesting doses of the water back to back. At first, there was no clear winner, but after Julian had just one more drink, Sebastien began doing all sorts of crazy stunts, cursing Julian all the while."

The whole mind control bit was beyond me; it didn't seem like something I would be likely to want to be involved in. I was more curious about the prospect of living eternally. There was just one thing that bothered me.

"Why did my parents die? If they were immortal…"

"Memento Mori. It's Julian's private joke, and our way of saying 'be careful'. It means 'remember you are mortal'. Any of us could die at any time. We carry the vials with us for that reason. It would save you from the brink of death, but Thomas and Rose were killed on impact. They never had time to take into account the vials. I'm so sorry, sweetie."

I flinched at the mention of my parents. Questions of every sort ran through my head. Everything began to take shape.

"What about your neighbors and the people who live around here? Don't they get suspicious that you never age?"

"We do most of our shopping out of town, and only venture into Panacea in an emergency. People around here don't ask questions. They respect the privacy of this house and our beach.

"The tinted windows make it impossible for anyone to see who is driving the cars. We hire an outside staff to come monthly, but they are hired from out of town, and usually out of the country. The crew that comes to tend to the grounds and do all of the other day-to-day cleaning and laundry are people sent directly to us from Henry. He sends the staff too, but on a different scale. They are hand-picked, and they sign year long contracts. He puts them through intense questioning before they are allowed to come. It wouldn't surprise me if most of the day-to-day staff are Henry's personal spies to make sure we all abide by the rules. As I said before, he knows everything, and I mean *everything* about what goes on here."

"I can't believe all of this. Seriously?"

I was a little scared zombies were going to crawl out of the walls at any minute. Nothing seemed ridiculous anymore. I second guessed every myth and legend I ever heard.

"That's it. I assure you everything is like I just told you. No more secrets."

"I trust you, but you promise, no more surprises?" I asked warily.

"Well, my name is not really Ava. My real name is Abigail Virginia." She scrunched her face and stuck out her tongue.

"Oh, and I was engaged to Doug."

NEMESIS

"What?" I shrieked. Of all the unbelievable things Ava told me, this was the most far-fetched of all.

"I don't want to talk about it, but I'll give you a quick, and I mean very quick version. I fell for him when we went to his house for the first time to meet Thomas' mother. I thought he was cute when I tagged along for your parents' first date, but when I saw how sweet and gentle he treated Millie, I fell hard."

I guessed Uncle Doug probably was good-looking in his day. I had never thought of it before. I remembered his soft, easy face in my mind's eye, and I tried to picture him twenty years younger. He was tall and thin, and he kept in shape from working such long hours. I still couldn't make out how Ava must have seen him in the glory of his youth. He was my uncle for goodness' sake, and I guess you can never really see those things. Yuck. I almost laughed out loud.

"I'm sorry, but you *have* to tell me. You aren't getting out of this. Why did you break up?"

"Because he is a cold, heartless ass whose only redeeming quality is the fact that he raised my niece."

"Not good enough…" I sang.

Ava sighed. "Because he was supposed to come to Eden to see

where I we would be living and help me plan our wedding. Thomas went to pick him up and bring him, but your father returned alone. Doug didn't even have the heart to tell me in person. Thomas relayed the message. I didn't see him again until the day I met you at Millicent's, and there was no love lost between us. That's it. No more."

"Why would he do that to you? Uncle Doug never went on one date in all those years."

She looked off into the distance, and I wasn't sure if she looked sad or irritated.

"Okay, okay. I'm dropping it. I want to get out of here and process everything. It's hard to think in this mist," I told Ava, swiping my hand in front of my face to clear the air.

We exited the room, and Julian stood right outside the door kinda doing a hopping dance from one leg to another. He was a very collected person from what I gathered, but now he was almost giddy.

"What did you think?" Julian asked excitedly.

"It's a lot to take in. I'm not sure what to think."

Julian's face fell.

"Don't be upset. I mean, come on. You have the Fountain of freaking Youth in your house. Of course, it's the coolest thing ever."

Julian beamed. "We would have told you sooner, but we like to ease people into it. Ava didn't want you to run screaming from the house and have us all committed."

"I think that's probably enough, Julian. Arianna has much to consider." Ava turned to me. "Do you want us to leave you for a little while?"

"I am sort of tired. I think I'll go take a nap." Without another word, I went upstairs. It *was* a lot to take in. In the back of my mind, I still thought I was nuts. I wasn't really tired, I just wanted to think, so I was shocked to find myself waking several hours later.

I rolled out of bed and started downstairs. I went toward the den, when I heard a shrill voice in the main entrance.

"I'm home!"

I rounded the corner to see everyone gathered to greet the visitor. I stopped in an alcove to watch in privacy. The tiny blond, Savannah, ran into the arms of Sebastien.

"I missed you," Sebastien told her. He stared straight into her eyes before dropping a light kiss on her temple. It was almost moving to watch them. I had never seen two people more in love.

"We were starting to wonder if you were ever coming home, Jade. How long have you been gone? Three months now?" Walker asked the girl with the piercing voice.

Jade came into view. She was as beautiful as Ava described her. She had long black tumbly hair and green eyes that slanted upward just a bit at the corners, adding to her exotic mystique. I was intrigued. From the history Ava relayed, there was not much of a friendship between the two of them.

"For your information, I was gone four months. It's so nice to know you were keeping track. I visited a few friends in St. Tropez, and from there I traveled to Monte Carlo. I met Savannah in Brazil to deliver to Silas, when I decided it was time to come home."

I guessed correctly that Silas must be as filthy rich as Julian.

"Did you miss me, Julian?" She flashed him a hopeful smile.

"I missed you as much as anyone would miss a splinter in their finger," he told her.

"Funny." She laughed and rolled her eyes, but I doubted Julian was kidding. Jade turned her eyes to the plant I was hiding behind in the alcove. "You. Go get my bags out of my trunk." She pointed her finger rudely at me. I stood still, and she snapped her fingers. "Now," she demanded.

Ethan stepped forward. "Arianna isn't staff, Jade. She lives here."

I was stunned he would stand up for me after he had treated me like I had the plague up to then. I chalked it up to the fact that everyone must hate Jade as much as Ava.

"By whose authority?" Jade asked Ethan.

"Mine." Ava walked in front of me, guarding me protectively.

"Arianna chose to visit Ava for the summer, but she has charmed us all entirely. I speak for everyone when I say we would like for her to maintain Eden as her permanent residence," Julian told Jade.

"She's my niece. Arianna is Rose's daughter." Ava backed closer into me.

"What?" Jade asked, her voice sizzling with fury. "You cannot be serious. *Rose*," she spat the word, "almost ruined everything. She was a manipulative whore. Isn't this lovely? No wonder she left. She went and got herself knocked up!"

"My mother was not a whore!" I shouted.

"How dare you speak to me? This is *my* house," Jade volleyed.

Ava ground her teeth together. "Julian, you had better take care of her, because if I get my hands around her throat..." Ava circled her hands together threateningly.

"If you ever dare to speak to another of my guests in such a way, you will never set foot in this house again. You are dead wrong, Jade. This is *my* house. I choose to allow you the *privilege* of rooming here."

Ava guided me to the staircase. "Come on. Let's get you ready," she prompted. "We will be having dinner," she turned and yelled at Jade, "OUT!"

I was fuming by the time I reached my room. My mother was a saint by all accounts. She gave up everything, including her perfect life, to make a safe home for me. The nerve of Jade to say such a nasty and untrue thing about my mama. That conversation was far from over, but I let it go for Ava's sake. I showered and blocked her words from my mind.

Ava and I decided on fresh seafood for dinner, along with Sebastien and Savannah. We went to a beachside crab shack a few towns past Panacea.

I found Savannah to be shy and quiet, but she lived up to all the wonderful things I heard about her. Our conversation turned to the evening's events.

"So why is Jade still living there? She seems to be the black sheep of the group. Why does Julian put up with her?" I demanded.

Sebastian's face grew somber as he spoke. "Because we're indebted to Jade. On a delivery in Rio, where Silas lives, Walker was incarcerated for the contents of the vial. He drew much attention when he came to the city, much like he does everywhere he goes, and the police were looking for a reason to detain him. His hotel was illegally searched, the vial was found, and they took him into custody.

"Jade was intrigued by Walker, and she convinced her lover, the Chief of Police, to allow her to examine the vial herself. Jade is very clever, and sly when she needs to be. She discover the powers of the liquid, and she craved more.

"She smuggled the keys to open the cell where Walker was held, and he released himself while she seduced the night guard. By the time it was discovered Walker was missing, he was well on his way out of the country. Our secret could have been exposed, but Jade's cunning saved us all. In a pre-conceived location, Jade met with Walker and flew back to Eden.

Begrudgingly, yes, but we owe our continued existence to Jade."

Ava spoke up. "Jade is power hungry. She's been after Julian all the years she's spent with us. Don't let her quick temper fool you. She is a force to be reckoned with. Julian readily accepted her because of her knowledge, and she has proven herself to be valuable to us more than once."

She quieted when the waiter brought us plates of steamed oysters and crab legs. Our waiter lingered far too long at the booth we were seated in because of Ava and Savannah. I was a little envious of the way Ava flirted with him so easily, but I resigned myself to watching a million men throw themselves at the girls' feet if it meant spending the summer with the people who were quickly becoming my adopted family.

That night, I discovered a newfound taste for seafood. Ellaville's offering of marine cuisine consisted of catfish and crawfish, both of which could be found at the barbeque restaurant. I was seriously lacking in my worldly experience in all areas, including food.

"Enough talk about Jade. I spent more time with her on this last delivery than I could ever want in a million years. I'm tired of her." The tiny angelic Savannah turned to me. "I want to hear all about you. I was so excited when Sebastien told me you decided to come. I loved you from the second I saw you at your school. I'm so excited to have a new member of the family. I was the last one to join." Savannah turned up the corners of her mouth. She had to have been a goddess in a former life. Her soft curls bounced when she spoke.

"There isn't much to tell," I told her.

I relayed the contents of my quiet life in Ellaville, and she listened intently. Sebastien asked questions, as did Ava, and I told them all the minute details of my boring hometown.

Ava tossed a mind boggling tip on the table for the waiter, and we returned to Eden.

*****

We spent the next several weeks playing in the sun. I grew accustomed to having someone take care of all my needs. My laundry was always done. My bed was always made. My room was always clean when I returned from my afternoon adventures, on the beach or otherwise. Savannah spoiled all of us, but she never accepted help. It was just her way.

The grounds were beautifully maintained. There were always tons of groceries, so we only had to venture out a few times. No one on the staff dared to speak to any of us if we saw them. I only caught a glimpse of a black-haired girl once and a short, red-complexioned man twice. They scurried around like mice, all but invisible.

Ava and I grew closer, and I loved the late night chats we had in her room. Her bright yellow walls were so happy and sunny. A white Siam canopy hung above her bed. The picture of me Millie had given her on the day I first met her was prominently matted and framed on the center of the only bare wall. Bright Moroccan quilts with sequins and embroidery were thrown about. Rich, chocolate wooden statues stood on the floor. She told me once they were a gift from a dignitary in India. Her life reminded me of one of her quilts. Bright, vibrant, and beautiful, exactly like Ava.

Savannah would bring in chips and drinks, and we would sometimes stay up until dawn talking. I usually just listened. I didn't have anything of importance to say compared to them, and I could almost see the places and people they had seen from the way they described them.

One of my favorite times in Eden was the night Ava pulled out her picture albums. I traced my fingertips along my parents' figures, and Savannah held my hand while Ava told me about her happiest memories of them.

A time or two, even Sebastien joined in our talks. He never grew tired of being with Savannah. He shared some too, mostly adventurous stories about dangers he faced on deliveries over the years, but I always felt as if they were edited for my sake.

Julian and I continued our secret meetings at the pool a few nights a week, and he always had a steady flow of questions to ask me.

"What's on your playlist?" he asked me one night when I came outside listening to my MP3.

I rattled off a few of my favorite bands, and he seemed to know at least one song from each group.

"What about you? You've lived through every decade. You probably listen to eighties love ballads," I teased.

"I'm more of a My Chem, MSI kind of guy."

That seemed fitting on so many levels.

"Now *I* get to ask the questions. What is your last name?" I asked.

"Davenport." He crossed his arms.

"When is your birthday?"

His expression softened. "The day I met you is the only day that has mattered in a century."

I rolled my eyes, but I was deeply touched by his reply.

"What was it like to live through so many times?" I could hear my voice fill up with excitement over the thought of seeing so much. "I would kill to see the Beatles play live, or look up at the moon knowing someone was up there right then." I tipped my head upwards and gazed at the dim orb that lit my nights with Julian. "World Wars, Woodstock, integration, the invention of the television, new episodes of I Love Lucy..." I secretly loved Lucy, but I wasn't about to tell him *that*.

"It was lonely to live through all of that because I had no one to share it with." His expression was so sad, my heart cramped. "Very lonely. I'm a prisoner here. My life has been lived through my imprisonment. It never really bothered me, though, because there was never anyone I wanted to share it all with anyway. Not until I met you."

I shivered as the wind began to whip around me.

He knew more about me than anyone now, except Gabriel. And Gabriel was the one tiny detail I decided to omit from any questions concerning my old life. I hadn't spoken his name since I arrived, and for the first time I missed the way it felt to say his name aloud.

Julian did not kiss me again, and I was torn between disappointment and relief.

*****

I soon discovered that it rained in Florida almost every day. For an hour or so each afternoon, we were forced inside by thunderstorms lasting through early evening. Florida had the ability to coax me into a nap every day while the rain fell late into dusk. We resumed our play as soon as the inevitable showers dissipated at night.

Sometimes, before I met up with Julian at the pool, I loved to curl up into one of the oversized leather chairs in the library and read the classics. I was fascinated by the library; Ellaville didn't even boast a bookstore, and there was never enough money to spend on extravagantly expensive first editions of some of the classics. Julian owned everything from Shakespeare to Twain, and I was reading an average of three or four books a week.

Sometimes, if it rained through the night, Julian would come and find me there. We would sprawl out on the floor in front of the fireplace, and he would stretch out his long legs and read to me. I discovered we both had a passion for tragedies, and no matter how romantic they were, Julian's interest didn't wane. More than once, Julian's dark voice led me to get teary-eyed at the most heartbreaking parts.

Life in Eden was very strange to me. We took the longest possible amount of time to do anything. I noticed things I never took the time to detect in Ellaville. The itchy first mosquito bite of the summer. The sick pleasure I found peeling my sunburned skin. How the tropical smell of tanning oil would from then on be my favorite scent in the world.

Jade steered clear of me most of the time. She wasn't openly hostile; she would shove me with her shoulders in the hallway when we passed each other and there was no one else around. She would will me to drop dead every time I spoke to Julian. I could almost feel her mind control at work. The first several times it gave me a mind-numbing headache to be near her, but eventually it tapered into an almost unnoticeable throb lasting only a few seconds.

Ava showed me the ropes on my personal jet ski, and it wasn't long before I was a seasoned pro. Savannah always begged off, claiming seasickness if she so much as stood too close to the water, but I was pretty sure she didn't want to intrude into my time with just Ava and I. Julian rode with us one day, and he held me tightly around my waist.

"Ready?" He smiled.

I nodded, and we sped off in spraying sea foam. I turned and watched Julian's dark hair blow, setting off his eyes the same color as the water. He held me closer, and his scent hypnotized me as it had the first night in my dreams, only now I could savor every second. He smelled like fresh air, summer rain, the first cool autumn night. He smelled of everything pure and beautiful. Life.

Julian was as fearless as Ava described. He jumped waves at ninety degree angles, until I was sure we would flip. I was never afraid, though. Julian never failed to make me feel safe. He clung to me tightly, and I vowed to never forget the moment.

One night Walker came home from a weekend trip and brought a hot pink flyer home and set it on one of the end tables in the den. "Seventies night at Screwdriver. Pull out your platforms, baby. We're going out."

I took a large bite of the orange I was peeling. "Seventies? Ugh," I said with my mouth full. "What's Screwdriver?" I was totally unimpressed with anything involving platform shoes.

"Absolutely not. Arianna is too young." Ava crossed her arms.

"Come on. She's eighteen. Why can't she come? Oh yeah, I went the other night, and that guy was there. The one you went to that hotel room with-"

"Another word, Walker, and you won't be going to the bar tonight or any other night," Ava snapped. I was sure she wasn't kidding.

"Screwdriver's a bar?" I asked.

"More of a club," Sebastien told me. "It's one of the closest nightclubs that is far enough out of town that we won't see anyone from around here. They do theme nights sometimes, and we always go. I don't care for the disco scene and didn't even when it was new, but we'll have a good time."

"Can't we go?" I pleaded. I changed my mind. Anything deemed cool by Sebastien's standards was sure to blow my mind.

"No. It gets crazy at Screwdriver sometimes, and I don't want to have to hurt someone." Ava was unmoving.

"It does *not* get crazy. You're just worried about what every man in the bar would be thinking when they saw this one." Walker motioned his arms up and down me, as if I was a prize in a game show. "Of course, you could always leave her here alone with Julian." It sounded more like a threat than a solution.

Ava was suddenly panic-stricken. "Get dressed Arianna. We're going out."

*****

A small fleet of identical black BMWs gets attention. We drove for what seemed like an eternity, but later I learned it was only a couple of hours away. Ava wore a skin tight gold metallic tube dress, and I wore a matching one in silver that Savannah let me borrow. I rode with Ava and Ethan.

Savannah rode with Sebastien, of course, and Walker rode with Jade.   Ethan

was indiscernibly silent the entire way, and I would have killed for a glimpse

into his mind. He still refused to speak to me. He sat as far back in his back

seat as he could. He looked almost as tortured as Julian did sometimes. I

never ceased to be amazed that rich people could be so miserable. Ava

ignored his behavior and talked the entire way there about what a great time

we would have. We pulled in the parking lot, and everyone outside the purple

velvet rope gaped at the beautiful throng entering the club.

Ava air kissed the bouncer on the lips, and we all strode in ahead of

the people who were dying for an invitation to go inside. The music was

definitely not disco, as seventies night implied, but everyone was dressed

appropriately for the theme. We were shown to a corner booth in a private

room upstairs for VIP. The walls in our room were padded in purple velvet. A

waiter entered the room to take the drink order.

Ava ordered water, as did I. I would have loved to try a cotton candy

martini like the one Savannah ordered, but I didn't dare. Millie would have had

my hide for being this place, and I knew how she felt about drinking. Though

she did turn a blind eye to Uncle Doug stocking the fridge with beer for his

fishing trips with Gabriel's dad…

I pushed the thought of Gabriel from my mind, and zoned out to the

punk rock music.

"Let's go dance," Ava suggested.

We walked down the stairs and stepped onto the dance floor. A hip hop song played next, and Walker was in his element. I was amazed at his movements. He was the best dancer I had ever seen. Ava and I spun each other and threw our hands up when we swayed to the music. Every few songs, a guy would bravely try to squeeze his way between Ava and I. She was shameless in declining their advances. Ethan shockingly joined in wedging his way between us, and the men Ava constantly fought off stepped away permanently. I guessed he could endure being close to me, at least for a little while, just to get to dance with his friends. I noticed that Sebastien and Savannah were so in tune with each others' bodies, the song playing must have been written for them. We herded upstairs for a drink to cool off after an hour or so, and by that time, Jade had become loud and drunk. I was her target.

"What do *you* have little girl? Julian loves *me*." She pointed at me and teetered from side to side. She suddenly put her head in her hands.

"Walker, take her home. She's had enough for tonight," Sebastien said.

"You don't tell me what." Her nonsensical words slurred, and she stood up in the booth. My face flamed when she turned to me. She rocked back and forth. "Arianna here is a fake. She is a *liar*." Jade tipped over and fell face first into the table. She sat up and laughed a pitiful laugh.

Walker lifted her upright and led her out. "Come on girl. We're going home," he told her.

"To Julian?" she asked.

"Yes. To Julian." Walker shook his head in pity and left.

"We need to be going, too. I'm tired," Savannah admitted.

I left Screwdriver, tingling with my first bar experience. I finally felt like an adult, but Julian weighed heavily on my mind. I wondered how grown up I'd feel once I got around him again.

Upon our return to Eden everyone gathered in the den for a movie. I begged off, claiming mock exhaustion, and laid in bed waiting for what seemed like forever to hear Ava's padded footsteps on her way to her room.

When she finally retired for the night, I threw on a bikini and slipped down to the pool. I wanted to see Julian again, but swore this to be the last of our late meetings. I was intimidated by Jade, there was no denying it. I wasn't sure how far she would eventually go to keep me away from him. I heard voices by the pool, and I crept into the shadows to eavesdrop. Peeking to see who was there, I saw Jade step into the pool and tousle Julian's hair.

"You know you want me Julian," she told him. Her drunken stupor had waned, but it was still apparent from her unsteady gait.

Her shiny, red one-piece revealed more than any of my bikinis. She was dark and tempting to any man who happened across her path.

"Jade, don't do this. You know nothing between us has changed,"

Julian said. I listened in silence. "You don't love me. You don't even really know me. You're drunk. All you see is the power I have and choose not to exploit."

"The night I left, you responded to me. I felt it." Jade's voice was pleading.

"I wanted you to take a vacation to get over this silly infatuation. This has gone on long enough. It's been nearly thirty years. Once maybe, I would have sacrificed companionship for love. It's not the case. Nothing changed. I never confessed feelings or desire for you."

"When did you become such a romantic? It's her isn't it? I saw it in your eyes. You are not seriously considering Arianna. No way. She's an innocent child." Jade laughed a humorless, empty laugh.

"My relationship with her is not on trial, nor is it your concern."

I stepped closer, trying to gain a better spot for listening. I promptly knocked over a potted plant, and sent it cracking all over the clean concrete. I fumbled with the plant idiotically, but I knew I was busted.

"My Arianna," he said brightly. "Taking a midnight swim?" Julian summoned me to him.

"I-I wasn't listening to you. I was going to bed. I'm sorry I interrupted." I walked quickly backwards in the direction of my room, but was halted by Jade's voice.

"My hat's off to you, Arianna. He's been discreet with his women all these years. Maybe they weren't so ready to put it all out there like you. You must have learned from the best." Jade pulled out of the pool, and glared at me. "I'm positive Ava would just *love* to hear that her precious niece is alone with Julian in the pool in the middle of the night," she said pointedly. She mumbled something that sounded like "whore" and sauntered into the house.

"Come here, love," Julian wagged his finger at me. I strode into the pool. "How much did you hear?" Julian prodded.

"Enough to know Jade has a thing for you. Why *don't* you have feelings for her? She's gorgeous and sophisticated and worldly…"

"And rude, and arrogant, and fake, and selfish," he finished. "She treats everyone as if they were beneath her. She gets whatever she wants whenever she wants it. She isn't used to hearing no, and that's the reason for her obsession with me. She wants what she can't have. I'm sure Ava told you Jade is power hungry. I encouraged her extended vacation because I thought she would find someone else. I was glad, though, that she was gone when you got here. I knew she wouldn't be particularly welcoming to you."

"Why would she save you though? She could have blackmailed you or exposed your secrets."

"She was intimidated by the size of our family, and taken with me. I don't completely trust her, but she isn't all evil villain. She's scared and lonely. Jade has never loved or been loved. She doesn't understand what it means. Neither did I, until you."

I pondered what he said for a minute. I knew what family was, what it meant to love. Millie and Doug's faces flashed in my mind, as did the portrait of my parents in my room. All of them loved me, and I loved all of them.

"Did you have fun tonight?" Julian inquired.

"I did," I confessed.

"Did Ava make sure no one laid a finger on you?"

"Not one." I smiled. I paused for a moment, and cocked my head to the side. I wanted to ask The Question. Was I the only one? "Have you ever been in love?"

"Once. Have you?"

My heart dropped. "I thought I was in love with someone, but it was unrequited."

My stomach flipped when I remembered I had forgotten all about Gabriel again. On the other hand, I didn't care. He said we were just friends, and left me no reason to remain in contact with him. Best friends usually moved on after high school. It was time for me to do the same. I needed to let go of my childish dream of Gabriel and I being more than friends. Right?

"I have a hard time believing that someone could turn you down." Julian turned down the corners of his mouth.

"Who were you in love with? What was she like?" I asked curiously, and at the same time not wanting to know.

"Let's see." Julian scratched his chin. Stubble had just began to grow along his sharp jaw line, I noticed. His dark sexiness just got sexier. Something I didn't think was possible. "She had long brown hair." He pulled two handfuls of hair from my back to my chest. "She had big green eyes, and freckles on her nose." He ran his fingertips across the bridge of my nose. "She was honest and innocent." He stared in my eyes. "She kissed me once, and I cannot stop thinking about her since she did. I think I might still be in love with her."

Julian pulled me to him. He kissed me upwards, from the base of my neck to the bottom of my ear. I grabbed his face and kissed him hungrily.

"Julian?" A deep voice called out.

We instantly jerked away from each other as if a lightning bolt hit the ground directly between us. Walker stood a few feet away, staring in shock.

"I didn't mean to interrupt anything, but Ava is on her way down. When we all took off to bed, I overheard Jade tell her you two were down here, and that you were... uh, doing what you were doing," Walker said.

"You mean swimming? Isn't that what we were doing?" I smiled at Walker and winked. My heart was thudding uncontrollably. "You were with us the whole time Walker." I shot him a pleading look.

"The whole time," Walker winked back, and did a cannonball into the pool. I swam away from Julian, and Walker picked me up and tossed me into the water. I emerged, sputtering and giggling just as Ava walked outside with Jade in all her exotic glory. Jade's self-righteous face fell when she saw that Walker had joined us. Nobody was compromising my virtue, obviously. The scene was just as it appeared. A few friends taking a late night dip in the pool on a hot summer night. Nope, there was nothing wrong with that at all.

"You brought me down here for me to see Arianna getting tossed into the pool by *Walker*? Again, *Walker*. Not *Julian*, but *Walker*. Jade, this is a new low. You are making up lies about her now? How dare you? You've had too much to drink. I *knew* you were lying. So? What am I supposed to be seeing? Why did you bring me down here?" Ava glowered at Jade.

Jade cut her eyes at me. "This is not over." She hurried inside.

"Julian, I can't take her anymore. I talked to Dave Mathis earlier this week. He set me up to look at the three properties a few days from now."

She turned to see my blank expression. I had no clue who Dave Mathis was.

"Do you want to go to Miami with me, Arianna? Julian is looking into buying some real estate down there. I need to get my hair cut anyway, and we can do some shopping. We can leave first thing tomorrow. Don't even worry about packing. We can buy anything we need on the road. What do you say?"

"Of course I want to go! I'll go to bed right now." I got out of the pool and grabbed a towel to dry off. I gave Ava a quick kiss on the cheek. "Goodnight." I threw up my hand to Julian and Walker and ran up to my room. I shut the door behind me and leaned my back to it. I slid down to the floor with a sigh of relief. Thank God Walker had the sense to warn us. I didn't want to dream up all the ways Ava would slaughter Julian if she found us together alone.

I decided to pack a few things, even though Ava told me not to. I pulled out my duffel bag I had brought from home. I was putting my toothbrush in the side compartment when my hands touched something that crinkled. I pulled out the note Gabriel gave me the night before I left.

I sat on my knees in the floor, and gazed at his spidery handwriting spelling out my name on the outside of the card. The outside of the envelope had a picture of a pretty little bird and scrolling letters that spelled out "Congratulations". I tossed the note aside, my final purging of the boy who didn't love me back. I went to bed without thinking of Gabriel again.

My room was void of clocks (as was the entire house), so I didn't have a guideline to a particular time to wake up. Who would set a clock if you have an infinite number of days? What purpose would time serve? Time was a man-made concept to make sure everything was accomplished when it needed to be. But here, there was really nothing to accomplish that had time constraints. Even a delivery was done on the Keepers' own time. They all had told me about stopping to see the sights of whatever city they were in before visiting Julian's friends and dropping off the vials. There was no rush for anything, especially in Eden. Evenings ran through the night, and most mornings didn't begin until after noon.

I woke up earlier than usual, my internal clock knowing I needed to be up and about. I greeted everyone, minus Jade, in the den. Julian's mood was brooding. His face was tumultuous, and I sensed that I wanted to leave him probably as much as he wanted me to leave. I would miss him, yes, but I wanted to go to Miami very badly.

"Here she is. Ready?" Ava asked.

"I brought a carry-on," I told her, holding up my bag.

Savannah stepped forward. "I would love to go. I wanted to spend some time with you, but I can't bear to leave Sebastien again so soon and tag along." Savannah's eyes locked with Sebastien's, and it made my chest hurt to see how in love they were.

"I'll be back in a few days," I assured her with a pointed glance at Julian.

"I speak for everyone when I say you will be missed. Hurry home." Ethan touched my shoulder in a big brother gesture, but somehow it felt more intimate.

I almost dropped dead at his familiarity. No doubt Walker relayed the previous night's events to his friend. There was no question in anyone's eyes as to the current state between Julian and I. Ethan must have felt sorry for me at that point. It was easy to see why he had treated me like a pariah. Julian was playing games, or better yet, acting like Jade. Wanting what he couldn't ever have. It only took one look at the other Keepers to see that I was ugly. Only Ava seemed not to have a firm grasp on my plainness.

"Memento Mori, Arianna." Julian slid a cold, hard object between my fingers. It was my vial. I was aghast at how he obtained it. I was positive I left it in my bathroom the night before. That meant he must have entered my room sometime during the night. I was humiliated at the thought of him seeing me in my most vulnerable state. I had a horrible habit of drooling on my pillowcase and talking loudly in my sleep. Millie alerted me to it countless times.

My vial's picture of the tree and water was a detail off from any of the others. Each one displayed a specific embossing on the lid. I noticed Ava's vial boasted an elaborate detail of the zodiac signs when she wore it over her blouse at the restaurant. I vaguely recalled my father's having a map of the world as one continent, which jarred my mind to the day Ava told me about the Fountain originating in biblical Eden.

I searched Julian's face. It appeared darker and far more torrid than usual.

"Let's hit the road." She nodded to her BMW waiting outside. "See you later," Ava told my new family. "Memento Mori."

Ava and I rode in her car, and she relayed the message that mine would be fetched from Ellaville that weekend by Walker, and would await me when we returned. I worried about him introducing himself to Millie; I didn't want her to think I was living with some guy. On second thought, I brought my only car key from Ellaville to Eden. Walker was used to sneaking around after all, so I figured there was only the slightest chance his path would cross with Millie's or Uncle Doug's.

We made our way along the Florida coastline, stopping for the night in a town called St. Petersburg. We stayed in a pretty nice hotel, but Ava assured me that it was no match for the one booked in Miami.

We arrived at our destination the following evening, and we checked into a beachfront hotel famous for its name and celebrity clientele. The hotel was not even half as nice as the comforts of Eden, but it was a palace compared to my house in Ellaville. The only luxuries offered there that Eden lacked were room service and valet. Ava and I chose to stay in and rest after our long drive. We ate the pasta room service brought us and snuggled up in terrycloth robes also provided with our lavish suite.

We met with Dave Mathis the next afternoon and looked at the properties Julian selected. Dave was a balding, middle-aged man who was as nice as could be. The first house he showed us was out of the question because it didn't have a fireplace. I wondered how many times it would actually be cold enough to use a fireplace in Miami, but I remained quiet. I didn't care for it either, it was too white. The walls, floors, countertops, rugs- they were all the color of snow. I was terrified of ruining the carpet just by stepping into it. I shuddered when I imagined having to eat in a place the color of a sheet of notebook paper. One speck of food would stick out like a sore thumb in the pristine house. I laughed to myself thinking that *I* was the speck of food. Compared to everyone else in Eden, I was a big hunk of chocolate cake on an otherwise flawlessly white canvas.

The second house had a castle-like turret in the front. It wasn't as nice as the white house, but I liked it much better. Ava told Mr. Mathis no to the second house too, because she said Julian would hate the floors. Since Julian never left Eden, it seemed silly to not purchase a house because the floors, which Julian would never see, weren't up to his standards. At this rate, we were going to be in Miami a long, long time.

The final house was absolutely breathtaking. It was a ways outside Miami, but it was close enough to enjoy all the perks of city life while maintaining the privacy of suburbia. Later, I would realize it was just a few feet from Miami compared to the multiple road trips I had to endure just to eat out or catch a movie and at the same time maintain the imperative privacy of Eden.

As soon as we entered the drive of the third house, I knew Ava would give it an instant no. The picture she had made it look much, much larger. Even so, I fell in love at first sight with the home. It was cozy inside, with bright, red and white gingham accents in the living room, and a sunflower yellow kitchen. It was somewhere I could imagine Millie baking fresh cookies. I wandered upstairs, and found a large bedroom decorated in green toile. My favorite part of the house was a window seat that overlooked a bay. It was a cloudy day, and I curled up in the seat and let my mind wander while Ava inspected the house.

"Arianna, are you ready? This house is ridiculously small, and the person who shot the pictures of it should be hung for how deceitful they were."

Ava and Dave walked into the room and found me perched by the window.

"I really like this house," I told them. "I know it's not good enough for Julian, but I love it here. It feels like home to me."

Ava smiled. "Well then, we'll see what we can do."

I knew she was just trying to pacify me; I had no business offering my opinion about real estate anyway. Ava took a few pictures of more houses that Dave offered, and we returned to the hotel.

The next morning Ava visited her favorite hairdresser, a flamboyant man who was well-dressed and handsome. He wore a paisley print shirt, and his hair was jet black with white chunks. The salon was all metallic and futuristic inside.

A short, cherry red-haired girl came to the chair I was perched in beside Ava. "So, what are we doing to you today?" She wrapped me in a black silk smock.

I looked at Ava for guidance. "Do you want your hair done too?" Ava asked me.

"What do you think?" I hadn't cut my hair since the Ellaville barber scalped me in the third grade. Millie trimmed my hair every few months, but beyond that, amazing hairstyles were elusive things found only in celebrity gossip magazines.

"I think you should style your hair however you want, but I think you're perfect just like you are," Ava copped out.

I stared in the mirror for a long time. The red-haired girl waited patiently, no doubt she knew from Ava's regular stylist's experience that Ava's tip would pay her rent for months.

"Be creative." I threw all caution to the pair of silver scissors the stylist wielded.

She made small talk while examining my head from all angles. The gesture was making me extremely nervous. "My name is Lauren. Do you live in Miami?"

Lauren and I gossiped back and forth along with Ava and her stylist. I learned his name was Patrick, and he gushed every detail of his fast life. Lauren and Patrick regaled us with stories of the Miami nightlife, and after the initial nervousness, I didn't even dwell on what she was doing to my hair. Lauren turned my chair away from the mirror for my blowout, so the final product was a complete surprise.

I closed my eyes tight, and opened when I faced the mirror to see myself. My hair was a little above the middle of my back, and had been chemically lightened to the same pale blond color as Ava's. A few blue strands peeked out from beneath my ear. I looked sophisticated and worldly. I was one step closer to feeling like I belonged in Ava's life.

"I love it!" I exclaimed.

"Your hair is perfect! I want mine like that," Ava whined and fluffed her pin straight bob. Sometimes she sounded about as old as she looked. On the other hand, she mostly sounded like a cool version of a mom.

As predicted, she left ridiculously humongous tips for Patrick and Lauren and promised to return soon.

We hit Saks at Dadeland Mall; Ava declared beforehand that we could shop until our bags were too heavy to carry. We filled at least ten bags with an assortment of clothes, shoes, jewelry, and anything else that was beautiful we found and wanted.

I finished the day for the second time since my vacation with Ava, with my belly full of fresh seafood.

The next day, we spent our time on the crowded and starlet filled Miami Beach. Ava was approached more than once by men. Some of them claimed to be producers, or actors- any profession they deemed stimulating enough to attract Ava's attention.

She waved them all off, claiming an impending marriage. I laughed every time, secretly envisioning Doug and Ava at the altar.

We stayed a few more days, living life on the sun-filled beaches I never tired of. We did, in fact, shop until our trunk nearly burst with all the trinkets we stuffed inside. I experienced my first day at a spa, and I fell instantly in love with all the pampering. I had never felt so clean and relaxed. Ava talked me into parasailing, and promised scuba diving in the Caribbean whenever I gave the word.

The last day, over a room service breakfast of kiwi and bacon (Ava's odd choice), we opted to return to Eden on a whim.

The truth was, I missed everyone, especially Julian. We checked out of the hotel and jumped into Ava's car. It should have been stifling hot in the summer Florida sun, but the valet had cooled it before we entered. I thought I'd never grow tired of or used to the opulence of my new life.

We hit the road, stopping only for the night in the same hotel in as we did on the way down there. I was giddy to return to Eden, especially because I hadn't spoken to or heard from any of them the entire time we were gone.

Ava's cell never rang once. Ava muttered something about not being a fan of telephones when I probed her for news from Panacea. In turn, I told her I was hurt no one seemed to miss us. I must have harassed the information out of her, because she admitted she kept her phone on silent the whole time.

"I'm sorry, Arianna. I didn't mean for you to think no one cared about us. I'm just being selfish. I knew when we got back to Eden, we wouldn't have much time for just the two of us. This is exactly what drove Rose away. I expected her to always allow me to monopolize her time. It's just that I don't have anyone else I really care about. You have Millie and Doug, but I only have you."

I felt horrible to have even brought up Eden. "Oh, Ava! I didn't mean that! I was just curious why nobody even checked on us." *Well, why Julian hadn't checked on us anyway.* "It doesn't make me feel really great about you going on deliveries either, if no one knows if you're okay or not."

"I didn't mean to put a guilt trip on you, honey. I'm very overbearing at times, and I have to check myself. Julian has called me repeatedly, and I'm sure he's probably gathering an army to find us by now."

My heart leapt at the news. *He called! He called!*

I bounded from the car when we pulled into the cobblestone drive. I noticed my car parked next to the others, my Georgia license plate sticking out like a sore thumb. My car looked at home here, a sharp contrast to it being parked outside our tumble-down house in Ellaville.

I raced inside and was greeted by silence. It was pretty late when we arrived, but everyone normally stayed up all hours of the night.

"Glad to be back to all this silence?" Ava asked me sarcastically. She laughed. "This is a nice welcome. Where's my marching band?" Her voice echoed in the room.

"I'll go get the bags," I offered.

"No, the guys enjoy chivalry. Julian would have a fit if I allowed you to lift a finger. Let's get into our jammies and meet me down here for a midnight snack. There has to be something left from dinner. I'm starving."

I dragged upstairs, and flipped on the light in my closet. I emptied the contents of one of my drawers. All my comfy clothes were still in Ava's trunk. I regretted not listening to her about buying whatever I needed along the way. I opened the dreaded lingerie drawer Ava and Savannah loaded for me. I only opened it once before, when I was poking through all my new things. I'd slammed it shut when I realized the tiny bits of silk and lace inside were meant to clothe me.

I chose the most modest piece, a satin periwinkle nightgown that was more of a slip than something to sleep in. *Good thing no one's up*, I thought. I shrugged on a matching gauzy wrapper that covered absolutely nothing, but made me feel less self-conscious all the same.

I crept down to the kitchen, but Ava wasn't there. I heard voices in the den, so I poked my head into the doorway to see if Ava was in there waiting for me. All of the residents of Eden were gathered inside. I immediately noticed Julian sitting down in all his dark glory. He was leaning forward, his folded hands limply hanging between his long legs. His eyes snapped up to meet mine when he heard me enter. A new resident that I didn't immediately recognize was present, one whom I learned later Jade lured there under false pretenses.

Abandoning the insecurity of my attire, I strode into the room.

"Hello, Gabriel."

UNEXPECTED

Gabriel stood when I entered the room. "You. Cut. Your. Hair." He ground out the words.

I pulled a piece of my hair toward my face. It seemed like the thing to do, but in hindsight, it hardly mattered. "What difference does my hair make? What are you even doing here?" I asked in shock.

"You promised me…" he started, but stopped short to gape in horror at my attire. "What are you *wearing*!? You dress like *that* in front of these, these, men?" he shot back. "You don't even *look* the same. You've been gone for almost two months without a word. Do you even care how worried we all were? Millie's been out of her mind. All this time you've been here," he lifted his hands, and gestured to the fresco on the ceiling, "with these people."

"How did you know how to find me anyway?" I demanded. I tried to think of anything, *anything* to take the focus off me.

Jade cackled with laughter, and Gabriel shot a finger at her. "She brought me here. She told me she would bring me to you."

"So you skip town with any woman at the first mention of some girl's name?" I accused.

"Yes. *Your* name. How could you have changed so much?" Gabriel marveled, his brown eyes flashing with rage.

"Me? What about you? Since when did you trade your Converse for Italian leather?" I gestured to his shoes, definitely not something he bought in Ellaville.

"Apparently, this is what you like. Your boyfriend over here looks jealous." Gabriel motioned to Julian.

Julian stood abruptly, looking as if he were about to burst with anger. "Who is this *boy*, Arianna?"

Ava blinked, and then she saw it. They all saw what we had tried so hard to conceal, mostly from each other. We were in love. The nightgown aside, I felt as if I were naked in front of them all. Gabriel had seen my hidden feelings right off the bat. Of course Gabriel had seen.

"Oh, God, Julian. No. You couldn't possibly, she is my *niece*. She is Rose's *daughter*." Ava wrung her hands.

"He's my-my best friend," I sputtered.

"Oh, we're putting labels on it now." Gabriel's tone had gone from an angry, accusing hiss to an irate howl. "You *knew* I loved you. I showed you every day. Did you even read the card I gave you?" His voice broke.

"No, I didn't read it. You let me go. You wanted me to come here." I choked up along with him, unable to speak.

"Get out of my house," Julian ground out.

"Fine," Gabriel snapped. "Go get your things, Arianna. Let's go."

"Like hell she will! She's not going anywhere," Julian roared.

"I don't want to go with you, Gabriel. I want to stay here with Ava," I protested.

"Are you kidding me? Again, do you even *care* how upset Millie is? Doug wants to notify the authorities. We've all been out of our minds worrying about you. Stop messing around, and come on."

"I'm not leaving with you. I like my life here. Why don't you just stay with me. I promise I'll call Millie and Doug right now," I swore.

"That is out of the question. Gabriel cannot stay here," Julian intervened.

Gabriel drew up to his full six-foot-two inch height and stood nose to nose with Julian. Neither of them blinked, and none of the rest of us breathed.

"I'll go, but I'll be back. I'm sure everyone will want to know all about what you're hiding. I will stop at nothing to make sure the entire world hears about your magic water."

Julian started toward us, but stopped in his tracks at the revelation of Gabriel's knowledge. Gabriel could have knocked him over with one finger at that point. Julian stared at Jade, expressionless. "You didn't. You wouldn't have."

"How quickly your princess falls from grace. Don't look at me. You know better," Jade said smugly. "Guess she kept in touch more than they are letting on." Her sugar-coated tone suddenly became sour. "Stop this nonsense, Julian. Kick them both out."

The pieces of the puzzle began to put themselves together in my head. "This was your plan all along," I sputtered. "You went to my home and brought Gabriel here to make Julian angry. For what? Did you think Julian would run into your arms?" I barked through angry tears.

"How did you know about the water?" Julian demanded from Gabriel.

Gabriel didn't back down. "Ava sent a vial of it to Arianna just before she left to come here. We got curious. Arianna left and never called except once to tell Millie she arrived safely. I almost let your little secret slip then." Gabriel turned to me. "Jade came and asked if I wanted to see you. She said you sent her to bring me to you. We pulled in just a few hours before you and Ava got here. Jade told me you were out and would be back sometime this week. She told everyone here that I was her chosen one, or something like that. I started to worry, but I didn't ask any questions until I saw you." He steered the conversation to quietly include only the two of us. "I didn't mean to cause trouble. I just wanted to see you." Gabriel's eyes were sincere. "Come home," he pleaded.

I pieced together snippets of the argument flying all around. Jade went to Ellaville to do an in-person background check to dig up dirt on me to make me less appealing to Julian. She got suspicious when she saw Gabriel at my house every day and confronted him after I left. She must have returned to Eden to tell Julian she had chosen someone to live with her, which was what she knew he wanted so she would finally leave him alone. She lured Gabriel here by telling him she would bring him to me. She assumed that once we were reunited, maybe Julian would see that he didn't stand a chance. Jade had done her homework alright. She just finished telling Julian about our night at prom with more than a few intimate embellishments.

Julian's face was so purple, I thought he would surely explode. I ignored his fierce expression, and begged. "Please let Gabriel stay, Julian. I'm sorry all of this happened, but he is my family. I won't stay without him. I can't. Where he goes I go. My home is his home." I did like my life in Eden, but I couldn't let Gabriel go again. He came for me, and I wouldn't stay without him. He was my family. The only one I knew before I came.

Silence filled the room. Even Walker didn't have anything humorous to say to lighten the mood. Ethan stepped forward and said the words Julian couldn't. "Come on Gabriel, let me show you to your room."

I found out later on that Gabriel was staying downstairs, as far as possible from me. His room was far less elaborate than anyone else's. I remembered thinking how small the bedroom was in comparison to all the others when Ava took me on my initial tour. Compared to the rest, he might as well have slept on a rock. There were plenty of beautiful unused rooms upstairs, but Julian childishly refused to let Gabriel and I sleep on the same floor of the house.

Gabriel gaped at the invitation. He took my hand in his and squeezed it tight. "I don't want to be here Arianna," he said seriously, his big brown eyes that so often reminded me of a lost puppy were wide with indignation. "I am only staying until you come to your senses and come back to Ellaville with me."

I snatched my hand from his, and hugged him close. "Thank you Gabriel. This means so much to me."

Ethan led him from the den, and the room was clothed in stunned silence. Julian averted his gaze, refusing to meet my eyes. His dark demeanor turned somber, as though the whole time he had expected the events of the night to turn in the atomic direction they had.

"Goodnight," I said lamely, to anyone who was listening.

I was so tired I don't remember my head hitting the pillow. I was finally at peace. My archangel was nearby.

I awoke late the following afternoon. My bleary eyes took a moment to register the lavish surroundings. Eden. I was back in Eden. Gabriel was in Eden. *Gabriel was in Eden!*

I threw back the covers, and raced downstairs. He was in the kitchen, sitting at the breakfast bar, speaking in hushed voices with Ava, Savannah, and Sebastien.

"You're still here!" I squealed. I ran across the kitchen and hugged him, almost knocking over his cup of coffee.

"I think we should leave for the afternoon," Ava told me. "We're glad Gabriel has come to join us, but I'm afraid of Julian's reaction to him being here. This goes against every rule we have. Technically Jade chose him, but she tricked him into coming, and in doing so she put all of us in danger. Henry will have a field day with this."

"Maybe we *should* go back." I dropped my head.

"If anyone leaves, it will be Jade. Neither you nor Gabriel holds any responsibility in this mess. No one is holding you accountable." Sebastien stood and pushed his chair in. "I spoke with Julian briefly, and though he is not thrilled with the relationship you and Gabriel share, he doesn't blame either of you for last night. In fact, he begged me to reassure you, Arianna, that this is still your home as long as you choose for it to be."

Walker listened at the doorway. He came to me and patted my shoulder. "We're your family too, and we stick by our family. You haven't done anything wrong. We love you, and we stand behind you. As for you, Gabriel, anyone who captures such loyalty from our Arianna must be deserving indeed. We welcome you."

I was blown away by his gallant speech. His light green eyes danced as he smiled at me.

"Thank you. I love you too." I was so proud to have Gabriel with me.

Gabriel smiled at the occupants of the kitchen. "I can only hope to live up to the expectations you have for me. My only happiness in this world comes from Arianna. She is the reason I live. To make her happy and protect her."

"As do we all." Savannah stood and grinned. Ava and Sebastien followed suit.

"I suppose we need to visit the car dealership before we go to lunch. You'll need a car. The transportation of choice, of course," she said referring to our fleet of Beamers. "Welcome home, Gabriel. Arianna's family is our family. We take care of each other," Ava said.

"Nononono. I don't need a car. I did just fine without one for this long. I won't accept anything more than your hospitality," Gabriel told them. "And maybe some lunch. I'm hungry." He patted his stomach. "By the time Arianna wakes up, you are probably all half-dead with starvation."

Everyone smiled and we went to get ready. Upon Gabriel's insistence, I called Millie before we left for lunch at a diner. She wasn't angry, just worried. I promised to call every day and check in. I changed from my gauzy nightgown, but I chose my least favorite pair of plain shorts and an old shirt. I felt so much at home with Gabriel, I abandoned the need to dress and act as sophisticated as the rest of the occupants of Eden.

Everyone was instantly charmed with Gabriel's easy wit and striking good looks. He blended in easily with the Keepers of such a Fountain, but I still felt like the ugly duckling. Ethan joined us for lunch too, and Walker and Gabriel entered into a playful banter analyzing who knew more about pop culture.

Our waitress was a friendly twenty-something who looked like she was about to give birth any moment. Savannah asked her how far along she was, and she said her due date was only a few days away. The waitress asked

168

if she had any children, and Savannah looked like she was about to cry.

"No. I don't have any."

Sebastien squeezed her hand, and looked almost as sad as she did.

"Do you *want* kids?" I asked them.

"More than anything," Sebastien replied.

"I know Julian has all these self-imposed restrictions, but he wouldn't really make you guys leave," I protested.

"Julian wouldn't but Henry would," Walker interjected.

Sebastien explained for Gabriel's sake. "Henry keeps close tabs on all the comings and goings of Eden. He owns almost as much stake in the property as Julian. Julian may be intimidating at times, but he is nothing compared to Henry. Henry is as cold-blooded and calculating as they come. Truth be told, he is the male equivalent of Jade, but on a much larger scale. He went after your parents full fury, but Julian is the one who stopped him from hurting them after they left. None of us know what was done, but Henry hasn't been the same since. He would never in a million years hesitate to throw us out on the streets if Savannah was pregnant."

I was suddenly angry. There were no better suited parents in the world. Savannah and Sebastien were the halves of each others' whole. They barely took their eyes off each other. Sebastien was doting, to say the least. I regularly found him rubbing her back, or bringing her something to drink, or snuggling with her on the couch watching a chick flick. He was intensely protective of her, and I was sure he would give even the cruelest man in the world a run for his money if he dared to touch his tiny blond doll.

"There has to be another way! You could run! Why don't you leave?" I thought about how romantic it all was. I wished then and there I loved someone enough to run away with them and throw all caution to the wind.

"Do you think we haven't thought of everything? I can give her anything but that. Having a child is the one thing the Fount-" Sebastien cleared his throat when he looked at Gabriel and changed gears, "Savannah would have the safest pregnancy in the world. But. It is also the only thing that would require one of us to seek medical attention. Your mother had you almost twenty years ago, and things were much different then. With all the blood tests they do now, there is no telling what they would find in her system because of the water she has already ingested.

"I even offered to sacrifice my share of Eden, but obviously that is not an option." He raked his fingers over his cropped brown hair.

I smiled sadly as I watched her lay her head on his shoulder.

"So, are you guys married?" Gabriel asked. He tried to appear nonchalant, but I knew his mind was whirring with questions about life-giving water, blood tests, and what could possibly show up in Savannah's system.

Ava told me before I met them that Savannah was simply his girlfriend but it seemed inconceivable that two people so in love would not have tied the knot in all the years they had been together.

Sebastien laughed. "Yes, we're married. We didn't want to scare you guys off, that's why we stuck to the girlfriend/boyfriend thing. We know we look too young be married. After we dated for six months, we decided to go to the mountains one fall morning, and we rented a cabin. I figured if she could accept all the secrets that surrounded me, she could endure anything life threw our way. We went hiking, and I dropped to one knee in the middle of the forest. We said our vows in front of a minister in his picturesque church with only his wife as a witness."

"It was so pretty, Arianna. I have a few snapshots the minister's wife took," Savannah said. "I'll show them to you. I got married in a simple white dress we bought from a vintage shop. It was perfect."

She never took her eyes off Sebastien while she talked about it. He kissed her on the top of her head, but he flexed his hand, and I could see the anger at their un-justice in his eyes. Sure, the wedding sounded great and all, but they were going to have all their dreams come true if I had to sacrifice myself to make it happen.

I left the diner feeling depressed about the situation. Why would you want to live that way? If everyone dictated your every move, what was the point in it all?

Neither Jade nor Julian ventured downstairs all day. After lunch I took Gabriel for a ride on my jet ski and showed off my new skills. He took a turn, and I was amazed by how fast he learned. He wasn't as good as Julian, but he did exceptionally well for a rookie.

I went to take Julian a plate of food for dinner, since I knew he hadn't eaten. It was really just an excuse to see for myself how mad he was about Gabriel.

"Julian?" I whispered after several knocks. I turned the handle, and it opened easily.

He lay sleeping in a pool of moonlight. His dark demeanor held more anguish than I thought a human could endure. He was more beautiful when he slept than when he was awake, except that the blue of his eyes could not be seen. He stirred.

"Do you want something to eat?" I asked.

"Why are you in here? Please leave. Now. I don't need your pity."

"What's wrong? Why are you angry with me? If this is about Gabriel, you have it all wrong. You don't know anything."

Julian touched my face. "Go to bed. It's late. You have no business being in my room."

"I want to be here." I slid onto the covers next to him. "I missed you all day."

"Arianna, I mean no disrespect to you, but please, leave."

I rolled to face him. "If I don't?"

Julian smiled and his dimples deepened. There was something else, though. His smile didn't quite reach his eyes. He lunged for me and kissed me, grinding his mouth into mine. He bit my lower lip so hard I tasted blood.

"Julian, you're hurting me," I cried. I writhed in his bed, under his strength.

"What did you mean coming here and getting into my bed? You have no idea about the way the world works. I am a man, and you are just a child. Get out, Arianna. *I mean it!*" he roared.

I was playing with fire, and I knew when the lit tip of the match was drawing too close to my fingers. I literally ran. I slammed the door behind me, and raced into the comfort of privacy in my room. I took a long, hot bath, contemplating the severity of the situation at hand. I didn't think Gabriel was in imminent danger, but I did understand that by visiting Julian I was making the situation worse.

Thunder rumbled in the distance, and lightning cast jagged shadows across the floor. I dragged the corner table closer to my bed. Flipping on the lamp, I opened a book I discovered in the library. When we were in Miami, Ava hounded me to read it and I quickly lost myself in the pages that night. I missed the husky sound of Julian's velvet voice reading to me, candlelight flickering off his long dark hair. I remembered the way he kissed me for the first time in my room, just a few feet away from me.

A soft knock and the turn of my door handle pulled me from Julian's arms and back to reality. I jumped nearly a foot off the bed.

Gabriel appeared in the doorway. "Thank God. I already woke up

Ethan trying to find your bedroom. How do you find your way around? I thought I'd never get to the right room. I was scared to death I'd wake up Julian."

I already took care of that, I thought.

I patted the bed, and Gabriel curled up next to me. He had a thin frame, but he was so tall, he nearly took up the whole bed. I rolled to one side to make room and propped up my head on my elbow. "You couldn't sleep either?"

"I wanted to see you alone." He held up a piece of my blue hair. We both laughed. "I guess I can get used to this."

"Why didn't you want me to cut my hair by the way? I forgot I promised you I wouldn't. If I had known you would be so upset I wouldn't have done it."

"You are the only girl I know that is completely real. You are who you are, and you don't try to act any certain way to impress anyone. I guess I figured your hair was part of your purity. I liked it long and wild. I guess I expected too much." I opened my mouth to speak, but he waved a hand to convey he wasn't done.

"I have always put you on a pedestal. My ideals of you were not far from reality. You are the most perfect person alive to me. I don't want to see you tainted by anyone's opinion of how you should be. I want you to be my Arianna all the time." He twirled my now blond and blue hair in his hands. The mix of the colors swirled together like that made it look like a piece of bright candy. His face grew suddenly serious, and I felt my stomach flip, knowing what was coming next. I gulped.

"What is Julian to you?"

I contemplated my words carefully before I spoke. "He became a good friend to me, but he has obviously kept his distance from all of us since you got here. I don't understand why he's so attached to me, but to be honest, I'm equally attached to him." I hung my head, and glanced up to gauge his reaction.

"As what? A friend? More?" Gabriel's eyes searched mine, and he visibly braced himself.

I chose my words carefully. I wanted to tell him the truth, but I didn't want to hurt him. "A kindred spirit. We both seem to be searching for something, but neither of us have figured out what it is. I care a lot about Julian, but my fear is that his feelings are deeper. Much deeper. He's really... *into* me. I wanted to stay here, but I was apprehensive without you being here too."

He knew there was more   to the story than I was telling him. "You *cannot* get serious about Julian. This house, the money... it's all his."

"So I'm not good enough for him?" His feelings mirrored mine, but they still hurt. I knew I was out of my league playing around with Julian.

"That is *not* what I said. He's just very different from you. Julian is cold and dark and mean. I refuse to believe you could have feelings for someone like him."

"I came here for you, and I'm staying here for Ava. Julian is not a major part of my life right now."

I hated being put on trial. As vehemently as I wanted to deny him, Julian was always somewhere in my thoughts. I didn't want to discuss Julian with Gabriel. It made me feel low, like I was being unfaithful to Julian. When I was with Julian, I felt unfaithful to Gabriel.

I should be so lucky to have either one of them really want me, I thought. *Gabriel is just comfortable with you, and you're just a new toy to Julian*, I told myself.

"It's really late. Do you need me to show you how to get back to your room?" I asked.

"I don't want to leave you. I missed you so much. Please let me stay with you tonight," Gabriel begged.

I crumpled inside. I could never turn down Gabriel. I pressed his face to my chest, and began humming an old song Millie sang to me as a child. I will never know which one of us fell prey to sleep first. I held Gabriel tight all night long.

Ava barged in sometime after noon, and we woke up lazily. I stretched and yawned. Gabriel must have been tired, I'd bet this was the first time he'd ever slept this late. I wasn't afraid of being caught with Gabriel. Ava held no judgment about things like that. In my mind, I figured she would much rather discover me sleeping with Gabriel than Julian. I welcomed her appearance with a sleepy grin.

"Good morning my angels. Would you like to race with us today? Walker will stand guard while we face off." Ava slashed an invisible sword. "Fight to the death on jet skis." She laughed.

"Right now?" I asked.

"As soon as you're up and about, meet us at the dock. We will explain the rules."

DUEL

Gabriel and I readily accepted the challenge. I took Gabriel downstairs to his room so he could change, and I grabbed two energy drinks out of the fridge.

Everyone (save Walker and Julian) was out at the dock. Eight jet skis were tied down, and the boat was moved onto the beach. The sun was bright, the sky cloudless.

"Okay, here are the rules." Ava held a piece of paper high enough for all of us to see. "We race in teams of two, and the winner advances to the next round. Ethan and Sebastien set up ten anchored floating markers beginning on each side of the dock." She gestured to the red and white striped buoys lined up in the water. "Each person must navigate between the buoys. You are not allowed to skip a marker, or you are disqualified. At the last marker, circle around and make your way back around the markers. The first one back to the dock moves to the next round." That seemed easy enough. I nodded my comprehension.

"The markers are progressively closer together. The last two are extremely hard to pass through and maintain your speed at the same time. This paper is the lineup. Ladies first, of course. I'll be racing first against Savannah.

" These are the stakes: the winner gets one request from any person in the house. No matter what is asked, if you are chosen to fulfill it, you must comply. Got it?"

"Got it," Gabriel and I answered in unison.

Julian ambled out to the dock to join the rest of us. He wore dark gray shorts, and the sun gleamed off his muscular chest. He walked slowly. There was purpose in his arrogant gait. I was petrified. The stakes had just risen.

"Do you have room for one more?" he asked.

"Of course," Ethan replied. He looked unsure, but he wasn't about to argue with Julian.

We all watched Julian apprehensively, but he continued to stare directly at Gabriel. I moved in front of him as if to guard him from the sadistic things Julian had in mind for him.

Ava and Savannah mounted their jet skis on their respective sides of the dock. Savannah looked so tiny and childlike. Her blond ringlets shone in the sunshine. Ava handed me a checkered flag. "You do the honors."

I stood at the end of the dock and held the flag high in the air. "Go!" I dropped the flag, and the girls took off in a flash.

From the beginning, it was no contest. Ava won easily. Savannah was slow and careful not to miss any markers, while Ava was confident and fast.

Sebastien helped Savannah onto the deck. "Good job, baby." He kissed her forehead.

"Yeah, yeah. Ava's too tough for me, besides it makes me queasy being on those things." Savannah smiled.

Ethan held up the paper. "Arianna, you're next and then Jade will match up with the winner."

I prayed a silent prayer I wouldn't win so I wouldn't have to face off with Jade. At the same time, I wanted to give it my best effort. I slung one leg over my jet ski, and turned the key. Ava winked at me from across the dock. Savannah held the flag high.

Savannah's big blue eyes filled with excitement. "Go!"

I twisted the handlebar that controlled the throttle as hard as I could. The first few markers were a breeze. Ava and I were neck in neck. The further the markers, the closer and more dangerous they became. I slowed down to keep from flipping when I passed through the last two. Ava's speed never faltered, and she hit the finish line while I still had two more markers to pass through.

Gabriel helped me up, and spun me around. "If Ava here wasn't such a show off, maybe you would have a chance," he grinned.

Ava pinched his arm. "Show off huh? You just wait until the last round. I'll show you show off," she laughed.

"Are you last?" I asked Gabriel. I took the sheet from Ethan. "Yep. Jade's next, then Ethan, Sebastien, Julian…" My voice trailed off. Oh, no. I knew where this was going.

"I will compete in the last round," Julian said. "I hold a partcular interest in the game." He turned up the corners of his mouth diabolically. Great.

"Go!"

I heard Savannah yell, and two jet skis pelted me with sea spray. Ava and Jade were moving at the same speed, in complete sync. The entire race appeared choreographed. It wasn't until they were a few yards away when we could clearly tell who was the victor.

Ava slammed into the dock, and raised her fists. "Whew." Jade bumped the dock a split second after Ava. The jet ski hit the dock so hard it shook. "Good game girl. Close, but you have a long way to go." Ethan threw Ava a high five.

Jade actually smiled. "We'll see next time. I demand a rematch."

"You ought to be all worn out by now, Ava. Take it easy on me," Ethan said.

"You wish," Ava called back.   "Let's see what you got. Stop delaying the inevitable. I'm going to slaughter you. Let's get on with it."

Ethan miscalculated, and skipped the last marker. He swung out too far and passed the last marker by what appeared to be millimeters. Ava spotted his mistake instantly and drove back up to the dock at the speed of a snail. She was standing up pumping her fist in the air while doing a little dance, all the while holding on to rev the engine, creeping up in a crawl.

Ethan pulled in ahead of her. "You won by default. I had you and you know it."

"What? I can't hear for all your sore losing," Ava drawled jokingly.

"Are you having fun?" I asked Gabriel. I was having such a great time, I hadn't spoken a word. My stomach clenched in each race, nervously awaiting the outcome.

"Yeah. I just can't wait to see who I'm up against. Ava's tough. I'm nowhere near as good as she is."

I knew who Gabriel was up against. He hadn't seen Julian race. Julian had his arms crossed, his eyes boring holes in Gabriel's loathed head.

Sebastien sat down, and Savannah leaned down to kiss him. "For luck." I envied their easy ways of reassuring their love for one another.

Savannah's luck must have rubbed off, because Ava flipped. I ran so close the edge of the dock, I almost fell in. Ava popped her head out of the water, and Sebastien pulled next to her and helped her back on. She remounted and allowed Sebastien to go on and win the race.

"That was the nicest thing I've ever seen," I said to Savannah.

"He knows what would happen if he left my best friend to help herself back up. He won fair and square. There would be no point in winning if it meant becoming less of a gentleman."

Savannah was a lucky, lucky girl. She expected nothing less than perfection from one of the only men perfect enough to offer it. They were so old- fashioned sometimes.

"You're up rookie," Sebastien called to Gabriel.

My palms were sweaty. Savannah dropped the flag, and they sped away. Sebastien moved through the flags gracefully, but Gabriel's undying sense of pride assured his speed never faltered.

Five more to go. Four more to go. My heart was pounding. Gabriel was no rookie out there. He hit the dock half a second before Sebastien. I screamed, and pounced on him as soon as he stepped up.

"Rookie? What was that Sebastien? You got beat by a newcomer," I jeered.

"I believe I have the honor of racing the top competitor. Funny it should be you." Julian stood inches from Gabriel's face. He laughed, and stepped off the dock to mount up. The determination in Julian's eyes gave me chills despite the sweltering heat.

"May the best man win," Gabriel challenged.

Savannah swooped the flag, and I covered my eyes. I spread my fingers open slowly after several moments. Julian was not only passing through his markers, but Gabriel's too. Gabriel followed suit, and I was shocked they didn't crash with each passing second.

Julian clipped Gabriel's side, and sent him hurtling far out of the range of play. Gabriel quickly recovered, and smashed into the back of Julian's jet ski. I was afraid we were going to be picking body parts out of the water if they continued.

Gabriel and Julian rounded the last marker, and they crashed into the dock with such force, it lurched with a groan.

"Who won?" Gabriel asked.

"Who won? You idiot! You could have been killed. Have you lost your mind!?" I screamed.

"We were just having fun. It's a game, come on," Gabriel said to pacify me. I spun on my heel and turned toward the house. "Come back. I'm sorry. What about him? He did the same thing, and you aren't mad at him." Gabriel pointed an accusing finger at Julian.

"*He* can't *die*. Well, he could theoretically, but that issue is not on trial. You stupid, careless-" I shoved Gabriel with all my might, and he fell backward into the water.

He came up sputtering. "Oooh," he said mocking me in the most girlish voice he could muster. "You pushed me in the ocean. You are *so* big and bad." Gabriel smiled, but I was not in the mood to play any more games. Ever.

"We'll see who's big and bad. I'm calling Millie," I threatened.

"You wouldn't dare."

I ran to the house, taking full advantage of my head start. I slid on the marble floor into the hall, and snatched the phone from the receiver. Gabriel tackled me and wrestled the phone away.

"Let go, and I'll spare you payback," I teased. I twisted my legs around his to keep him from moving.

"Never. I'm bigger, and I *will* win." Gabriel wrenched free of my leg lock, and raced up the stairs with the only phone I knew how to locate.

I tripped on a rug when I stood, and was embarrassed to find everyone lingering in the hallway watching us. I ignored them all, and flew upstairs to find Gabriel. He slammed the door to my room, but I twisted the handle just in time to prevent him from locking it. It was a battle of strength, and I knew Gabriel would be able to keep me from opening the door. I bumped it with my hip.

"Open the door."

"No."

Ava crept up behind me. "I drink from the Fountain." She winked, and gave the door a tiny shove.

Gabriel fell backward onto the floor, dazed, as he looked at the open door. I pried the phone easily from his fingers.

"I won't call Millie if you end this war with Julian. Now." My tone was serious, and he sat up.

"How did you…" He saw that I was unrelenting, and he smiled. "No more battles. I promise." He waved an invisible white flag.

I squeezed his hand and helped him up. "Now go. I need a shower, and so do you. I'm hungry and salty."

Gabriel kissed my cheek. "I am so glad I have you back."

He let go of my hand, and bumped face first into Julian. Their jaws clicked on contact, and Gabriel rubbed the back of his hand against his face.

We were both unaware of his presence until then, and his face was like a dark thundercloud. "I don't want to interrupt anything. I wasn't aware you frequented each other's bedrooms, but that must have been standard procedure back home." Julian gave a slight bow and stalked out of the doorway.

I was angry at the insult; he knew that wasn't true. Anything that happened between Gabriel and I was innocent. Even the kiss we shared at the mall before graduation was G-rated compared to the ones I shared with Julian.

Gabriel left my room quietly, but not without saying, "You had better be glad I made you that promise."

Walker picked up lunch while everyone showered, and we ate in the den. A storm rolled in off the Gulf, as one did almost every day, so we decided to watch a movie while the rain pelted the windows full fury. Endless shelves of movies made it seem like all the movies ever made were lined up on shelves on one of the massive walls of the den, so we all finally settled on a new one that was still out in theatres. Not surprisingly, Julian was absent from the group. Walker suggested a bonfire on the beach after dinner, and we all agreed.

At dusk, we walked out to the beach. The sky was clear except for the moon and the sparkling stars. Not a single cloud could be found in the humid southern sky. We spread blankets out on the sand, and I wrapped up like a burrito in one. The night air was colder than normal, because the rain had stayed late into the afternoon. I shimmied closer to the fire. The sky looked more like a high ceiling than a sky. The stars looked like light bulbs high above our heads, and I marveled at my presence in such a place in that moment. Gabriel wrapped my blanket even closer to me.

I couldn't help but think that Julian must have been starved, because he hadn't left his room since discovering Gabriel in my mine. Jade wasn't even so brave as to venture upstairs to visit Julian. Let him wallow in his misery. I was still pissed at his comment.

I pressed him far from my mind, and snuggled closer to my archangel. The fire flickered in Gabriel's eyes. His coarse, curly blond hair had grown longer than it was before I came, but his chestnut brown eyes still held the warmth that kept me going all through my life.

I took in all the sights around me with wonder and appreciation. Whatever I had done to deserve such magnificence, I couldn't tell. The smoke from the fire rose and curled like a ghost. The waves ebbed far back into the sea marking the climax of low tide. Amid all the new senses around me, I took a moment to study the faces of my new family.

Savannah was every bit a porcelain doll. I looked at Ethan and Sebastien, the identical twins, who were as different to me as two people could be. Ethan was devastatingly cool. His patchwork plaid shorts and navy blue polo could have launched a thousand ad campaigns and sold a thousand times that many replicas of his outfit. We still weren't on speaking terms. He avoided me at all costs, but still, I had to admit, he held an allure most men would never know how to capture. Sebastien was warm and friendly and romantic and devoted. And Ethan's polar opposite. He sent Savannah a bouquet of gerber daisies twice since I had been in Eden. Ava, the most beautiful, by far, of all of them sat twirling her short, silvery blond hair cross-legged in the sand. Jade in her dark beauty and evil temptress ways that scared me to death, even felt like someone familiar to me that night. And finally Walker, the jokester who looked like a star from one of Millie's soap operas.

I got a good look at "the boat" now that I was close enough to it without the prospect of swimming or riding my jet ski to distract me. It was more of a yacht, now that I paid closer attention. It was moved back to its position, tied to the dock. The jet skis were gone, the guys had probably moved them to the boathouse on the far side of the sprawling mansion.

"So, do I finally get a clue of what's going on here?" Gabriel asked. "I know you have some kind of magic water, but that's the least of my questions. First of all-"

Ava interjected, and explained the Fountain in much the same way she explained it to me.

Gabriel laughed heartily. "The Fountain of Youth? Like Ponce de Leon? Are you people nuts? That's a myth. Right?" We all fidgeted uncomfortably. "Right?"

"*Apparently*, it's *not* a myth. Ponce de Leon's quest to find our treasure is also a legend. Most historians accept it as false, and yet it's taught in every fifth grade schoolbook across the country. We haven't asked you to drink from it, so I wouldn't be so coy," Jade snarled.

"I didn't mean to make fun of you. But that's just a little far-fetched don't ya' think? How does it supposedly work? It makes you younger? So if you drink too much will you end up as a toddler?" No one else seemed to think his musings were funny.

"We are only allowed to drink every so often. We have no idea what it would do if ingested in large doses. We do know it would greatly increase your strength, but no, it would not make you regress in mentality or shrink in height," Ethan said. "As Ava told you, it makes you beautiful and increases your strength. We don't necessarily want to be supernaturally strong, or control people's minds. We simply want an indefinite life span. We are allowed one vial at a time. It's not a science experiment, it's our lifestyle choice."

Savannah interrupted, and I was surprised. She so rarely spoke out of turn, and not much at that, but Ethan was getting hot-headed with Gabriel's flippant attitude about something they all took so seriously. "I didn't believe it at first either. I almost ran from Sebastien when he told me. I had finally met the man of my dreams, and I thought he was insane. I've met my fair share of men, and if they're single, there is usually a reason why." The couple smiled identical smiles at each other. "I accepted his wild stories with as much conviction as I would take a cartoon, but I'm glad I stayed. My life is perfect here.

"Gabriel, let me ask you," she continued, "how much different would your life be if you were certain you would never grow old? If dying was more difficult a task to accomplish than living? Because we are born knowing our days are numbered, human beings tend to rush through life. Death is the ultimate fear. How much more pleasure would you take in the small things if you didn't rush them?"

Gabriel immediately interrupted to argue his point. "I disagree. I take much more pleasure in the small things knowing that one day I won't be around to see them. What do you have to look forward to? You have everything, but none of you will ever know the joy in seeing your child's first smile. None of you will sit on a rocking chair when you are old and gray next to the person who saw it all with you.

"What fun is life without the knowledge that one day it will be your last? I love the fragility of life. What's the point of playing cards if you always have all four aces? I'm sorry, but I wouldn't drink from your Fountain even if I were on my deathbed." Gabriel gave us all a curt nod, and returned to the house.

I openly disagreed with him just like everyone else. Why did there have to be an end to it all? Gabriel would say it was the natural progression of things and humans shouldn't interrupt that, but why? I could never let Gabriel's life end if I had the power to prolong it.

Ethan spoke. "A small part of me agrees with him. Gabriel is wise beyond his years, and Arianna is too. He doesn't have the hardness of a cynic. He is so full of love, and he truly believes in the good of humanity. We shouldn't criticize that," Ethan said soberly.

I was bowled over at his compliment. I couldn't believe Ethan thought I was mature. "I think he might be a little freaked out. I'll go talk to him," I said.

I wandered into the house to search for Gabriel. I found him in the den, sitting in darkness. The TV was turned off, and not one of the lamps was lit.

"Are you okay?" I asked. "I know it's a lot to take in." I plopped down on the brown leather sectional next to him.

The others crept in one by one to gauge Gabriel's mood with the excuse of telling us they were going to bed. Ava and Savannah whispered a sweet goodnight to us, but I was glad they left us to speak privately. It was late, and I wanted to talk to Gabriel alone, so we went up to my room just to make sure we weren't interrupted.

"I'm not sorry I came, and that's all that matters. You are here with me right this second. But you belong here. I don't."

"So you're leaving? Just like that? Please stay with me. I want you here. I can't be without you again."

He squeezed my hand and kissed my knuckles. "What's going on between you and Julian? I thought we had something. You can't tell me you love him."

The truth was, I couldn't tell Gabriel I loved Julian. I didn't know what I felt for him besides the flattery that came with his attention. I loved and adored Gabriel, and it was a fact I was sure of. But what about Julian? I just flat out didn't know.

"Love is irrelevant, but I do need to tell you something. I kissed him. More than once." Gabriel's expression was pained, but I kept going. "You left me with no promises, and it's unfair for you to want me to wait around. You left me, Gabriel. That day at the mall, you left me. I kissed you and you left me. I wanted us to be together," I choked the last word.

"You're my best friend. Julian will never dance with me at prom. We will never sweep pizza dust from the checkered floors at work together. Julian doesn't know what it's like to live in a run-down neighborhood and not care what anyone thinks. Julian does not know love. He knows loyalty and control."

The unspoken lingering fact was that Julian knew much more than I let on. He knew how to make me forget all those things- Millie's decorating the Christmas tree in tacky red tinsel, Uncle Doug taking us fishing at the creek, Gabriel spending his lunch money in the gumball machine at the local dollar store to buy me a quarter ring when we were little. All my memories became a blur of almost white-blue eyes rimmed in cerulean and fringed with jet black lashes. One glimpse of Julian made my simple life undeniably complicated.

"Let me stay with you again." Gabriel's voice startled me.

"You aren't mad?"

He shook his head. "I guess you're right. It was wrong of me to expect you to wait around. I'm sorry. I don't want to leave you. Besides, I pretty much figured out what was going on."

My jaw dropped. "How?"

He laughed. "Arianna, you wear guilt all over your face." He touched the tip of my nose. "Like I said, it doesn't bother me... much. Now move over." He tried to wedge himself onto the side of the mattress he always slept on.

I was still unsure about the whole mess. I didn't want to go into anything further with Gabriel until I laid all my cards on the table. "I don't know if I want you to stay, Gabriel, if you aren't sure about the whole thing. I'm going to be perfectly honest. I've been thinking, and Julian cut me deeper than I want to admit. I did- I do really care about him. I don't want anyone to think you and I are... you know. I hate sneaking around." I turned away, and it was silent for a few moments.

"I've been thinking, too. I never repaid you for pushing me off the dock." Gabriel had a wicked gleam in his eyes.

"No. Uh-uh."

Gabriel tossed me over his shoulder, dragged me out of my warm bed, and I squealed all the way to the pool.

He stood at the edge of the pool and teetered back and forth for dramatic effect.

"The water is probably freezing, and I'm completely dressed. Don't you dare, Gabriel Bennett."

He tossed me in, and I shrieked just before I hit the water. The strong taste of chlorine drifted up my nostrils and burned through to my throat as I kicked my legs to bring me back up. I stuck a out my hand and caught the leg of Gabriel's pants. I pulled with all my might, and he splashed in behind me.

"Now I owe you double." Gabriel pushed my head under. I emerged and he stopped suddenly.

Julian peered down at us from the patio. "I'm so sorry to disturb you once again." He laughed bitterly, and I winced. "Arianna, I'm disappointed you brought a friend. I thought you would expect me here by now. We met often enough. You must be confusing your midnight affairs."

"What is he talking about?" His eyes volleyed from me to Julian. "Why are you following us?" Gabriel studied us back and forth.

"Julian you have no right to judge me. I'm just a little girl, remember? What have you ever cared about me?"

Julian flinched. I threw out my arms to challenge his previous statement. He started inside, and I chased after him. I caught up with him outside of the room containing the Fountain. I was sopping wet, and dripped water all over the floors.

"I didn't ask for this." I grabbed his arm, and spun him around. "I didn't ask to be brought here. All I wanted was to spend the summer at my aunt's beach house, not to get tangled up in something I don't pretend to understand. I tried to talk to you and explain myself. If you would open up, maybe you would realize not everyone wants to use you. I don't want your money or the promise of living forever." I grabbed two fists full of hair from my scalp and tugged, trying to think of a way to make him see my side.

"I *dreamed* of you. We shared a connection more powerful than money or," I gestured to the door of the Fountain, "water. So go ahead, Julian. I can't *imagine* why you never fell in love before," I said, my voice riddled with sarcasm. "You don't know what it means to love, and you have no clue what it means to *be* loved. I feel sorry for you."

I left him to stew over what I said. I meant every word, and I hoped my voice echoed in his head every night when he tried to sleep. God knew, I had stayed up plenty of nights trying to decipher the sincerity of his words to me.

I fought off my tears and fetched Gabriel from the pool. "I changed my mind. Come to bed."

PREDICTION

Gabriel slipped into my room, and instantly laid down on one of my pillows. He held my hand until he fell asleep. I watched him for a long time. His chest rose and fell, and I marveled at how close one person could feel to another. My claim on Gabriel was nameless. We weren't lovers. We weren't friends. "Soulmates" was too bourgeois and cliché.

Archangel. He always found a way to save me. Coming here was such a sacrifice of his pride, and yet he took it all in stride just to be near me. I knew it stung him to the core to be so reliant on someone whom I had fallen for, and to see Julian give me all the things he couldn't give me. The truth was, Julian could give me the world, but Gabriel could and did give me something Julian couldn't. Love.

He twisted a lock of his curly, dark blond hair in his sleep. His lavender eyelids flickered, rendering him the captive of deep sleep. He was so beautiful, so mortal. I watched him for a long time that night. I marveled at his beauty. Natural. Real. Gabriel was perfect without the water, even though I imagined when Julian was sleeping, he was abnormally gorgeous in his own right.

Gabriel looked so childlike. He mumbled incoherent words from time to time, and I wanted so badly to enter into his head and dream his pretty dreams.

"Memento Mori," I whispered in his ear, and fell prey to sleep myself.

Ava awoke us the next morning the same way as the afternoon before. "Gabriel," she rolled her eyes, "you have your own bed, you know." She shut the door quietly.

Ava invited us on an outing to Panama City Beach. Walker and Ethan were gone on a delivery to Henry, and they were making their voyage to one of his private residences in Spain.

Jade supposedly went on a shopping trip out of state, and we found this as the perfect excuse to give Savannah and Sebastien some private time. Ava told Julian about our plans, and she said he promised her to stay out on the beach all day. Ava nudged Sebastien on the way out the door.

"Don't get used to this, but we'll stay out *extra* late."

Savannah's face purpled with embarrassment, but I heard her whisper, "Thank you," in Ava's ear when we departed.

If Gabriel had charmed Ava before we left, she was smitten by the time we got there. I was virtually silent the entire way. I loved to close my eyes when I rode in the sunlight. The trees on the highway passed so fast. The sunlight sparkled through my closed eyes, and lit them up with bright orange flickers of light. I listened to Gabriel's husky voice talk about my home. He spoke about our lives in Ellaville with such conviction I felt a sudden pang of homesickness.

"I bet I sent that town into a flurry," Ava said wistfully. "The last time I went to Ellaville to see Doug-"

Gabriel choked on his soda. "Uncle Doug? As in Arianna's uncle?"

I shifted in my seat to dodge the imaginary daggers I could feel radiating off Ava. "Sometimes I forget how long ago it all happened. I was engaged to him once. He was supposed to come to live with me in Eden, but he never showed. Thomas broke it off for his spineless brother. Whoever she was that made him stay with her, I hope she made him happy."

"Uncle Doug never dated anyone," I whispered quietly. She suddenly got very still, and I saw her jaw line harden. "Well, I guess not, but then again, I didn't know anything about you or Eden either."

Gabriel changed the subject. "So, you only wear your vials when you leave Eden. How do you protect them? What if they fell off or were lost?"

"That's a chance we take. The benefits to having them outweigh the risks by far. We try very hard to ensure our secret is not compromised. There are no guarantees, but that's why we don't accept outsiders. It's the main reason Walker, Ethan, and I never chose anyone to live with us. Of course, Arianna was my ultimate choice. Technically, Jade didn't get a choice because we didn't hand pick her. Savannah doesn't get a choice either, since Sebastien chose her. Jade put us all in danger by asking you out of spite. We are very lucky you are a decent and discreet person."

I was bothered badly by that. I was chosen by Ava, so I guessed I didn't get a choice either. What if I did fall in love with Julian one day? Or

Gabriel? I wouldn't be able to have children, just like Savannah. I tried to focus on what Gabriel was saying, and pressed the issue far from my mind. I knew it wouldn't be the last time I thought of it, but I didn't want to struggle to have a good day because I was "borrowing trouble," as Millie always said.

"I would never tell your secret. Arianna is the reason I get up in the mornings," he said proudly. "I should have waited for her to call me before showing up, but I missed her so much. I'm sorry to have caused so much trouble." Gabriel leaned in between the front seats and curled his hand around mine.

"Jade was the source of any conflict arising from your arrival. We all accept you. Eden has never been so filled with happiness. You two have brought light to our home. Thomas and Rose's deaths filled our house in sorrow until Sebastien met Savannah and brought her to us. But you brought us *real* youth. The Fountain offers us a façade of being young, but you changed the way we all look at ourselves. Even Julian had to rethink the basis on which we allow newcomers."

"Why doesn't he allow you to have children?" Gabriel asked. "I can almost see his reasoning behind not exposing or draining the Fountain, but is it really worth the sacrifice?"

"Not for me. Not now. Arianna, you have permanently altered my reasoning." Ava brushed my cheek with her hand. "Nothing is worth the sacrifice of not being there to watch you grow up. Nothing is worth the sacrifice of missing out on having great-nephews or nieces. I have no desire to have children at my age, but I would so love for you to have children if you wanted."

"At your age." Gabriel barked in laughter. "You are *so* old Ava. I constantly forget that any of you are older than us."

"Gabriel, if you weren't in love with my niece, I would snatch you up myself," Ava joked. She turned her car into a parking place on the strip. "Welcome to Spring Break heaven."

"Where to?" I asked Ava.

"Wherever. I just wanted to get away. Panama City was close, and I would like to get a chance to get to know Gabriel a little better. Anything in particular you wanted to do?" she asked us.

I was still feeling a pang of nostalgia from Gabriel's colorful stories of home. I wanted to leave Ellaville so badly, but when I actually left, I realized my home had made me who I was.

"Can we go into one of the shops? I want to send Grandma Millie a postcard." I purposefully omitted Uncle Doug even though I wanted to send him one too.

We ducked into a cheesy beach shop, and I picked out a postcard for Millie displaying the gorgeous Florida sunset I had grown so accustomed to. I selected one for Uncle Doug with a well endowed woman's chest in a tiny triangle top that read "Panama City or *Bust*." I snickered to myself, thinking I should probably have sent him a picture of Ava in a bikini to really knock his socks off. The multiple pierced and tattooed cashier of the shop directed me to a nearby post office. I silently prayed Uncle Doug would be checking the mail when the postcard arrived so Millie wouldn't chew me out about inappropriate mailings. I scribbled a quick note telling them I missed them and would see them soon.

We passed by a palm reader's shop, and Ava suggested we should go and find out what our futures held. The "Genuine Romany Clairvoyant," according to the sign, took us back through her beaded curtain one at a time. Ava emerged after thirty or so minutes, and exclaimed that an old flame would soon be rekindled.

Gabriel announced his opinion that it was all a waste of time and ridiculous, but when he emerged from Madame Zoya's beaded curtain his face was pale. He refused to tell us what she predicted, and I knew his mannerisms enough to assume he must have held some stock in what she said.

Madame Zoya was an old woman with blue painted eyelids and fried red hair that was obviously dyed to hide the gray that was peeking out at her roots. Her hands were filled with silver rings, with two or more on her pinkies.

I went back to her chamber cautiously, and she told me to hold out the hand opposite of the one that was my dominant hand. Being a lefty, I produced my right hand. She took my hand in her weathered grasp. Her wrinkled brow furrowed as she concentrated on my palm.

"Your life line looks much like your friend in there. Hers seems to have no end. It loops all the way around. I have never seen anything like it,"

Madame Zoya said ominously. She flipped through a stack of   tarot cards that

I vaguely remembered Millie had warned me were "the devil's toys" when I was

a child.

She splayed the deck and instructed me to select seven cards. I did as

she said, and she flipped them in a pattern on a black cloth.

"You are at a crossroad. You will have to decide between two people

you are very loyal to. Each card of the tarot represents a positive and a

negative. You are in great danger. You will soon have to choose between

darkness and light. These two people are not necessarily representative of

good and evil, though everyone may advise you they are. You will face many

obstacles in either case. Light may seem the easiest decision, but a life with

the dark one you dreamed of may lead to an adventure that will bring you true

happiness."

How the heck did she know that?

"You will return to your true home very soon. You are faced with life

changing choices. A life of excitement, or the familiarity and comfort of the life

you have resigned yourself to.

"The dark one holds a strong connection with you. He appeared in

your mind's most private corner. Your dreams overlap. That is not an ordinary

occurrence. That implies a crossing of your stars. When your stars were

crossed, a space in your heart was filled, along with his. This supernatural occurrence is rare. Most people's hearts are never filled. They are constantly searching." She coughed, and her raspy voice once again filled the air.

"Do not let this information interfere with the one of light. He brought you life when you knew death. Without him, your life would have ended shortly after your great loss."

I always thought of my parents' death as my great loss, and I shuddered at how much she seemed to know about me.

"Your life is intertwined with the one who is your angel. I told him the same thing." Zoya motioned to the front. "Do not allow yourself to be separated from him. He is your life and you are his. The two of you are interchangeable.

"Either choice will result in your ultimate destiny. You alone know where your destiny lies. Choose wisely, Arianna. The dark one and the one of light both care deeply for you. It is up to you to design the course of your life."

I gaped at the woman. Unsure of how she knew my name, I guessed she heard Ava speaking to me while Gabriel's future was being told. Either way, I was totally freaked out.

Ava never called me by my name, I thought. *I know she didn't.* I revisited our conversation in my mind. I was aghast in her knowledge of my dreams of Julian. I walked up front to see Ava lounged with her legs tucked under her, sprawled in a cozy but gaudy velour chair.

"What does your future hold?" Gabriel asked. There was a nervous edge to his voice.

I rubbed my forehead as I scanned my brain for an answer to let them know the visit to the palm reader was nonsense. "I'll soon be changing my major in college." I plastered on a reassuring smile, trying to convince them that I thought it was all a big joke.

"I told you this stuff is fake," Gabriel said. He let out a long, relieved breath.

"Fine," Ava retorted, defeated. She looked very disappointed her flame rekindling was a farce. "No more fortune telling. Let's go."

We ate burgers and onion rings for lunch, and Ava and I bought souvenir tank tops and beach towels. Panama City was a beautiful place and the people were friendly. The city seemed like it would burst from the energy all around me. I loved it. We stayed all day until dark clouds rolled in, and we started home.

The rain was late that day, I noted. Angry drops pelted the windshield, and I couldn't help but dwell on the fortune teller's admonition. *It is up to you to design the course of your life*. Her words rang in my ears.

It was unusually quiet when we arrived. Savannah and Sebastien were holed up in their room, I was sure.

"I'm going to check in with Julian. To tell him we're home, you know..." I trailed off.

Gabriel squeezed my hand. "I'm going to go to bed. My bed," he assured Ava. She nodded her approval and obvious relief.

I tiptoed to Julian's room. I barged in the door without waiting for him to grant me entrance. He sat before the unlit fireplace.

"I'm sorry," I said and waited impatiently for him to acknowledge me. "It's your turn. You are supposed to apologize to me now."

Julian took a deep breath. "I'm sorry to have gotten in your way. I'm sorry I offended you. I'm sorry I forced your parents to leave, resulting in their deaths. I'm sorry that I am the direct cause of everything bad that has ever happened to you."

I knelt beside him, and tears sprang to my eyes. I grabbed his chin and turned it to mine. "I'm sorry you feel responsible for events you had no control over. I'm sorry that you feel sorry for yourself and push everyone away. I'm sorry you blame yourself, too, but that was no reason to make me believe you cared about me." I pulled out the key to the Fountain he gave me in my dream. I placed it in his hand, the same way he gave it to me. "Playing games with me makes it worse, Julian."

I hurried to bed, and cried myself to sleep. I was glad to sleep alone.

Tensions increased over the next few weeks. Julian and Gabriel wisely steered clear of each other, but there were a few altercations. One night at dinner they got into a screaming philosophical argument over Julian's prized Fountain. It was more of a "who can take better care of Arianna" debate, hidden under the guise of whether or not drinking from the Fountain was a mortal sin. Gabriel argued that anything that would eternally separate you from the Almighty would land you in hell one day, and Julian stood beside his point that not partaking in something that could potentially keep him with me for eternity was a mortal sin in his book. I tried to stand between them, but when Gabriel threw his shirt off, I pulled him back. At one point I thought Julian was going to throttle Gabriel, but Gabriel eventually backed off on his own.

Other than the stress of trying to keep them apart, life was pretty much perfect. Gabriel and I spent every waking moment together, and everyone seemed to succumb to Gabriel's magnetism. Jade took every opportunity to take Julian his meals and anything else he might need, so she wasn't around to antagonize me. For a while, I wondered if the two of them didn't actually have something going on.

I woke up one morning after an almost all-night drive home from a late movie in a far off town. I looked like a big mess, and I knew it. I didn't attempt to brush out my tangles, or any other method of making myself more presentable. My face was puffy and swollen. I wore a huge shirt I brought from Ellaville that belonged to Uncle Doug. It had paint splatters all over it, but it brought me a measure of comfort when I was upset as a kid. My pajama pants were too short, and I was too groggy to put on my makeup. I plopped down next to Gabriel in a stool at the breakfast bar, and was humiliated, but not concerned, to see an unfamiliar man and woman staring at me.

The man was handsome, but not nearly as beautiful as the men residing in Eden, Gabriel included of course. He had beady brown eyes and mousy brown hair. He would normally have struck me as attractive, but my standards in men was increasingly high with each day I spent with the likes of Julian, Gabriel, Sebastien, Ethan, and Walker. The woman was almost as tiny as Savannah. Her hair was the color of cinnamon, and her dark green eyes held sadness. In a strange way, she reminded me of Julian. I decided after a split second that it was because she shared the same moping look on Julian's face he had worn since Gabriel's arrival here. She looked like a fairytale princess in her gauzy peach sundress. A sad fairytale princess.

"You must be Arianna." She looked confused.

I was too tired for friendly gestures. Their presence should have struck me as odd, but my mind was muddled from exhaustion.

"Uh-huh."

"It is so nice to meet you," she gushed. "My name is Emily Goss, and this is my husband Edgar. We have heard so much about you." For a moment I wondered why she seemed to be almost in awe of me.

Oh no. This was Emily!? The one Julian was supposed to marry? She was breathtaking, of course. Just my stupid luck.

"Of course you're Emily. This is poetic justice." I climbed down from my chair.

"Arianna, why are you being so rude?" Gabriel whispered. "I'm sorry about her. We stayed up really late," he told them trying to disguise my rudeness for my exhaustion. He pinched the skin above my elbow discreetly.

"I have heard so much about you. You are all Julian talks about," Emily said.

"That's funny because he never said anything about you," I countered.

"Arianna? What's wrong with you?" Ava sashayed into the room. "Emily is our guest." Ava stopped and searched my face. "Unless she did something wrong?" She glared at Emily.

Emily's perfect little heart shaped mouth became pinched with alarm.

"I'm sorry, Emily," I told her, trying as I might to ignore how magnificent her complexion was compared to mine. "We did stay up really late. I didn't expect for you to be so, um, well, I wasn't expecting you."

"It's all right." Emily flashed me a bright smile.

I pinched the bridge of my nose, but the gesture did little to conceal the agitation I felt with Julian's ex sitting next to me. I did not for the life of me know why I was being so sour. I always tried to go out of my way to be nice to everyone.

It hit me suddenly. I was jealous of Emily. I tried not to imagine why... Everyone at Eden was beautiful, and Ava had already told me she was married to Edgar, so she obviously drank from the Fountain to have lived so long. I should have expected no less from her than perfection, but it made me even angrier at Julian. If he couldn't fall for her, there was no doubt he was just playing with me to assuage the unfounded guilt he felt over my parents' passing.

Oh, right, and, there was the underlying fact that I was just the teensiest bit jealous of Julian.

Jade flounced in the kitchen. That must have not been a very successful shopping trip if she was back so soon. She stopped short. "Emily," she bit off.

"It is very nice to see you, Jade." Emily's cool smile did not quite reach her eyes. I liked her a little bit better already.

Julian strode in wearing a crisp white shirt. His black hair tumbled into his baby blue eyes, and I mentally slapped myself from noticing. "Edgar, I am so pleased you have come to see us. Emily you truly have not aged a day," he said.

"Thanks to you." She clasped Julian's hands in hers.

Something flickered in Julian's eyes. Regret? That wasn't likely. Emily's passion for him was written all over her face, not to mention she was leaning as close into him as possible. She would surely have dropped Edgar like a hot coal if Julian gave her any indication that he wanted her.

"It is a good thing you are so *happily* married Emily," Jade said, her velvet voice dripping with sarcasm. "We would all think you still held a candle for our Julian, the way you greet him, even though we all know his affections are elsewhere," she said coldly and clung to Julian's arm possessively.

Julian shrugged her off. "And happily married Emily is. Edgar is a wonderful friend."

Edgar seemed blind to the entire situation, he was too busy pining over his bride of almost a hundred years. Edgar slapped Julian on the back just a smidgen too hard. "I'd like to see our Fountain. It never ceases to capture me. I still remember the first time we saw it." He raised his nasally voice even louder and spoke to the rest of us. "Did you know a hurricane passed through and almost took the whole house down? I was worried sick about losing the Fountain-"

Emily broke in. "And Julian, of course."

"Oh, honey, sure I was concerned for Julian." He waved his hand in irritation. "I tell you, when Okeechobee blew in I thought I'd seen the last days of my youth."

Edgar most definitely showed an affinity for using his outside voice. The man talked louder than I could yell. None of the Fountain drinkers gave the impression that they were any older than they looked. They all held maturity and worldliness and eloquence about them that was rare in anyone my age, but Edgar just seemed downright old. He even sounded like a dull, old man. He was boring and dry, and his one-sided conversation droned on.

"As engrossed in your story as we are Edgar, we all must be getting hungry. Why don't you get refreshed in your room, and we will have lunch as soon as you are ready." Julian pointedly ended Edgar's lackluster rambling, and left no room for argument.

I went into my bright white bathroom and took a long, hot bath. I laid back against the base of the tub and opened my eyes under water. I let out a blood curdling scream to alleviate the stress I felt. The only sound was bubbles that burst at the surface with muffled frustration. I wrapped my hair in a fluffy towel and selected a long halter sundress to wear.

I went into the bathroom and combed my hair. I wiped the steam off of the mirror in a spot just large enough so I could see my reflection. I stared at the girl in the mirror. Gone was the poor, gangly orphan from Ellaville with the bony legs and tangled hair. My pale skin was a golden, sun-baked bronze. My blue chunks of hair were funky and young, and I had grown curves in all the right places. I may not ever feel like I belonged in Eden, but I would have stood out in Ellaville.

I scrunched my hair, and my wild natural curls sprang to life. I swiped on a smoky eyeshadow and slipped my feet into a pair of wedged sandals. I left my room feeling more self-confident than I had ever felt. This newfound empowerment was not found in Gabriel or Julian's attentions, but in knowing that I came a long way and stepped out of my self-imposed box. I had found myself, and I was strong enough to make myself happy without anyone else's help.

I came upon a heated conversation at the base of the stairs.

"If you think your coming here will sway Julian into wanting what he already gave up, you are *dead* wrong," Jade hissed.

Emily was backed into a wall, Jade's finger pointed an inch or so from her. Her face was moist with fresh, Jade induced tears.

"It was Edgar's idea to come. You know better than anyone how much it hurts to be so close to Julian knowing he loves someone else. It's just the way things have to be. Arianna is meant for him. You know she is, and you can't change it. I would never leave Edgar. I love my husband. I do!" Emily sobbed.

"Julian loves *me*. If you and that whore Arianna would stop parading yourselves around him he would see that."

"How dare you Jade?" I stepped out of the shadows into the sunlight. I gave her a little push directly in the center of her chest. "You are delusional. Julian and everyone else in this house only puts up with you because they feel obligated. No one else is brave enough to stand up to you, so I will.

"You saved them once, but they continue to save you. You are never here, except long enough to wreak havoc and upset us all. You blow through Julian's money, and you act like you own the place. I'm calling your bluff. If you want to expose us, go ahead. Everyone who has ever met you will vouch for the fact that you are a half-crazed lunatic with no friends, and you are in love with your boss who is clearly out of your league."

Jade's mouth was agape, and it took her several moments to recover. "You think you can come here and do as you please? I haven't dealt with you yet, and your days have been numbered since I first heard your name. I hate you just like I hated your filthy mother."

I slapped her hard across her bony face. What in the world made me ever see Jade as beautiful was beyond me. Jade was the ugliest, most repugnant human being I would ever have the displeasure of viewing. She was visibly shaking with rage. She took a few steps backward, and ice cold water raced through my veins. I was actually scared, but I showed no sign of fear. I raised my jaw, and she scampered away.

Emily fell to the ground, sobbing. "You didn't have to take up for me. She's right. I do love Julian after all this time. I try to love Edgar, and I do, in a way. I'm a failure to him. I know Julian doesn't love me, but I can't let go." She wept harder.

I lifted Emily's face with my fingers and looked her in her eyes. "It is just way things have to be. You said it yourself. He hypnotizes people like us, and manipulates us into believing we are special enough to capture him. Julian is feral. He can't be captured or caged. No one woman will ever be enough for him."

She spoke in broken sobs. "But you're wrong, Arianna. Julian has always loved you. You are the one. When he broke off our engagement, he told me he had a soul mate, the one who had the power to change his life. You have the power to break his darkness. His father was so cruel to him, and all he knows is pain and loss. He refuses to attach himself to anyone because he is afraid of losing them." I tried to break in, but she continued.

"His eyes, Arianna. They change when he's around you. The

turbulence turns into majesty. You are the one for him. Please don't let go. I love him. I will never be able to release him until I know he's happy. He has loved you for a hundred years, and you know it. Julian knew you would come someday, and that's why I let him go. Because I knew he'd be happier with the person that was meant for him. You."

Emily stroked my cheek and disappeared into the annals of the great house.

CONFIDENCES

I went out to the beach alone, and sat in the sand to think. Ethan came and sat down next to me. His silence mortified me. To be perfectly honest, I was petrified of him. He never spoke to me, and he acted as if I were a filthy stain on the perfection of Eden.

Somewhere in the silence that followed, I found that being next to him was a little comforting. I couldn't figure out why he didn't speak, or why the fact that him being there felt a lot like having Gabriel beside me. It was one of those times when I didn't have to talk, but someone was there to listen if I wanted to.

"Don't you get lonely?" I asked him finally . "I don't mean to pry, but why haven't you found someone to bring here with you? Don't you ever envy your brother? He is so happy with Savannah."

Ethan smiled. "It would be extremely hard not to be envious of what my brother shares with Savannah. There have been women, but none who I wanted to spend an eternity with. 'Till death do us part' doesn't apply to us. Our lives will span centuries, ages, eons. Not one girl has captured me entirely enough to spend that long with her. There is always some quirk or another that eats me up.

"I don't want perfection so much as sanity. The last girl I was with talked nonstop about how fat she was. She was probably a hundred-thirty pounds." His brown eyes flashed in disgust.

"How do you know you're making the right choice?"

"In your situation, the right choice will be whatever you decide. They're both wonderful. My loyalties lie with Julian, but Gabriel is a genuine person. He's real."

He continued, "Arianna, I think I need to come clean." He scrubbed his freshly shaved head with his palm, trying to coax a sugar coated version of what he was about to say out of his head. "Julian and Gabriel weren't- aren't the only ones who are infatuated with you. I struggled from the beginning to separate myself from you because of Julian's feelings."

My cheeks flamed in the awkwardness of the moment. Ethan was every girl's dream. He was the celebrity that made your chest ache with the beauty of him, even though you would never even get close enough to touch him.

"Julian doesn't want me. He wants to make up for what he imagines he did to my parents," I sneered. "Gabriel is comfortable with me, because he doesn't know anything else."

I paused, and decided to go for it. I had to know. "Why do you hate me so much?"

"Hate you? Is that what you think?" He buried his head between his knees and rocked back and forth. He reached for me, but stopped short from my shoulder like he was scared to touch me.

"Arianna, I don't know what you see when you look at yourself, but you are dead wrong if you think any of us had the ability to hate you. Each one of us was drawn to you in ways we don't understand.

"Your parents both drank from the Fountain, which we know gives us certain abilities above the natural realm. We are stronger mentally and physically. In turn, those gifts were somewhat passed to you at conception. Do you understand?"

I rolled my eyes. "I could barely lift my book bag in high school, and I certainly have no control over anyone's life, including my own."

Ethan shook his head. "How can I explain this? Gabriel sheltered you from the brunt of others' desire to possess you. Your powers are not like any of those that we can lay claim to. You are a magnet. None of us can resist the pull. Even Jade feels it, and it makes her angry. Regardless of her obsession with Julian, her hate for you runs as deep as the love the rest of us feel for you."

"Why didn't you use the mind control on us? I've thought about that. I mean, why doesn't Julian make Gabriel leave?"

"What I am going to tell you is in confidence. It may scare you, but you must promise to keep this quiet."

"I promise," I said, and meant it.

"From the time we met Julian, he rebuffed all female attention. He always spoke of a girl in his dreams he could never quite catch. He vowed to remain alone until the one day he met the girl; he claimed she was too real to be a dream. Julian said the girl was his soul mate, and he wouldn't settle for anything less than the magical girl he was waiting to meet. He swore she wasn't some run of the mill fantasy. We all thought he was nuts, of course, but he was very serious.

"The day Ava returned to Eden and confirmed your existence, she brought a picture of you that your grandmother gave her. Julian was dumbfounded, and he confided in Sebastien and I later that night that you were the girl. You were the reason he couldn't marry Emily, the reason he rejected Jade so many times. *You*."

I sifted sand through my fingers, thinking hard on all Ethan was telling me. "So, Julian got in my head? I dreamed of him too."

"Julian told me about your shared dreams. This is where it gets complicated. We have a theory, like pretty much everything else around here, that Gabriel is some sort of protector. We all know you had a separation with Gabriel. It was the only reason we could deem that Julian was able to draw you to him in your dreams. We were unaware of Gabriel at the time, but we guessed correctly there was an unseen force guarding your mind. At first, we imagined it was because your parents were Keepers, and their minds were off limits, but we soon discovered there must have been a reason he was able to bring you here twice and not again."

"We did have a separation if that's what you want to call it. I mean, we had a dumb fight at school. I had never gotten into an argument with Gabriel before then."

"If I'm correct, Julian contacted you a second time, but only for a few moments."

"Yeah. I dreamed of him again, but I was pulled away. It was so weird. I mean, he was there and he gave me, um…a gift. When I woke up, I was still holding it."

"You are equally linked with Julian and Gabriel, I think. Gabriel protects you, and Julian is able to cross the threshold of your mind. Weak-minded people are very easy to control, but when we first drink we are the most physically powerful. The strongest-minded person in the world would succumb to our wills.

"I shudder to think what fate Julian would have carried out had he been able to enter Gabriel's mind, and the same goes for you versus Jade."

"So I protect Gabriel too?" I asked anxiously.

"You seem to function as one. We can't penetrate either of you because of the other."

"But I was upset with Gabriel when I arrived. No one got into my head then," I protested.

Or did they? I thought. I met Julian every night at the pool. I kissed him, several times.

"I think that was a mutual attraction," Ethan laughed. "And I can't read minds, if that's what you think, but I can read expressions very well."

My face tinged pink with embarrassment. "So you tried. You tried to control my mind?" I swallowed hard. I didn't know whether to be angry or flattered. Extremely flattered.

"The night you came, Sebastien and I got into a huge argument. I fought the urge so hard, but my head screamed to bring you to me. At Screwdriver, it almost killed me to be dancing so close to you.

"Ava turned a blind eye, but in hindsight, she had to know. I didn't sleep for days. I don't mean to scare you. I mean, I wasn't some hormone-crazed teenager. Seeing your face was a drop of ice water on a black flame. I can't stand to imagine what Julian endured."

My mind wandered to the first night I met him. He had pushed the wall and panted after we kissed, like he was in pain. "Nobody in Ellaville seemed to be impacted by me," I muttered. I thought for a moment. "And what about Walker and Sebastien?"

"Walker was able to take out his, uh- frustrations on a girl he was seeing in Tampa as early as the first night," he told me suggestively. "I'm not the kind of guy who 'takes out his frustrations' if you know what I mean." He bent two fingers on each hand to emphasize his quote. "Sebastien felt the pull, but on the same level as Savannah and Ava. You see, he's in love with Savannah, so his attraction is more family-oriented and protective. Not so...physical." He quickly changed the subject. "Again, Arianna, Gabriel is your protector. We will probably never fully understand it, but as long as he's close to you, you cannot be harmed."

"So Ethan and Walker, along with Julian were out of their minds with lust? For me?" I burst into laughter. Finally able to compose myself, I went on, but still chuckling, "You are still forgetting what I told you. I was angry with him when I came here. Gabriel wasn't protecting me."

"When Jade went to find Gabriel, he was utterly destroyed with the loss of you. He never completely resigned himself to let you go, no matter what your feelings at the time. Even when Julian was able to make you dream of him, it was only a dream. It wasn't strong enough to bring you here in person. And believe me, he tried. You came here of your own free will to try to create a relationship with your aunt. If Gabriel was to release your spirit completely, you would be in grave danger," he told me in a dark tone.

"In danger? Of what?"

"You're still forgetting what *I* told *you*. You're a magnet. Every person alive would be drawn to you. I shudder to think what vile and horrific things people would plot to have you."

"Ethan," I stood up and brushed the sand off my bottom. "This has been a lovely chat, but I can't believe any of this. I've always been scrawny, and too tall, my hair is always a tangled mess, I drool when I sleep, and not to mention I only have a basic understanding of general math. I am not a genius, or beautiful, and of all the things I've been told here, this is the most ridiculous.

Own me? There were times in my life I would have had to pay for a date." I was beyond irritated.

"Let's say I believe you. Why are you all so drawn to my magnet and everyone else in the world all but ignores me?"

Ethan scrambled up to stand beside me. "Drinking the water of the Fountain makes us more susceptible to any force natural or otherwise. Henry was able to instantly discern that Sebastien and I, and also your mother and Ava would not tell our secret."

"That *so* doesn't answer my question, but I'll humor you. You have a sixth sense. Yeah, okay. So here's the flaw in your theory. What about Jade? Didn't you know as soon as she set foot in this house she was evil?"

Ethan shook his finger at me. "Not so fast. Jade was an exception in the first place, which I'm sure you have been informed of. She is here by default, but Walker would never have brought her here if he sensed anything amiss. Jade is many things, but indiscreet is not one of them. She is in love with Julian, and that makes a difference, but she is predominantly shallow. Jade is a narcissist, she puts herself first. The Fountain is to Jade what Gabriel is to you. It's what she lives for."

Okay, I was listening. Jade? Shallow? That definitely made sense.

"The only way she would risk exposing us is for Julian. Her obsession with him is unhealthy, and she's not used to hearing no. I believe she would die for Julian. Not only because she loves him, but without him her beauty would be futile. No man in this world will satisfy Jade but Julian. He is the one thing she can't have."

"Really, Ethan. Give me a break. I'm tired of talking about Julian and Jade, and I'm sick of everyone trying to give me undeserved importance. I'm not Ava. I'm not Jade. I'm not Savannah. And I am sure as hell not my mother. I don't belong here. I know it as well as you and everyone else. You are just making this up to make me feel, I don't know, more included. I think you really believe all this, though, and that's ridiculous."

Ethan balked. "This is *not* how I wanted this conversation to go. Ava begged me to talk to you about this and let you know the severity of the situation, but I can see I was wrong. The Fountain of Youth didn't freak you out, but being told you are potentially the most sought after woman in the universe does?"

I laughed. "Yes. Something like that." Severity. What a load of crap.

"I had no intention of talking about this with you today, but I'm not sorry I did no matter what you say." He hesitated for a moment, and it scared me a little bit.

"But there is something else. I need to warn you of one more thing."

"And what could it *possibly* be?" My voice dripped with sarcasm.

"Julian won the race fair and square. You were too busy with Gabriel to notice Julian's devil horns coming out," Ethan joked, trying to lighten the situation before adopting a more serious tone when he got to the heart of things. "Julian hit the dock a split second before Gabriel. He knows he won. He is just waiting. He wants something from you, and God help us all when he makes his request."

The sun was disappearing quickly behind the clouds of late afternoon. I was hungry, and it was about to rain. Chill bumps raised on my arms at Ethan's last warning. I shivered.

"I'm sure I'll be fine." I raised my chin high to convey my false bravery. "Walk me inside?" I tucked my hand in the crook of Ethan's arm, and strode into Eden. No matter what happened, it was my destiny.

NINETEEN

Emily and Edgar stayed with us for several more weeks. We watched the Fourth of July fireworks display over the ocean, and celebrated America's birthday with a cookout. I remembered the sparklers Uncle Doug used to light for Gabriel and I every year. Sometimes I couldn't fathom how much grander of a scale my life was on now.

The last night Edgar and Emily were with us, we ventured to Screwdriver to celebrate the year's most important date in my book- Gabriel's birthday. I planned meticulously for the big day, buying out all the stores with every stitch of clothing and electronic gadget known to man. The big day dawned, and we had a private lunch together just a few miles out of town.

We returned to Eden, and Gabriel opened his gifts from everyone. Ava insisted he close his eyes for his last present, and we were led outside onto the lawn.

A black, top of the line BMW SUV with a huge blue bow sat in the center of the circular drive. Even I was surprised. Ava lowered her hands from around his eyes to allow him to see her gift.

"I told you, I don't want anything from you. Ava, I can't accept this," Gabriel said, but the shock on his face gave away the fact that he wanted it. I could almost hear him drooling.

"You are as much my nephew as Arianna is my niece. I bought this with my money, and I won't take no for an answer. It's completely different from our cars, so I thought you would be a little more inclined to accept it."

Gabriel pondered her statement for a few moments. He wrapped his muscular arms around her thin frame. "Thank you so much, Ava. Thank you."

We all gathered to get a closer look. The interior was decked out, even more so than my car. I was so proud for Gabriel to have something so nice to call his own.

Walker bought him a video game console for his room. Sebastien and Savannah bought him an MP3 hookup for his car dash. Ethan bought him a pair of couture aviator sunglasses, way nicer than his knockoff signature pair. Edgar and Emily produced a pair of airline tickets, and asked him to bring me to visit them in Ireland whenever we wished. Even Jade bought him a gift card to a popular electronics store.

He opened my gifts to him last, and claimed to love every one. The last thing he opened was a leather bound journal with his initials on the front.

On the inside cover I inscribed, "My Archangel, for all your thoughts. Memento Mori, all my love."

He squeezed my hand and kissed my cheek. "Thank you. I will never be able to repay you for all that you've done for me. And for Arianna," he added to everyone else. His eyes scanned the room, and he nodded his appreciation to everyone.

The only person missing was Julian, as he was most of the time these days. I was angry at him as much for his spiteful words as his self-confinement, but I missed him nonetheless.

Emily and Edgar said their goodbyes and hurried off to the airport. Emily hugged me before she departed and whispered in my ear, "He loves you. Don't let him go."

My lips twitched to respond, but the words never quite made it to my mouth. *I won't*, I thought as I watched them leave. We were a sad bunch. The woman who loved the man who loved me, and the man who was so blinded by love for his wife and his friend he never suspected a thing. I felt sorry for Edgar, not because Emily didn't love him, but because he would never have all of her heart.

I swallowed the thought that I was doing the same thing to Gabriel and Julian. Neither one could have all of me. Each one was a special part of me, and as much as I hated to admit it, I was dependent on them both for different reasons.

Sebastien helped Gabriel load his gifts into his room, which again, was outlandishly smaller and less lavish than the rest of ours. I sat on his tiny blue cotton blanketed bed when Sebastien left us, and toyed with one of the gadgets I bought him.

"Did you get everything you wanted?" I asked.

"Almost." Gabriel was a fraction of an inch from my face, his eyes pleading. "Can I kiss you Arianna? I promise not to run away this time."

I knew better than to let him. I should have left from the room, but my mind exploded, bursting with memories.

Gabriel was six years old kissing my knee when I fell off my bike. He was ten, and he spent his allowance on a sparkly hair clip I wanted instead of the remote control truck he was saving for. He was sixteen, and we cried together when Millie told us she had cancer.

Gabriel *was* me. I looked into his eyes and saw raw, unadulterated need. He was always there for me, and he needed me now. If I was honest with myself at the time, I would have admitted that I needed him too, way sooner that I did.

I kissed him. He kissed me. We tore at each others' bodies in the rush to be fulfilled by the other.

There would have been no stopping. We had passed the point of no return. A knock at the door broke our embrace.

"It's me," Ava said from the other side of the door.

"Come in," Gabriel called in a hoarse voice.

I pulled my shirt down, and adjusted my skirt.

Ava frowned, but gave no other indication she had witnessed anything between us. "We wanted to know if you were ready to go to Screwdriver?"

Gabriel's face twisted in confusion.

"It's a nightclub," I told him. "They play rock and hip hop, but it makes complete sense. I went there not too long before you got here. I think you'd like it. We were going to surprise you, but your real party is going to be there," I told him.

"Sure." He grinned his sparkling smile. "Why not?"

I dressed excitedly for the occasion. I bought a new dress online ages ago, and it was perfect.

Julian decided to make an entrance just before I came downstairs. I ignored his envious stare when I stepped into the foyer, clothed in my tight-as-a-glove banana yellow dress. I'll admit, I took the last few stairs slowly, letting him eat his heart out. I wanted him to know what he was missing out on. Little girl, ha! He ate those words that night. The dress was about the size of a cocktail napkin, and I was restless and ready to party. Ava's dress wasn't much larger, and it was black and white patterned houndstooth in a simple sheath cut.

Ethan and I had found a new comradeship in each other, and he drove Gabriel, Ava, and me to the nightclub.

We arrived and stepped ahead of the waiting crowd, drawing as much attention as we had the last time. We were herded to our same designated VIP booth. Sebastien, Walker, Jade, and Savannah were right behind us.

The music was loud and right on par with what we typically listened to. The same waiter we previously had approached our table.

"What can I get you?" I could tell he was nervous.

Ava ordered a rum and coke, and all the guys except Ethan and Walker, who were driving, ordered beer. Gabriel followed suit, which surprised me, and Savannah and Jade ordered lollipop martinis.

"Ava, um, do you care…"

She smiled. "You are a big girl. Get what you want."

I felt a twinge of guilt, but bravely ordered the martini that Savannah and Jade wanted. My conscience screamed at me. Millie's face loomed in my mind, reminding me of all of the evils of alcohol. She would kill me. She hated drinking.

I pushed her from my mind, and sipped the candy-flavored drink set before me.

"Do you wanna dance?" Gabriel yelled above the noise.

"This is way different from prom, huh?" I said.

Gabriel led me to the shiny floor and we began to dance. The waiter kept a steady flow of our vices of choice, even on the dance floor. Three drinks later, my inhibitions were slowing way down. Six drinks later, my inhibitions were nonexistent.

I ground my hips into Gabriel's, the sounds of a familiar song ringing in my head. Sometime during our night, we started making out like crazy on the dance floor. We returned to our VIP booth breathless, tired, and turned on.

Everyone gathered upstairs, and the waiter brought out a huge birthday cake with candles that sparked like pyrotechnics at a rock concert.

The deejay announced Gabriel's birthday, and everyone gazed up at us from the dance floor. Gabriel dipped me, and kissed me in front of everyone. The crowd went crazy, everyone clapped and cheered.

"Well isn't this something?" Jade slurred. "I knew when I went to dig up trash on you that Mr. Gabriel here would be a black smear on your snow-white record. Julian will *love* to hear this story."

Gabriel put his arm around me. "Go ahead, Jade. What do we care what Julian thinks?" He kissed me on the lips, his beer breath tasted sweet on my mouth.

I sobered somewhat at the sound of Julian's name. The guilty feeling crept up my neck, leaving unease in my bones.

I cared what Julian thought. Great.

We got back to Eden late, and I fell into Gabriel's bed. My head was literally swimming, and I was out cold in nothing flat.

The usual staff chose that particular morning after to come and mow the lawn. The air was abuzz with noisy machines inside and out, cleaning, cutting, and washing. Nausea and a razor sharp pain in my head awoke me. "Gabriel?" I mumbled. I could barely move my head. "It hurts. Everything hurts." I buried my face in the pillow.

"It's a hangover. You'll be fine."

Three days later, none of my symptoms had subsided. Sebastien moved me into my bed sometime the first day, and Gabriel kept vigil day and night. The guys and Ava and Savannah came to check on me regularly.

The mention of food Ethan originally came up to suggest, sent me hugging the toilet for an hour. The endless supply of crackers turned to sawdust in my mouth, and the ginger ale had the consistency of sludge. My fever raged, and I refused a doctor.

Savannah forced Gabriel to leave for a few minutes and get some air. After much protesting, he agreed.

"Please let us take you to the doctor. Julian's out of his mind with worry. He hasn't slept since you've been sick." Savannah's tiny porcelain face was wrought with anxiety, and I almost caved.

"He hasn't come to check on me once. Besides, I'm not dying. I have a hangover."

"Arianna, sweetie, hangovers don't last this long. They are usually gone by the next afternoon."

"I caught something then. I'll be fine."

"I wish you'd reconsider..." Savannah gently leaned me forward and fluffed my pillow.

She sponged my forehead with a cold towel, but Gabriel soon returned to take over.

Ava came in behind him and disappeared in my bathroom. She handed my vial to me.

"What is that for?"

232

"You're sick. Don't drink it if you don't want to, but the relief is instant. Come on, honey, please. I'll leave you now, but you need to try it. Remember your foot?" Ava kissed my cheek and motioned for Savannah to follow her outside, and they left Gabriel and me alone.

Gabriel unscrewed the lid and uncorked the vial.

"I've had enough to drink, thanks," I protested through gritted teeth.

"Suit yourself."

And so began a battle of wills.

He swung the vial back and forth on the necklace like he was trying to hypnotize me. He laid it next to my sick form, green with nausea. He swirled it over and over, but I didn't budge. As ailing as I was, I kept my lips sealed tight.

The next day I was even sicker, and Gabriel finally lost it.

"Arianna! Why won't you just drink the damned water? I can't stand this. You're just being stubborn. Even your Prince of Darkness is out pacing the floors," he said referring to Julian. "Why won't you please just drink it?"

"Because you'll think I'm a sellout," I whispered. "You said you don't want to live forever, and forever would be torture without you."

"Oh, baby. I was on a soapbox. I didn't mean what I said. Well, I did mean it, but you don't have to drink it every day. Just this one time? Please? If I get too old, you can hold me down and pour it in my mouth. Agreed?"

The fact that he called me baby was probably the deciding factor. Either that or the fact that I had to puke again. I carefully took the vial, and opened it.

"Cheers."

DEMAND

I emptied the contents into my mouth and squeezed my eyes as tight as I could. The water should have been room temperature, but it was ice cold. The taste was instantly addictive. It was a flavor not found anywhere in the world. Pure, natural, sweet. The taste of everything that was beautiful.

It was the taste of youth. The taste so many people craved- the sick, the old, the dying. The water coursed through my veins. I felt every blood vessel, every artery it entered. I felt alive.

When the sensations subsided, I slowly opened one eye. "Did it work?"

Gabriel fell off the side of the bed in loud guffaws.

"It didn't. I'm still plain and ugly." I was on the verge of tears. At least I felt better.

Gabriel laughed harder, and I was sure he was mocking me. "I'm sorry, I'm sorry." He looked at me and broke into laughter again.

"Gabriel Bennett, it's not funny!" I swatted at him.

"Of course it didn't work. You have always been the most beautiful girl in the world."

I leapt out of bed, forgetting the fact that my illness was completely cured. I gazed in the bathroom mirror, leaning close to get a good look.

Gabriel was wrong.

It was me, but it wasn't me. I barely recognized the girl in the mirror. Smoke from the misty water swirled about my body. The haze cast a spectral rainbow I hadn't been able to see before. My eyesight was so clear. Each one of my senses was magnified a million times. I smelled, saw, heard, tasted, and felt like never before.

The mark on my forehead from my childhood case of chickenpox was gone. The scar on my knee from a bicycle accident had disappeared. My ugly hands, ruined from years of knuckle cracking and cuticle biting were perfect. My hair was shinier, and my skin was cleared of the blemish I felt coming up on my chin earlier.

"It worked! You liar, it worked!" I ran from the bathroom and danced around the bed.

"Keep it down. Everyone has gone to bed by now."

"I'm sorry, I just feel... everything. Gabriel you have to try-"
He shook his head. "Not until I'm old and dying, remember? I'm glad you're better. I am going to go finally get some sleep." He squeezed my hand and kissed my cheek.

"I love you Arianna."

The words came naturally. "I love you too, Gabriel."

Gabriel closed the door behind him.

I felt too much alive to sleep, so I stole downstairs. I passed the pool and ran as fast as I could down the beach. The ache in my lungs I expected to come after I got winded never came. The exhaustion I should have felt from running after a sickness never surfaced. I kept running until I voluntarily collapsed in the sand.

I stared into the night sky for a long time searching for an answer to life. I brushed the sand off, and began to walk back. A dark figure walked toward me, and I recognized it immediately.

"Julian."

"You drank." He held out his hand and motioned to the rainbow mist. "It will wear off soon. Drinking it makes it last much longer than applying it to wounds."

"What are you doing out here?" I was mesmerized by the sight of him, but a little unnerved at the same time. We were supposed to be mad at each other.

"I should ask you the same thing."

"I came to get some air."

"I came to make my request." His lips curled upwards in a sardonic grin.

"Oh? And what would that be?" I raised my eyebrows.

"I want you to ask Gabriel to leave."

I gasped. "I can't- no, I won't do that. Gabriel and I are a package deal. If one goes, the other follows suit."

I reeled at the implications of his demand. I would no more ask Gabriel to leave than I would Ava. I was fuming. How dare he ask me something like that?

"I'm sorry you feel that way, but you must comply. You agreed to the terms when you entered the race."

"Not those terms! I won't do it. It was a stupid race, Julian. Not a life or death situation. How would you feel if you were forced to make me leave? You're wrong, Julian. I'll gather my things and leave when Gabriel wakes up in the morning."

"You will not leave me, Arianna. You cannot."

I ran from him. I flew into the premises of the secret hiding place of the Fountain of Youth, disgusted by the entire situation. I fell into my feather soft mattress, and buried my face in its depths. I screamed and railed, wanting someone to come up and check on me, but the response was silence. I grabbed my stomach. Nausea ripped through me. It seemed the Fountain's water cured everything but heartache.

At the first light of dawn, I opened my eyes. They should have been puffy and red with lack of sleep, but a closer inspection in the mirror revealed a pair of bright green eyes. I hated Julian for his demand, and I hated myself for the burning desire to comply with it.

I would never hurt Gabriel. Not at the expense of forbidding him from a house I hated more and more with each passing day. I was at a breaking point.

I wasn't too surprised with the gathering in the den so early. I was a late sleeper, so I was usually the last one to make it downstairs. I was surprised though, to see several suitcases lined along a wall.

Ava approached me. "Gabriel was right, honey. You look exactly the same."

I grinned at her bold faced lie. "*Sure* I do." I rolled my eyes, laughing and shaking my head. "Delivery?" I pointed to the bags.

Ava walked right up to me and whispered. "I need to talk to you. Alone. Is that okay?" Ava's face showed urgency.

The sound of her hushed tone should have been hard to hear, but the words were as loud as a normal conversation. The newfound super senses explained some lingering questions I had about the day Ava and Savannah came to my school. I remembered their lips moving quickly deep in conversation. Even in the dead silence as everyone stared at them, no sound was heard.

Ava took my arm an guided me to her room for privacy. I thought of all the happy times I spent in there with her and Savannah and Sebastien; it was easily on of my favorite rooms in the house.

I perched in a wicker chair. "What's up?"

"I know it's not any of my business, but the night of Gabriel's party I walked in on you two." She waved her hand to convey nonchalance, but I knew she was truly worried about my love life.

I was mortified.

"Have you ever- I don't mean to pry, but I promised Millie I wouldn't let you get into any trouble. It was a lapse in judgment for me to let you drink. It's so hard to see you as my niece and not one of my peers." She cleared her throat and looked everywhere in the room but at me.

"Anyway, that's not the point of   this talk. You are a smart girl, and you can decide what's best for you. My concern is about the stress Julian is putting on you."

"He's making me ask Gabriel to leave," I told her.

"He is not! Wait until I see him." Ava's nostrils flared, and I was comforted in knowing that breathing fire was not one of the special talents acquired by drinking from the Fountain.

"I care about Julian, though. I'm doing them both wrong."

"Have you made a commitment to either one of them?"

"No."

"I can see how much you love Gabriel. We all see it. But I also see how Julian seems to ignite a fire in you. The first time you rode with him on the jet ski, you practically floated back up to the dock.

"It's going to be a hard decision, but I think you might be being too hard on yourself. You didn't turn to Gabriel until you argued with Julian, right?"

"I have barely spoken to Julian since Gabriel got here, and when I have, it hasn't been pleasant."

"But you're sure you want to be with Gabriel," she prompted.

"No. Yes. I don't know. Gabriel can see what's between Julian and I. He knows, I've told him that much."

"I am *not* encouraging you to pursue Julian, but whatever decision you make is the one that's best for you. You aren't the kind of person to lead them both on, but you have the tendency to try to make everyone happy all the time. This time though, you can't do that. Often in life you have to let something go so you can hold on to something more important with both hands so it won't escape." We were both quiet for a moment, and I knew we were both thinking about how uncomfortable we were. "On that note, I didn't mean to hold you hostage all day. We can go."

"So, who's leaving to go on a delivery?" I remembered the luggage in the den.

Ava smacked her forehead lightly with her palm. "I almost forgot to tell you. That was the whole point of me talking to you about Julian. I need you to be here with him today. Alone.

"Well not completely alone, staff will be here."

I balked. Alone with Julian. The three most dangerous words in my mental dictionary when they were put together in just that order.

"Staff is coming back to finish some things in a few hours, so we need to scatter. The guys are going deep sea fishing, and I'm going on a delivery with Jade. Savannah is going to talk to Dave Mathis in Miami about acquiring our new residence there. I didn't want to tell you until I knew for sure, but we won't have to stay in a hotel next time. We're getting the house you wanted." She curled one side of her lip up in a sly smile.

My mind went far back to my trip to Miami with Ava. I had forgotten the whole thing. My cottage a little ways outside Miami. Home. At least, it felt like home when I was there. I imagined myself on my window seat at that second, dreaming away with a cup if chai tea. I was stunned. I could not believe they were buying a house that was completely unsuited for them just because I liked it.

As excited as I was, there was no way I was letting her off the hook so easily.

"Why can't I go with you? I would love to go away for a few days, just like Miami. Please, Ava, why does Jade have to go?" I protested.

"Because she's important to this one, and we need you here. Staff is usually different, but we've used these people several years ago. It's hard to find a new crew of discreet foreigners that we trust with everything we keep so secret here. Henry had a new staff for us, but when he used them at his home before sending them here, he found one of them plundering through his office. It's been close to ten years since this crew came last time. They are going to notice that we still look the same. You're a new face, and it helps us to maintain our privacy. We don't want to be seen very often by the same people."

"What about Julian?" I tried to sound indifferent, but I was hysterical about being alone with him.

"He stays in his room all day anyway, and they've never seen him. We need you to be here if they have any questions and to supervise the Fountain."

"I guess so, but I'm mad at him. He doesn't even want me here." She seemed stern about the decision, so I began to grasp at straws to get out of the task at hand. "Will I be able to call you if I need to?" I felt like a child being left for the first time with a babysitter, and I probably sounded like one too. I was whining and I knew it. Grrr. I used to look forward to being alone with Julian.

"I'll keep my phone close as I can." She gave a weak smile.

We went down to the first floor of the house, and I stopped in front of Gabriel. "Come back to me soon."

"I will. I don't feel comfortable leaving you here... with him," he murmured.

"I'll be- I'm fine," I stammered. "Go have fun. Hurry back, okay."

He squeezed my hand.

"Let's go guys," Sebastien hollered as he herded the boys outside to the boat. He kissed Savannah so gently my heart wrenched. "I envy every man in Miami who gets to see your face. Are you sure you want to go alone? I can come."

Savannah shooed him with her hands. "I want some time to myself," she said, but I knew better. She wanted Sebastien to spend some guy time with his brother and his friends.

Each person made their exit one at a time, slowly leaving me alone with *him*. Ava was the last to go, even though the guys were delayed thirty minutes or so by Gabriel's lingering. I started up to my room, deciding to retreat for the day.   Julian made his first official appearance leaning against my doorframe outside my room.

"Your boyfriend threatened my life if I touched you." He laughed bitterly. "Isn't that smart, biting the hand that feeds you."

"Could you please move?" I crossed my arms and sighed impatiently. "I haven't slept all night because you're a jerk."

"My being a jerk had nothing to do with your lack of sleep, so I won't apologize for that. But I could never ask him to leave, if that meant asking you to leave. I was wrong, and I'm sorry. I want to spend the day with you. That is my request." His turquoise eyes were sincere.

I was instantly suspicious. "All right. Let me get dressed."

Thunder rolled ominously in the distance.

ATONE

This was the day I forbid myself from dreaming of. A day with Julian, alone in his mythical playground. Eternal sun sacrificed itself that infamous day for storms, cultivating the perfect day with my dark angel.

I donned a black dress and my necklace with the black angel's wings Ava sent me, a lifetime ago it seemed, in Ellaville. It represented everything that was Julian. It was perfect. I wore the wings of my dark angel.

I almost jumped out of my skin when a dark-haired woman met me face to face outside my bedroom door when I opened it. She was plump, but she had a kind sort of face. She was way more terrified of me than I was of her.

"I'm so sorry to scare you ma'am, but Master Julian asked me to tell you he is waiting for you in the formal dining room," she said in a thick accent I could not quite place.

"Did you just say *Master* Julian?" She just stared.

Classic, I thought.

 A look of confusion swept across her face.

"Nevermind. Tell him I am taking a nap, and he will have to wait." She turned to relay the message, but I wasn't done. Julian was going to pay for the things he'd asked of me the night before. "Oh, and Julian wants all of his clothes donated to charity, he has a new wardrobe on the way. Throw out everything."

I smiled inside imagining the look on his face when he realized all of his clothes were gone. *Master* Julian. No doubt in my mind that he asked to be called that, the arrogant self absorbed... I couldn't think of a name shocking enough to label him with. Ha. Ha. A master with no clothes. Served him right.

I didn't want to ruin my outfit by sleeping, like I told the woman I would be doing, and I was shocked I wasn't tired after not going to bed all night. I wanted to keep him waiting though, so I finished several chapters of a book I was into. The heavy rain continued, and I was glad it wasn't sunny. I hated being cooped up indoors when I could be at the beach or the pool.

The house was full of people scrubbing things and running up and down the stairs with armfuls of dirty curtains and carts of cleaning supplies. The acrid smell of the disinfectant they used burned my nostrils. I said hello to all of the members of the staff as I passed, but they stayed as far away from me as possible. Julian probably demanded privacy at all costs.

It was around one before I went to see if Julian was still waiting for me in the dining room. He was. Just as stubborn as me. The candles that flickered across his dark face were melted almost all the way down. He had been waiting for quite a while.

"That was a long nap." There was a sharp edge to his voice.

"You shouldn't have waited," I said curtly.

"I want to spend time with you," he said softly.

"To degrade my relationship with Gabriel, and ask inappropriate questions about us." It wasn't a question.

A tall man came into the dining room with our first course. I was expecting breakfast since it was still early when Julian asked to see me, but I was delighted at the Caprese salad set before me. The balsamic vinegar perfectly balanced the sweet tomatoes and creamy mozzarella.

"Here's your big chance. What do you want to know?" I asked.

"Everything I haven't asked you before. I've told you all my stories, and you've told me none of yours. My life became important after I met you. You know everything that has happened since then."

Actually, he had never told me any of his stories, but he was trying to be honest with me. The realization that I could not say the same hit my stomach and took my breath right out of my chest. Julian made my life more important. More worth living. But circumstantially and financially so. Millie and Doug and Gabriel gave me a reason to wake up and go to bed with a smile almost every morning and night of my life.

"You must have loved your father very much to imprison yourself here for so long after he died." I knew I was opening a door to a very dark place. I wanted Julian to show me something about his feelings. Anything.

He flinched. "My *father*," he spat the word, "was a cruel and disgusting man whose evil ways killed my mother."

I swallowed. I got a response at least. "Literally?" I squeaked.

"Yes. She committed suicide when I was a teenager."

"Are- were you an only child?" I corrected myself.

"I had a brother. A younger brother. He was stillborn."

I remained silent. "So you see, Arianna, before I met you, I knew nothing but loss. You bring me light. I need you. As much as you need Gabriel. At the same time it drives me crazy for him to be here. You would hate me if you knew all the plans I concocted as revenge against him."

My heart twisted, and all the agitation I felt toward him melted. "I could never hate you Julian. And you could never hurt Gabriel."

"I wish I were as innocent as you think I am. I want him gone, and I want you to be the one that tells him to go. Not because I make you, but because you want to."

"I can't do that Julian. You know I can't." I stood from the table. "I fulfilled your wishes, now please let me go."

"You're excused." He complied easily, but not before he threw his linen napkin on the floor and walked out of the room before I did.

My heart broke at the sight of a person I cared so much about hurting so badly, and all at the expense of my cheap, fickle feelings. I was disgusted with myself. I was the source of all the hurt in the house. He did me wrong too, but only after he found out that I wasn't honest about having someone else back home. As much as I wanted to leave and be done with it all, I wanted most to stay.

I loved Ava. Millie raised me, and Uncle Doug looked after me, but Ava had become my sister. We were so close, and I trusted her. It would have been hard to see her as anything else because she appeared so young, but she was my big sister. She never judged me, or tried to sway my opinions.

On the other side of the scales was Gabriel. I had miserably failed any attempt to cut him out of my life. If I had been more reasonable, more mature, kept in touch, he wouldn't have come here. I wouldn't have to watch Julian suffer so much.

A scream sent me running upstairs. I tried to discern where the sound was coming from, and my heart stopped when I realized it came from Julian's room at the furthest stretch of the east wing. When I came upon him he stood in front of the maid who had cleaned my room earlier, his face ghost white. Her hands and apron sparkled with the rainbow haze that had become so familiar to me.

She knew, and she was about to ask a lot of questions.

FLIGHT

"Diablo," she accused, pointing her finger at Julian.

"No, you don't understand," he protested, stepping toward her, but she stepped back, shrinking from his presence, shielding her face from him.

She began yelling in Spanish. I hadn't recognized her language earlier. I only caught bits and pieces of her tirade. This was probably due to the fact that my high school Spanish class was not in-depth enough to understand simple directions, let alone the steady flow of angry words leaving her mouth.

Julian fired off for a moment in flawless Spanish, and she spoke back. She calmed down for a moment after they talked.

"Ella?" Julian asked. There was and edge to his voice.

"Si, si." Her finger pointed straight at me.

"You told her to throw my clothes away?" Uh-oh. His frosty eyes burned mine with their coldness. I felt like I was getting hypothermia just from looking at him.

I laughed weakly. "Heh, heh. Sorry. It was just a joke?"

"Do you know what could have happened?" he thundered.

My heart raced. How was I going to get out of this one? More so, how was *he* going to get *us* out of this one?

"Maria, you must have bumped your head hard when you fell. Are you dizzy? Let's get you down to the den and prop your feet up," he suggested in English.

She looked as confused as I did for a moment.

Julian flashed his perfect, dazzling smile and patted her back. "Come on, sweet lady, I'll take good care of you." He wrapped his arm under her knees, and carried her steadily down the stairs as if she weighed no more than a kitten.

The buxom woman grinned shyly, her wrinkles more pronounced. "Gracias, Master Julian."

I gasped. What just happened? She didn't fall. She was plundering in Julian's room, which I told her to do, and must have come upon Julian's vial.

I followed downstairs and watched "Master Julian" put on an Oscar worthy performance. He set her gently on the couch, and ordered a young staff boy to bring him something I didn't know the English interpretation for. The boy brought a pillow, and Julian fluffed it beneath her neck. He whispered something in her ear, and she laughed like a schoolgirl.

I tried hard not to gag. We left the room after she was placated, and Julian led me outside, grasping the top of my arm with a little too much force.

It was still storming, but I braved the pelting rain for solace from the hot and crowded house. The wind sent stiff raindrops into my arm that felt more like daggers. It was actually cold, a sensation I had not genuinely felt since last winter. But then I remembered how coldly Julian had just looked at me, and I got chills when I realized he wasn't far behind me.

"What happened in your room? The woman, she believed you?" I asked, shivering.

"*You* told her to relieve me of my hundred-thousand dollar wardrobe, and she stumbled across my vial, tucked into a box in the back of my closet. I hid it there because staff is always forbidden to enter my closet in addition to the Fountain room. She thought it was going to be thrown out, and she opened the vial because, as any person would be, she was curious. Do you *know* the danger you put us in?"

"But you told her she hit her head. Won't she question the fact that her hands look like a teenager?"

"Are you always so brainless? I *told* her she hit her head. She won't question anything I tell her. I made her believe that, because she would believe anything I told her. I can control her every thought. Didn't you pay attention when Ava showed you the Fountain? I could make her dance naked if it pleased me."

I curled my fists so tight, my nails dug holes in my palm. "You are disgusting. Too bad it doesn't work on me. You could control the whole world, but you only choose to control me. I won't make Gabriel leave, ever. He will go willingly when I *tell* him to. *With me*!" I yelled. "And furthermore, I am not brainless, I obviously have the sense to tell the good guys from the bad." I spun on my heel and fled up to my room.

I spun the dial to the shower as far as it would go to blast me with the water full force. I stripped down and hugged my knees in the painful water pressure, trying to drown my sobs. I turned the knob to the cold water all the way off and the knob to the hot water full fury. The water singed my skin, leaving bright red blotches. I couldn't get warm enough. Julian's icy blue stare chilled me to the bone.

My threats were idle. I couldn't leave. But I couldn't stay. I weighed the pros and cons of my options, and neither felt right. I sobbed harder. Julian would make my life hell as long as he thought I was in love with Gabriel, and Gabriel...well, Gabriel would never make my life hell, not even if I chose to be with Julian. He would be supportive no matter what I opted.

If I could find a way to show Julian I wanted him, he would let us both stay. I began to formulate an plot to stay in Eden with my new family, and keep my reason to live here with me.

I scrubbed my skin until it shone. I shaved carefully while I let my hair conditioner soak in. The blue strands were almost completely faded out; I needed to visit Patrick the hairdresser's shop in Miami very soon.

I picked through every inch of my closet searching for the perfect outfit. Nothing seemed appropriate, and I threw up my hands in defeat.

Where could I find something perfect? I sneaked past a maid and into Ava's room. I felt like I was committing a crime, even though Ava had offered me free reign of her closet many times.

It didn't take much plundering through Ava's clothes before I found exactly what I was looking for, a slick, black, off-the-shoulder nightgown. It had an empire waist, and hit my legs just below where my thighs met my hips. I wadded it up to conceal it if anyone caught me, and took the lingerie into my room. I heard Julian's voice booming authority from downstairs, and went to see what was going on.

"Thank you Juan," Julian said. All of the staff members were lined up, about to leave. For three months without cleaning, the house didn't look much different. Eden was always immaculate. The smell was the only thing that gave away the fact that intruders had been here. The scent of ammonia made me sneeze. Julian caught my eye out of the corner of his. He gave the young boy a thick padded envelope. I was sure it was filled with money. He continued to hand out the envelopes, and gave Maria her envelope last.

"My, you have lovely hands. I noticed them when you arrived. It must be a very special hand cream you use."

"How did you know Master Julian?" She blushed to the tips of her toes.

"Thank you all. We may require your services again soon." Julian bowed and the staff hurried out of the door.

The sound of the door being shut rang in my ears. Alone.

I went upstairs without saying a word to Julian and put on Ava's nightgown. I scattered every grooming product I owned on the bathroom counter, and put them all to use. My hands trembled so badly, I could barely blowdry my hair. Curling up on the bathroom floor, I lost all nerve. It seemed like an eternity before I could muster up the courage to pick myself off the floor and put my illicit plan into action. I crept down the hall to Julian's private chambers.

He was sitting on the edge of his bed with his head in his hands. He swirled amber liquid in a crystal brandy glass.

"Julian?" I stepped toward him, my gait as unsteady as my feelings about what I was going to do next.

"Arianna, what are you doing in here?" He raked his fingers roughly through his hair. "Please, not now."

I walked bravely to where he sat and removed the glass from his hand. The liquid bounced; my hands shook uncontrollably. I clamped my mouth shut to keep my teeth from chattering. I threw one leg over him, and straddled his lap. I pulled his face toward mine and opened my mouth, drawing him into a deep kiss. My nervousness faded immediately when his mouth opened into mine.

"What are you trying to do to me?" he asked. His breath was ragged, and there was a sexy rasp to his speech.

I kissed him again with more fire, more lust.

"I won't be able to stop," he said, pushing me away.

"I don't want you to stop." My voice was as smooth as silk when it left my lips, but chill bumps on the back of my neck belied my lack of confidence.

"Arianna," he breathed in my ear.

He flipped me backward onto his bed. Our bodies tangled, and I was unable to tell where he ended and I began. I arched my back, drawing myself up. Julian lifted my gown and kissed my hips and navel.

We moved dangerously close to everything I wanted, everything I hated myself for.

He ripped the gown in two pieces, from the embroidered bodice to the hemline. I gasped. The only thing between us now was a pair of gray boxers and a sheer black bra and underwear set that matched the gown that I would have to replace before Ava got suspicious. He ground his hips into mine, and my nails dug ditches in his back, eliciting a dark, hoarse moan.

"Do you want me, Arianna?"

"Yes. Yes," I growled.

He pulled away suddenly and looked into my eyes. His beauty made my heart ache.

"Tell me you love me."

I sat up, my back ramrod straight. "What?"

"Tell me you love me."

I knew what he was thinking, and I tried to explain. "Oh God, Julian. No!"

He jumped away from me as if I had suddenly changed into something repulsive, vile.

"You thought you could trick me. You thought if you made me believe you wanted me, I would let your precious Gabriel stay here." He emptied the contents of the brandy glass in his mouth and squeezed the glass so hard it exploded with a loud *pop!* Shards of glass lodged deep into his hands, and the blood began to flow.

His hand was covered in blood, but he didn't seem to notice. I rushed to him and pulled his hand into mine to examine the severity of his wounds, but he snatched away from my grasp.

"You don't understand," I told him. "It's not what you think."

If he heard me, he didn't let on. "I could have any woman I wanted." There was a frenzied edge to his voice and mannerisms. He swiped the back of his hand across his jaw, leaving a trail of blood across his face. He stared at the wound on his hand while he spoke. "I don't want your body, I wanted you to love me. *Damnit!*" He raked his arm across the decorations on the mantle of the fireplace and sent several priceless antiques across the marble floor.

"I believed you, and you never told me the truth. I'm a fool. I have *never* been loved."

"You're wrong Julian. Please, listen to me."

The door flew open.

I can only guess what Gabriel thought he was witnessing when he happened upon us that night. He must have heard the yelling, and everyone else must have been downstairs. All he saw was me, silent tears running down my face, shaking, my blood streaked hands, dripping with Julian's anguish.

"How dare you," Gabriel hissed. "What have you done to her?"

He grabbed Julian and threw him face first into the floor. "You filthy piece of -" Gabriel fired off a string of profanities, some of which I had never heard first person.

He punched Julian squarely in the face and kicked him in the stomach when he fell to the floor. He stomped Julian's face over and over. Every inch of Julian's body was covered in blood. I tried to intervene, but Gabriel shoved me back, hard.

"Do something Julian!" I pleaded.

Julian grinned. The spaces between his teeth bled. "I will fight for you Arianna, but never against you." Those were his final conscious words.

"Stop it Gabriel! You'll kill him!" I screamed.

"What's the commotion?" Ethan stopped short, dumbfounded by the scene. I flailed my arms at Gabriel, but he continued the massacre, even after Julian's mind had gone black.

Sebastien and Walker were right behind Ethan, and they pulled Gabriel off Julian. Gabriel fought against them, and they tackled him to the floor. Gabriel was no match for their strength.

Gabriel finally stilled, and Ethan spoke. "Julian will kill you when he comes to. You have to leave. Right now."

Walker fumbled in his pockets. The stench of fish from their deep sea fishing made me gag. Walker handed Gabriel a key to his car. "Take care of our girl."

Gabriel jogged down the hallway, but I stood frozen to my spot.

"Arianna, go with Gabriel," Ethan commanded.

I knelt beside Julian and kissed the corner of his blood stained mouth. I yanked the chain of my angel wings necklace until it snapped into my palm, and I placed it in his hand. "Memento Mori, Julian."

I ran to catch up with Gabriel. My body and mind were completely numb as I climbed into the passenger seat. Gabriel revved the engine and threw the car into drive.

The headlights did little to guide our path. The rain was coming down so hard, it was almost impossible to see the road. While Gabriel swerved and sped, I welcomed the thought of careening into a ditch and blacking out from the pain. Gabriel's safety was at risk too, though, so I broke the silence.

"You need to calm down. You're going to kill us."

"I should have killed *him* for what he did to you!" Gabriel screamed. He slammed both fists on the steering wheel.

"*I* came to *him* Gabriel. I went into his bedroom, I sought him out, and I initiated everything."

"Then why are you covered in blood? Why was he yelling at you?"

"He broke a glass in his hand. He was angry because I wouldn't tell him I loved him."

I began to cry, and I wiped my face with the short arm of the ruined gown. The gesture released the scent of Julian's cologne. I gagged again, the second time that night.

"Pull over," I said.

I got out onto the shoulder of the road and vomited, emptying the contents of my stomach onto the grassy shoulder of the road. I began to sob. I buried my face in my hands and let it all go. There, on a deserted Florida highway, I lost control. I mourned the loss of my new family, my new home, and the man who I had almost given myself to. Gabriel never came to console me. Minutes ticked by, and I finally managed to pull myself together and get back in the car.

"Do you love him?" Gabriel's voice cracked on the last word. He did not look at me.

I let the seat back and closed my eyes. The weight of the unanswered question was almost unbearable.

"Where are we going to go?" Gabriel asked.

I was unresponsive. Sometime during the dark and the quiet, I wondered if I still had a pulse. The only reminder that I was still alive was the hum of the highway that filled my ears, and the throbbing sound of my broken heart.

"We're almost out of gas. Arianna, please I don't know what to do. I don't have any money, and we're a long way from anything."

I wanted to hold his hand and tell him everything would be okay, but the words wouldn't come out, and I wasn't sure if I believed it myself.

Gabriel pulled into a gas station at the first sign of civilization. "We are driving on fumes. What are we going to do?"

He opened the glove compartment and the center console. The only things they produced were and owner's manual and a pair of women's thong underwear. Walker's car, go figure.

Gabriel sat back in his seat. I opened my eyes long enough to see him staring out the window watching the rain make small pools on the blacktop. We stayed that way for a long time.

My throat was raw and dry when I spoke. "Give me your shirt," I croaked.

"What?"

"I can't exactly go in there in a shredded nightgown and my underwear."

"What are you going to do?"

I sighed, exasperated. "Rob them with my pistol." Gabriel actually looked scared. "Seriously?" I challenged. "Are you kidding me? I don't have a gun. You know that. Give me the shirt."

He removed his shirt reluctantly, and I slipped it on after removing the gown. The tee shirt was just big enough to cover my bottom.

I walked barefooted into the store. It was vacant except for a chubby male clerk sitting behind the counter, flipping through a computer gaming magazine.

"Hello."

He stood at full attention. "What can I help you with?"

I mustered my courage. I knew it worked, I had seen it firsthand.

"I need some gas, and I seem to have lost my wallet." I flipped my palms upward and shrugged. I concentrated on the clerk, envisioning him succumbing to my needs. I pressed the thought of what I wanted into him. I could feel my mind stretch with the new sensation. The power came easily, but I was still dubious about whether or not it would work.

"I can take care of that for you. Fill it up."

I almost fell over in shock. I suppressed a grin. I leaned as far forward as the counter would allow and traced my fingers along his pink, hairy arm.

"I really need some money."

He pulled a Velcro wallet out of his back pocket. He produced a fistful of bills, and dropped them on the counter in front of me. I was disgusted with myself, but I was starving, and I knew Gabriel was hungry and tired.

"Thank you mister. If I ever go back to where I came from, I'll make sure you never have to worry about anything else."

He scribbled his phone number on a paper sack. "You c-can c-call me if you want," he stammered.

"Sure, sure," I agreed, with no intention of remembering the awful events that lead us to that godforsaken store afterwards. "Thanks again."

I walked back to the car, and instructed Gabriel to fill the tank. He got back in the car, eyeing me suspiciously. I produced the money.

"How did you get that?" he demanded.

"It doesn't matter now. Just drive us home. I want to go home."

ADRIFT

"Gabriel, can we please stop for the night?" I tried to reason with him. We were lost. We must have driven past the turnoff to Georgia, but the rain was so heavy we couldn't make out anything. The roads had recently changed, and Walker's GPS wasn't updated. We were lost and a long way from home. He stayed focused on the road, not even flinching. The odometer continued to rise, and I was worried about Gabriel driving under the circumstances. I was mentally fried, and I knew Gabriel must have felt much the same way.

"That guy gave me more than enough money for a hotel room and breakfast. We have to stop for clothes anyway. I can't go to Millie's like this." I gestured to his filthy shirt that still reeked of fish.

Gabriel touched the screen of the GPS. "There's a hotel seven miles from here."

The hotel was actually a motel, and a roach-filled one at that. Gabriel had to pay the sleazy clerk double because he didn't have his ID.

I fell into the bed, not caring how unclean the sheets were. The dingy walls held a faded print of a Southwestern desert. The bedspread was a stained floral print, and there were dead bugs in the bottom of the shower. I thought of the Egyptian cotton sheets awaiting me in Eden. Gabriel hesitated when I scooted to one side, leaving room for him. He turned away and settled down, curling in a ball on the floor without saying a word.

I flipped off the dim lamp, and after a few moments, I heard Gabriel's muffled crying. There were many things I could endure, but Gabriel's pain caused by me was not one of them.

I lay down beside him on the cold hard floor and held his hand while he cried. I smoothed his hair, and tears slid down my face as well.

My voice was shaky with grief, but I had to tell him. I wanted him to know what brought us to that point. "He wanted you to leave. I told him no, that you and I were a package deal, but he wouldn't let it go. I went to his room, thinking that if I could make him believe I wanted to be with him, he would let you stay. I wanted to stay there, with you and Ava, so I came up with the only way I knew to keep us together."

"So you sacrificed yourself to keep me with you? Arianna, I can hold my own with Julian. I would never have left, not until I made sure you had a secure future. Now your options are as limited as mine. There is nothing in Ellaville, there never was."

My heart surged when I heard the name of the town that held my true home. Resigning myself to it wasn't as hard as I'd thought it would be. I was relieved to be going somewhere so familiar. I had to tell him though, before we got home. The truth. It made my stomach do somersaults.

"I thought it was only about that Gabriel, but it wasn't. I... responded to him. I'm so sorry. I thought my feelings for Julian were gone."

Gabriel wrapped his arms around me. "Be quiet. I love you."

"I love you too."

*****

We slept on the floor until the maid woke us up ten minutes before check out. We headed to Ellaville, and made one last stop at a discount store so Gabriel could pick me up some clothes and toiletries. As I cleaned myself in a truck stop bathroom, I swore off any chances of returning to Eden, ever, if it would land me somewhere like this to clean myself up before going home. What should have been a joyful experience was a bitter one. Ellaville seemed like an exile, not a reprieve.

I looked halfway presentable when we pulled up at Millie's sometime midday. Uncle Doug's truck was in the yard, and my feeling of unease increased tenfold.

I knocked on the door. It felt strange just to open it after being gone so long.

"Who is it?" Uncle Doug barked.

"It's me." I heard him twist the deadbolt, and smiled to myself. There had never been a robbery in Ellaville that I'd heard of as long as I was alive.

"Arie?" His face broke into a wide grin.

"I'm home."

"It's about time! Hey Mama, Arie and Gabriel are home," he called over his shoulder.

Millie had never moved as fast as she did to get to the door that day. She snatched me inside so quickly my head spun. "My babies! Come in and sit down, you must be starving."

Leave it to Millie to worry about the condition of our stomachs before anything else. I was glad for the food, though. We didn't have enough cash for anything to eat after the shared toothbrushes, toothpaste, and deodorant.

"Arie, you look beautiful," Uncle Doug gushed.

I shifted uncomfortably in the worn sofa.

"Did you have fun? This is so unexpected," Millie said.

"I'm just glad to be home."

Gabriel sat next to me on the far side of the couch.

"Want me to unload for you?" Uncle Doug offered.

"We didn't bring anything back with us," Gabriel told him.

The silence went from uncomfortable to unbearable.

"Does the cat have your tongue? Gabriel, you don't look so well. What's wrong with you two? What in the world went on while you were gone?" Uncle Doug probed.

"Grandma Millie, do you mind if Gabriel and I take a nap? I'm really tired, and I promise to tell you everything, but please can I lay down for a while?"

Millie scrutinized us, her eyes wary. "Go right ahead, baby. Anything you want."

I burst into tears as soon as we shut the door to my room. Everything was exactly as I had left it, but it was still sparse, to say the least. I took all of my good clothes to Eden, most of which Ava sent anyway. The room was almost bare. It was as if Eden never existed.

Gabriel and I held each other close, and I drifted off into a thick, black sleep. Millie came to wake us up for dinner, but I couldn't keep my eyes open. Breakfast the next day went much in the same way. By dinner the next night, I woke up alone.

I slept again. I only got out of the bed to use the restroom once. I was drained, and sleep was the only thing that offered me peace.

I lost track of time; days and nights melted together. One cloudy morning Millie came in to wake me.

"Arianna, you have to eat. I will not leave this room until you take a bite."

The smell of the plate of food made me nauseas, but she was right. Eating, moving, doing anything but sleeping made me feel like I was letting it all go. Moving on. I wasn't ready to let go *or* to move on.

"What happened?" Millie asked quietly. "Are you pregnant?" she asked. Her eyes were kind, though narrowed, and I knew she would accept any explanation, so long as it was feasible to my condition.

I choked on the mouthful of green beans I had shoved into my mouth to placate her.

"Pregnant!? No!"

"Spill it. Something is going on, and it's high time you told me what."

"I-I-oh, Millie," I sobbed into her chest. "There was this guy-"

She broke in. "All the good cries start with something like that. Take all the time you need."

"He made me forget Gabriel, and when Gabriel came, he wanted to make him leave. We left in the middle of the night, and now I can't go back. It's over, Millie. It's all over."

Millie didn't understand, but she lifted my chin as if she had seen every glance, every moment that wrecked my life in the last three months. "It would help a great deal if I knew what went on at that place. I'm not a stupid woman full of nonsense. Ava hasn't changed in almost twenty years. There's all this money, and it doesn't come easy, I can tell you. I won't say I'm sorry I let you go, because I wanted you to experience the life I couldn't give you here. You deserve whatever luxuries Ava offered. But I *am* sorry I kept you from her. I was a selfish old woman who wanted her granddaughter to herself. Nothing is ever over, baby," she added. "Not unless you want it to be."

"I can't go back now." I lamented. "It's too far gone. I'm in too deep and there is no going back. I love my life in Ellaville, but I loved my life there, too."

271

"Not everything is black and white. It can't be as bad as all that."

That's what you think, I thought. I purposefully omitted the part about the Fountain of Youth, as to prevent her from thinking I was crazy. And I definitely left out the parts about my love affair with a billionaire man who was over a hundred years old.

I smiled at Millie, my first genuine smile since Eden. "I'm just glad to be home."

She left me then, and I went on shaky legs to shower. I smelled exactly how I should have anticipated to smell after not showering for X number of days. My eyes burned from the mixture of fluorescent light and late morning sun in the bathroom. The clouds were thickening to the east, but the sun shone brightly on the Bennett's house. I had a perfect view of it from my bathroom window when I opened the it to let out the hot steam from my shower.

My mind drifted to Gabriel. I wanted to know where and how he was at the moment. I went into the living room to ask if Uncle Doug or Millie knew Gabriel's whereabouts, but Millie was gone.

"Where did Millie go?" I asked Uncle Doug, looking at the clock on the cable box. It was noon.

"She went to the store to pick up some things and then she's going to get her hair done."

"Oh. Well, do you know where Gabriel is?" I tried to sound nonchalant.

Answering Millie's questions and still keeping the truth of what happened to myself had drained whatever energy I mustered upon waking. I didn't think I could take any more interrogation, and I didn't want to alert him as to how desperately I needed to see Gabriel.

"He left here when I was at work yesterday morning." He flipped through the channels with the remote so fast, he could not have possibly been able to focus on what was playing on any given station.

Yesterday? How long had I slept? I flopped down on the couch. I found comfort in his mindless surfing of the channels. I let my mind wander. *What would I be doing in Eden right now?*

"Why didn't you marry Ava?" I demanded suddenly.

"Ah, so she turned my niece against me."

"She waited for you."

"I went down there, you know. I went to Eden, or whatever they're calling the place nowadays. Your granddaddy died a few years before I met her, and I couldn't bring myself to leave Mama to fend for herself. I told Thomas to tell her it was over, because I couldn't just leave Mama all alone. I finally came to my senses and went to the address her letters came from. As soon as I saw the house, I left. I'd never have made enough money or class to compete with *that*. In a lot of ways, Ava was out of my league. I never forgave her for it."

"She never got over you, and I think you are perfect for each other."

He gave me a "mind your own business" look, and I crossed my arms and shot him an "I'm not letting this go" look right back.

He grunted and regressed to flipping channels again.

"I'm going to see if Gabriel's home." I gave him a wry grin and kissed him on the cheek on my way out. I would have sworn he looked almost wistful.

*****

I knocked on Gabriel's door, and his dad answered. "Hey, Mr. Bennett. Is Gabriel home?"

"Come in. He's on the computer I think."

Things were so back to normal, it unnerved me. His dad gave no indication that his son had just left one day and came back with no explanation. I walked down the hall and nervously twisted the knob to Gabriel's door.

He twirled around to face me in the shabby office chair in front of his computer. "What's up?"

"I came to see how you're holding up," I told him.

"I've had better days, but seeing you makes it perfect." He leaned back and gave my hand our special squeeze.

"Do you want to get lunch?"

"Yeah, I was just checking out a new game console."

I squinted in the bright light of the computer in the dim room. The video game was one I recognized from Walker's endless competitions.

"It's like culture shock isn't it?"

"What do you mean?" I asked.

"Coming back home after having all that."

I ruffled Gabriel's hair playfully. "It was a small price to pay to be with you."

"If I hadn't come, you would still be there."

"If you hadn't come, I would still miss you."

"Let's go eat. I haven't had pizza in a long time."

*****

We walked into the pizzeria, and I felt a sense of nostalgia. I smiled when I saw the cash register I stood at for countless hours, dreaming of Gabriel's kiss. The dry storage room, full of pizza boxes, to-go cups and plates, and napkins. It was there Gabriel and I would sneak a quick study break or listen to a few songs in the MP3 when we were slow.

There were two new faces replacing mine behind the register and Gabriel's in the kitchen. The boy baking pizza stared constantly at the girl making change, and I smiled to myself, thinking how far away that life seemed. I ordered cheese sticks and soda, and Gabriel and I laughed and talked about old times.

I wasn't surprised to see Brittany and two of her friends walk in, for lack of anything better to do in the small town.

"Look who's back from vacation!" she exclaimed. "Gabriel, it is so good to see you. I haven't seen you in months. Where have you been? The last time I talked to you was at my party."

I glowered at him. "Party?" I asked in a shrill voice, loud enough for everyone to hear.

"I was bored and you were gone. Let's not forget about what *you* were doing. Not that it matters, but nothing happened. She tried to kiss me, and I left," he muttered, even though I was sure Brittany heard every word.

"Look who else is here. She finally came crawling back," she said to her friends, pointing at me. "Arianna, aren't you supposed to be out of town for the summer? Guess everyone saw what a complete loser-" Brittany grabbed her throat, unable to speak.

"You know what Brittany? Why don't you take your self-absorbed ass back home and think about the way you treat people?" I was angry, no, I was livid. I took all my frustration out on the one troubled girl who ruined my life for far too long. "High school was your prime, right? Let me guess. You have no college prospects, and you have no real friends. Nobody likes you, and you will be sponging off your father for the rest of your life. Gabriel does not and will not ever lower himself to be attached to someone as shallow and unintelligent as you."

Brittany stumbled out of the restaurant with a confused but ghost-white look on her face.

"What did you do?" Gabriel demanded.

"Let's just say we will be having dinner here every night until she learns her lesson." I smiled a hateful smile. "On a good note, she will be learning that lesson very soon."

We did return to the pizza place that night, and Brittany wore a conspicuous ballcap.

"It's like I didn't even know what I was doing," she cried to her friends.

I smiled to myself. I knew her head was as bald as an onion. A shaved head in exchange for all the times she made fun of me in high school. Sounded fair to me.

"I'm not hungry anymore," Gabriel said almost instantly when he saw Brittany. He tossed a slice of pizza on his plate with a revolted look on his face.

"Why? What's wrong?" I followed him outside.

He quickly got into the passenger's seat of Walker's car. I was uneasy and unsure as to how long it would be before someone came to pick up the Beamer.

I tumbled in behind him and started home. "What could be wrong? Mad at me for giving Brittany a taste of her medicine? Don't forget how much she hates me. She taunted me for years," I reminded him. "The reason I had a fight with you to begin with was based on her belittling comments. She made me feel like crap about myself, and she got what she deserved."

He forced his way into my little justice speech. "All of you have such a sense of, I don't know, entitlement. You aren't gods because the man who happened upon a legendary fountain has filthy rich friends all over the world and he deems you important enough to drink from it. It wasn't right what you did to Brittany and it wasn't right what you did to that poor guy in the gas station . You are a beautiful girl Arianna, but I saw the glazed look in his eyes from outside. He didn't *see* you at all. You *made* him give us money. I would rather have slept on the streets than see you swindle him.

"And poor Brittany. I cannot believe you lowered yourself to her level. Showing off your car is one thing, but she doesn't deserve what you did to her. It was wrong. She won't ever, not even for a day, see the things you got to see, or do the things you got to do in Eden." He drew in a deep breath and kept on condemning my behavior.

"Your water will wear off soon, and I hope the new you does too. I miss Arianna. You are acting more like Jade."

We had long since pulled into the driveway, and I was dumbfounded by Gabriel's words. But…he was right. I was ashamed of myself.

He was right. Dang it. He was always right. Brittany didn't deserve public humiliation, even if she had done it to me. She only disliked me because Gabriel and I were so enamored with each other in high school. Gabriel was perfect, and she envied the fact that I was close to him and she wasn't. She didn't know me well enough not to like me.

I already promised myself to repay the guy at the gas station, and I silently vowed to do the same with Brittany.

I went to bed feeling low, and I tossed and turned for a while. I had just dozed off when I heard a rustling noise outside my window. I sat up, and my blood ran cold at the thought of an intruder. I made out the shape of a person trying to open my window.

"Arianna," a familiar voice whispered.

"Gabriel what the heck are you doing? Are you trying to scare me to death?" I whispered back.

I opened the window, and he fell inside. "I needed to tell you I'm sorry," he said, out of breath from his window crawl.

"For what? I got to thinking about it, and you were right as usual," I told him begrudgingly.

"You *have* changed, yes. But I like the change for the most part. You are more confident, and I'm glad you had the courage to stand up to her."

"After Jade, Brittany is a kitty cat."

We both laughed. "Move over," he said.

"No funny business," I insisted.

We went to bed giggling.

Gabriel was in the living room the next morning, talking with Millie over coffee. I breathed a sigh of relief. He must have sneaked out before Millie woke up. Everything picked up where it left off. Every passing day left me with the feeling that Eden had all been a dream.

One afternoon, Gabriel and I went out to the backyard and sat in seclusion under an ancient oak tree. The night before, I had been rummaging through my closet and found a book of short stories in my high school backpack. Gabriel began reading a story to me, and the wind blew dandelion wisps around us. It was the most beautiful moment of my life. They swirled around our faces, and I felt more alive than I ever had. Gabriel's argument held water. Literally.

Life was not about living forever. It was about living.

One morning, I asked Millie where my parents were buried. I had wanted to visit the place with Ava, but I wasn't waiting around for anyone anymore. No excuses. I tried to live every day as if it were my last.

With a weathered look, she directed me to a graveyard a few miles out of town, and Gabriel came with me for support. I squatted in between their resting places, put one of my hands on each of their graves and cried. It was the first time in thirteen years we were all together. I told my parents everything as if they were there with me. Maybe I didn't want to live forever after all, if it meant never seeing them again. We stayed for a long time, and I felt the peace only Gabriel's presence could give me, as it had the last time I was there.

The last few days of July's sweltering temperatures melted into the scorching heat of August. August bled slowly into September, and I could not shake the feeling that crept into me that something was terribly wrong.

I tried on several occasions to summon Julian into my dreams, if not to assure myself that it all really happened. I went to bed in deep concentration, but was unable to invoke any lucid dreams. I knew that as long as I had Gabriel's protection, I wouldn't be able to contact Julian, but I tried nonetheless.

Gabriel and I steered clear of conversations about Eden, Julian, and the like, and I considered the fact more than once that I was losing it. I was obsessed with a really long, beautiful and strange dream that turned into as nightmare at the end.

One night I was actually able to induce myself into my old stomping grounds. I was in my room. It was untouched, exactly as I left it, but something was amiss. There was an unrest within the house. The darkness was so pitch black, you could cut it with a knife. The walls groaned with it. I ran down the halls, but the house held only emptiness. There was no Julian, as I knew there wouldn't be, but something must have been strong enough to pull me there, even with Gabriel so close.

It weighed on my mind for weeks afterward, and I felt sick every time I thought of it. After the initial worry, I discontinued my quest. I knew how to get to Eden, and I was the one who ultimately controlled the decision not to return.

Gabriel was reinstated at the pizza place and was promoted to assistant manager, while I resigned myself to a life at the end of Millie's hallway. The money in my pizza place cashier/saving up for a new car before college account quickly ran out, and I was forced to take a long, hard look at my situation and means of getting by. I hadn't thought about the measly sum I had earned since I first saw the phenomenal amount in my account that Ava gave me.

I donated the last of my bank account to Brittany. We had become fast friends after her crew deserted her, college bound. After several "heart-to-hearts" as she called them, I discovered that she was lonely, to say the least, and her infatuation with Gabriel apparently stemmed from how wonderfully he treated me.

I called her up and offered her my last fifty bucks for a hair color appointment. Her hair grew back quickly, and a pixie cut suited her. She was as shallow as I originally thought, but I redeemed myself through long, boring hours on the phone discussing second-rate discount labels. I tried to quell my snobbery, thinking all the while how one of my handbags stashed away in my closet in Eden would buy about fifty outfits from one of the stores Brittany frequented.

One night, when I was on the phone with Brittany, I looked down at my worn top and laughed out loud. I might have *had* a million handbags once upon a time, but there was eighty cent left in my bank account at the time, and I would have been lucky to shop with Brittany.

Gabriel and I grew unnaturally close. He sneaked into my window every single night, even though Millie eventually told him to use the door because opening my window to him was making too much noise.

Everything was perfect again. Uncle Doug took us fishing, and asked us once to take a ride on the jet ski his friend had allowed him to use. We both declined vehemently, citing heat exhaustion as the reason for our refusal.

Gabriel applied to a college that wasn't too far away, and was accepted. His stellar grades in high school and an almost perfect score on the placement exam won him a full scholarship and a spot in fall enrollment, but he decided to wait until spring semester. I speculated that he put off signing up for classes because he didn't want to leave me. The college was still close enough to commute; we were used to that from having to drive out of town for absolutely everything in Eden. The problem was, in Gabriel's eyes, between working and going to school, it didn't leave much time for me. I brought it up to him repeatedly, but he denied that my involvement swayed his decision in any way.

Through it all, I sulked. I went from rags to riches and back again. I was content, but I wasn't happy. Not completely, anyway. I couldn't seem to anchor myself to a life in Ellaville. Sure, laying on the beach and sleeping until noon was a perfect sounding life, but I wasn't predominantly lazy. I didn't want to be a bum in Eden anymore than I wanted to be a bum in Ellaville, but I wanted more. The Fountain of Youth promised me a life of excitement, adventure, and travel others only dreamed of.

I never even got to go on a delivery. I never got to go visit Edgar and Emily in their Irish castle. I never got to apologize to Julian.

I could deal with being poor if I had the people I loved around me. I did it for eighteen years before I even knew Eden existed, and never thought too much about it. It wasn't the money, it was the thrill. I was bitter for a long time that that fabulous chance was taken from me, but ultimately the blame was found only in myself.

I went to bed late one night watching TV in my room with Gabriel. Millie woke me up by knocking on my door way too loudly and way too early the next morning. She barged in right before I opened the door, wringing her hands.

"There are," she cleared her throat nervously, "some people here for you."

"Tell them the car keys are on the kitchen counter." I yawned and snuggled closer to Gabriel.

"They're not here for the car. They're here for you."

URGENCY

"I don't know how to entertain these people. Please, hurry!" Millie urged, and quickly left the room.

I sat upright. I shook Gabriel awake. "Gabriel! They've sent the authorities! Oh, no. What if it's worse? What if Julian came to kill you? What's going to happen?"

"Calm down. Julian can't hurt us. Stop being so melodramatic. I'll get up and take care of it," Gabriel reassured me.

My heart suddenly surged. I wasn't crazy after all. It should have been as obvious as Walker's BMW in the drive. Someone from or sent from Eden was here! I jumped out of bed and scrambled on the floor for something presentable to wear.

I shimmied myself into my trusty old gray dress. I tiptoed into the bathroom, praying no one would see me and brushed my teeth and hair, adding only the pertinent makeup: black eyeliner. I smudged the cosmetic around my eyes, and ruffled my hair. As soon as I talked myself into it, I walked into the living room of my humble abode.

Ethan, Sebastien, Walker, Ava, and Savannah were all there. They were scattered about, standing coolly in various places- perched against the doorframe, leaning against the couch, propping up on the entertainment center.

"Here she is now," Millie said.

I rushed to greet them. "What are you doing here?" I asked. I was winded at the beauty of the throng.

Ava put her hands on my shoulder, but pulled back abruptly. "We came to talk to you about something very serious. Millie, would you give us a moment? I know this is your house, but there is a private matter we want to discuss with Arianna alone."

My cheeks flamed suddenly at the surroundings. Ellaville was as different from Eden as it could possibly be. I noticed for the first time the un-matching wood grain of the hand-me-down furniture. The smudges on the glass table. The strand of pine straw on the worn hardwood floor.

"Any matter important enough to speak to us about, is important enough to say in front of Arianna's grandmother. Don't you agree?" Gabriel crossed his arms.

Gabriel's intervention woke me up from my scrutiny. I was proud of my house and both the people who lived in it. Who cared about money? For the first time in a long time, not me.

"I want Grandma Millie to s-stay," I stammered. The quavering sound of my voice startled me.

"We would never have come if the matter wasn't of the utmost urgency-" Sebastien started.

"-but we want you to understand the severity of the situation," Savannah finished.

"Are you going to call the authorities? I mean, we would've brought it back, but we didn't have a way home. I didn't think it was that big of a deal. Walker gave us the keys and all…"

Everyone looked at me, dumbfounded.

"We aren't here for the car!" Ethan burst out, understanding the reason I thought they had all come. "We brought Gabriel's truck and your car back with us. I can't believe you thought we would do such a thing."

"Oh! Well, what *are* you doing here? What's wrong?"

Ava stepped forward and her face grew somber. "We have no right to ask this of you after the way you were treated, but please, Arianna, hear me out. I don't know what happened between you and, well, what happened the night you left, but we need your help."

Ethan spoke again. "We would never have come, but the situation is dire, and-"

"Ava will you just tell us what's wrong?" Gabriel demanded.

"Julian is dying."

REVELATIONS

My knees buckled, and I collapsed to the floor. It couldn't be true. Julian couldn't die. It was impossible. His life's work was to make sure it never ended.

"How?"

"He's done this since you left. He's eaten barely enough to stay alive, but now he won't even drink water. He says it's time for him to go. Please come. You are the only one who can help," Savannah plead.

"He refuses to drink any of the F-, uh, the f-f-fresh juice we bring him." Walker panicked at his almost slip up in front of Millie. "Fresh Juice. Yeah. He won't even drink his juice." He beamed at his pitiful excuse for a save.

"So why do you think I can help? He hates me after what happened. He'll never agree to me coming back," I protested dismally.

"He calls for you at night. He hasn't left his room since you were there. He clings to the necklace I gave you. You're the only thing that will bring him back," Ava said.

Sebastien made his final plea. "If you don't want to come, we understand. You don't owe any of us anything. If Julian did indeed hurt you the night you left, then we won't try to save him. We love you and support your decision, but we had to know. If he didn't hurt you, will you please help him.?"

Sebastien rested his hand on Savannah's arm. Her eyes welled up with hopeful tears.

"He never hurt me. Not physically," I admitted. "You don't understand what you saw that night. *I* went to *him*." I left it at that. Millie was in the room for goodness' sake.

I turned to Gabriel and raised my eyebrows for his approval or disapproval of returning.

He ran his thumb across my cheek. "Not this time. You have to do this alone. You don't have to put your dreams on hold for me anymore. I will always love you, but this is your path, not mine. Go."

I nodded, tears streaming down my cheeks. "I'll be home soon," I promised. I hugged him close and held his hand for what felt like the last time.

Leave it to Uncle Doug to always come bursting in at the most inopportune moments.

"What is this all about? I had to park on the street." He slung his tackle box on the table.

"Such a ray of sunshine, as usual," Ava growled sarcastically.

He made a ridiculous bow. "So sorry. I didn't know we had a *royal* procession visiting us. How lucky we are you have graced us with your presence, you ice cold-"

"Enough! This is my house, and these are my guests. I swear on your father, Doug, if you say one unkind thing to Ava or any of her friends..." Millie gave him "The Look" and crossed her arms. Ava mockingly batted her eyelashes to further antagonize him.

"We really need to get going." Ethan interrupted the childish display. "Every moment is vital."

"Is it really that bad?" I asked.

No one answered. They shooed me out of the door, and I was in the car before I knew it. Gabriel, Millie, and Uncle Doug each came around to my seat with a hug. Gabriel kissed my hand and wished me luck, and I told him I'd call him when I got there.

Spur of the moment decisions had not seemed to work out well for me thus far, but I found myself, once again, in a completely different environment than I would have envisioned myself the day before.

Walker brought Gabriel's SUV back to him to keep, so he was driving his own car back to Eden with Sebastien and Savannah. Ethan drove Ava and I as fast as my car would go (they brought it back for me anyway, just in case I didn't want to stay I'd still have my car). The speedometer was almost upside down at one point, and Ava told him if we didn't slow down, Julian's life wouldn't be the only one to hang in the balance.

"So he knows I'm coming?"

"No," they answered simultaneously.

"I'm supposed to be on a delivery to Peter with Ethan. Walker and Sebastien are supposed to be meeting Savannah in Miami to work out the last minute details on the house you wanted."

I couldn't believe they were still buying that house, even after I was gone.

"And Jade?"

"Jade has gone even further off the deep end lately. She won't leave the house, and she is almost always with Julian, even though he barely seems to notice her. Edgar and Emily are at the house right now, too, and they're in on our plan as well."

"How am I going to be able to help?" I asked, trying to divert my attention from the fear of crashing.

"We think you being there might make him change his mind about wanting to die. You are the only thing he lives for. You have to make him drink the water," Ava said simply, as if I could wave my magical wand and Julian would do anything I said.

"I can't get him to do anything he doesn't want to do. You need another tactic. I know him. He's not big on entrances, but he always, *always* has to make a dramatic exit," I told them.

"You may be right. We've tried everything." Ethan turned all the way around to the backseat to talk to me. I focused intently on the road, but he didn't sense any danger. "We put the water in his cups we brought to him, but the mist was too hard to hide. We put it in his food, but it had the same effect, and that's when he began refusing anything to eat or drink."

"That won't work with Julian. He distrusts everybody," I reminded them. "You will have to be cunning, like him."

""What do you suggest, Arianna? We're all ears." Ava gazed at me as if I held the answer she was looking for.

I remained silent for a few moments, but it wasn't hard to outsmart someone you knew so well. "Don't worry. I have a plan."

AMENDS

The instant we pulled around the driveway, I fell trying to scramble out of the car. I raced up to Julian's room, not even stopping to speak to Edgar and Emily at the base of the stairs. The second I rounded the last corner, I slammed hard into what felt like a brick wall. The brick wall was actually some*one*.

"What are you doing here?" Jade asked frigidly.

"Get out of my way." I shoved past her, and ran to Julian's bedside.

He looked as if he had already passed into the next life. His face was gaunt and pale. His eyes were sunk deep into their sockets, and I had to lean close to him to see if he was breathing. His normally tanned skin took on a bluish color noticeable even in the dark room.

He was still so beautiful it hurt to look at him.

"Julian?" I brushed the back of my hand along his jaw line.

"You have no business here," Jade hissed behind me. "I would rather see him dead than with you."

"You need to get some sleep, Jade," Ethan said, walking into the room with Ava. "Come on." He took her hand and tried to lead her from the room.

"No! She'll take all of the credit. I have been here the whole time. She's the one who did this to him." She thrashed against the strength of

Ethan's arms. "If she hadn't come…" Ethan led her down the hall and the sounds of her yelling faded away.

"She's right," I said to Ava. "If I hadn't come, he would still be okay."

"If you had never come, I would still be able to say I had never seen Julian smile."

Tears coursed down my cheeks. "Really?"

"Really," she said.

I heard the slamming of car doors. Ava slid the object I had requested as part of my scheme into my hand, but as soon as I grasped it, she tried to pull it away. Frenzied, she hopped from one foot to the other. "Everyone else must have been right behind us," she said, trying to distract me. She turned toward the door and back at me pleading. "Please don't do this, Arianna. You don't have to do this. There has got to be another way."

"Everything will be fine, you'll see. I *know* him."

"If you're sure, then I'll leave you. I'll see that you are left alone, and someone will be right outside if you need any of us." She closed the door behind her.

"Julian." I shook him. "You have to wake up."

He roused, but his eyes opened only to the width of tiny slits. The vibrant blue of his irises still made my heart lurch. "Mmmm…Am I in heaven?" He smiled groggily.

I slapped his face. Hard. "Get up. You're scaring me to death. Do you enjoy having everyone who cares about you worried sick? If you wanted to die, you would have found a quicker way to do it." I found the vial in a fold in the rumpled blankets. I snatched my necklace from his hand and replaced it with the vial. "Drink it. Now," I ordered.

"I was waiting to see you one last time. Without you, I have no reason to live."

"I'm right here, and I won't leave until you get well."

"I have to tell you something before I leave you. Under your bed. The combination is your birthday. The deed to Eden, other things, they're all inside. All of the banking information, the titles to our cars, boats, houses, it is all yours now." He began to babble, most of it incoherent. "In a safe beneath your bed... Your birthday to open... Everything now belongs to you...Yours..." He coughed. I pretended not to take his ramblings to heart, but I memorized the information in case this half-baked scheme of my failed.

"I don't want it! I don't want anything! Can't you see? It means nothing without you!"

"You belong to someone else." His words were garbled, and I knew he was struggling to speak. He took several moments in between words, and I was disgusted at the fact that he was doing this to himself.

If my actions induced this suicide, I was going to find a way to reverse it.

"I single-handedly ran off your parents, ultimately leading to their deaths. I was the wedge between you and your true love. I coveted something that was not mine. Eden was cursed in the Bible. Did you know that?" I didn't answer. "Eden was the birthplace of the curse placed on the entire earth, and I made the source of that curse on humanity my home." He tried to continue, but his breathing became so labored, he stopped trying.

"Drink the water Julian."

He shook his head.

I leaned in, an inch from his face. "If you don't drink, I don't drink, do you understand? I will not eat, I will not sleep. You die, I die."

"There is only one thing more important than finding a way to extend life." He patted his chest, and drew a vial out from under his shirt. "Having a way to end it." He uncorked the vial and emptied the contents into his mouth. Poison. The drink of choice for a dramatic exit. So predictable.

I kissed him deeply, and he instantly, if weakly, responded.

"Did you think I would let you leave me?" I opened my hand to reveal the object Ava had brought to me. I moved across the room out of his arm's reach. He would have to drink the water before he had enough strength to make it to me. I backed up against the wall farthest from me. I held the knife to my throat and plunged it into my flesh. I almost swooned at the sensation of the warm blood trickling down to my collarbone. I slid down the wall so slowly it almost seemed like a dream. My adrenaline ensured that the pain was nonexistent; the only thing I felt was my head flooding with the sound of a loud buzz.

"No. NO!"

He threw the vial filled with the Fountain's water bottoms up into the air, and the mist consumed him. The poison was no match for the water's effect.

I gurgled and tasted blood. It filled my mouth and I knew the end was coming. He would never have time to save me. I hadn't meant to cut quite so deep, but if I wouldn't have done it hard, I wouldn't have done it at all. Everything happened so fast at first, but it was all starting to go in slow motion.

Julian ran for the door, but Ava was waiting on the other side with Ethan, several vials in hand. They were so graceful they seemed to float toward me, even in a dead run. Ava tipped my head back and poured the water in my mouth, and Ethan poured another vial on the skin of my lacerated throat. Walker trembled while Edgar and Emily watched in horrific silence, and Savannah shrieked in terror when she saw me. Sebastien took her from the room to shield her from view, and Julian was standing in front of his fireplace screaming blood curdling screams in anguish at the top of his lungs.

It took me a minute to fully come to; I *must* have been on the brink of death for the water to take so long to work. Ethan cradled my head, and laid me down on the cool marble floor. My eyelids fluttered after a few moments, and I sat up straight. Julian continued to scream, and I covered my ears. The water made my hearing super sensitive, and I thought I would go deaf at the sound.

He suddenly stopped and turned his fury on me.

"Why would you do this?" he railed.

I stood to full height, and my mind was again bright and capable of understanding the severity of the situation. I laughed suddenly.

"Well *that* was close."

I was the only one laughing, to say the least. Julian ran toward me, but not because he was thrilled we were both alive and kicking. I let out a little yell and inched away from him, blocking my face with my hands. He held his arms toward me, but his shaky hands were poised in a clawing motion, and he snarled.

"Julian, what are you doing?" I backed away faster and faster.

He let out a guttural moan. I was terrified.

He darted toward me, and I ran as fast as I could down the hall. My room was my ultimate destination, but he caught me just before I could shut and lock my door.

He threw me on the bed, and the house exploded with the sound of the others racing to catch up with us. I thought the floor would fall through the noise was so loud. It sounded like a thousand elephants hopping up and down on the second floor. Julian pinned my arms high above my head, and held me down with the weight of him. The mist sparkled a thousand facets around us, and everyone stopped short at the foot of my bed.

"If you want to pick up where we left off, I would rather not have an audience," I spat.

"Who told you to come here!? You weren't wanted." He averted his eyes.

"You're a liar. You *just* told me you were waiting on me! Tell me you don't love me. Look at me and say you didn't want me to come."

"I wanted to die! I wanted you and Gabriel to have the life that I dreamed of for *us*! I tried to leave so I wouldn't interfere, but you came back here and destroyed everything!"

"I was invited here. And where is Gabriel now, Julian? Is he here? Did I bring him with me? No. I came for you. You." I stared into his eyes, but I was not going to be intimidated. "I knew you would have some hidden method to leave with a grand and dramatic exit, but you forgot. I held the trump card. *I know you.*"

I wriggled under his weight, trying to free myself, but he tightened his grasp. My body was splayed before him, and he lost focus when he became aware if it. He inhaled deeply, and breathed down my neck. He again inhaled as if the smell of my body and blood were an intoxicating perfume, and he could not get enough of it. The blood was still warm on my throat in some places where it previously poured thick. In others, it was burgundy and dry. The metallic taste of it still lingered in my nose and mouth where it flowed generously from the wound the knife inflicted.

I smiled his smile. The evil smile that was at the same time taunting and seductive. "Don't you have anything to say? Make. Me. Leave." It was a challenge.

Julian wrapped his hands around my throat. "You took everything when you left me. There is a price going to be paid."

"Go ahead. Pay up." I lifted my chin.

"Enough, Julian. Let her go," Walker commanded.

Julian paused for a long moment before he dismounted, the display of his thin frame echoed in my mind for months after. He wore dark gray (his color of choice) drawstring linen pants, and his pelvic bones thrust through his pale skin. He clenched his fists and panted.

"You're right. She isn't worth it."

Ethan jumped him. He punched him squarely in the face, knocking him down. His knees buckled when he tried to stand, but this time I stood between Julian and the self-inflicted abuse he acquired through his disgusting response. All of a sudden Julian's face went from furious to repentant. He spun around and pulled me down to the floor with him and held me.

"What have I done now? I waited so long, and you came back to me. I love you. I'm so sorry. I love you." Julian wept, and I wrapped him in my arms. The burden of separation from Julian I had been forced to endure the last few months was lifted. I motioned for everyone to leave us. He shook violently.

"I know."

I clenched his face until he became still. We found our way to the bed, and I held him until he slept. I walked downstairs and with a weary smile, assured everyone he was okay.

Emily began to cry. "Thank you, Arianna. We all owe you a lifetime of gratitude."

I rubbed my eyes. "Ava, I'm ready to go when you are."

"You want to go home. To Ellaville. Of course, yes." She looked around.

Sebastien put his arm around Savannah's waist and pulled her close to him. Walker stared off into the distance, and Edgar, for once, was quiet. Ethan's face paled, and I was compelled to once again make a lame speech. I hated that I was always expected to say something to fill these awkward silences. Gabriel stood in for me when he was around, but I was on my own once again. They deserved something, though. The whole thing was my fault.

"I never meant to cause any of this." I hung my head in shame. "I am so sorry I agreed to come in the first place. Because of me, you all put yourselves in danger. I can promise you that Gabriel and I won't tell anyone about anything we've seen here. So goodbye, and good luck to all of you." I turned toward the foyer and opened the grand front doors to wait for Ava to meet me in her car for the long drive home.

I guess I knew all along, in the back of my mind, I wouldn't be staying in Eden. There was too much water under the bridge- it was washed completely away this time. I did what I had come there to do, and now it was time to return to real life. For good.

Ava stepped forward. "Arianna, wait. Nobody here blames you for anything. I don't want you to feel obligated, but I speak for us all when I say that I love you. Everything with Julian, that's my fault and mine alone. I was responsible for you, and I failed miserably. I respect your decision, but I'm begging you to stay. We love you. You are more a part of Eden than all of us combined. *This* is your home. We all in agree. For however long the Fountain stands, Eden is yours."

I searched their faces. There were no signs of animosity toward me, no matter how much I knew I deserved it. I remembered the first time I met each of them not so many months ago. Each one's beauty was as bright as ever. Savannah was so tiny, her blond curls made her look like more of a china doll than the real thing. Sebastien and Ethan, the identical twins whom I couldn't tell the difference between at first, stood side by side. Their baby faces were perfect and kind and brave. Emily, in all her fiery red-haired glory, was held in the arms of her loud but sweet knight in shining armor. Walker's caramel eyes smoldered, leaving even the most unsuspecting starlet at Screwdriver or elsewhere panting for more. Ava was the substance of fairy tale princesses. Her face was the one I had come to love most of all. I had to say though, she did always look like she was up to something. Her bubblegum pink lips curled just a little bit on their own. No man stood a chance.

Reflecting on all my experiences, I loved them all in their own respect. Not because of their beauty, but because of how they stood by me, even though I was wrong on so many levels. The only thing that had seemed to change while I was gone was the weather. It seemed the sun was not as endless as I thought. The doors were opened wide, and the sea breeze brought a chill with it in the early October air.

"Whatdya say, girl? Will you stay with us? Give us another chance?" Walker winked at me.

"If you'll have me, I would love to stay, but I don't think Julian will stand for it. I'm not so sure he wants me here as much as you. And, um, I thought he was going to freaking *kill* me a few minutes ago."

"Julian would never be able to hurt you. He wants you here. More than anyone else in this house. More than anyone in this world," said a voice from behind me. I turned to see Julian, leaning against the banister. His posture was as aloof as ever, but his eyes were pleading. "I promise, if you stay, everything will be different. Better." He came to me and took my hands in his.

"It doesn't get much better than this," I whispered breathlessly to him. I forgot why I would ever want to leave when he was so close.

"Gabriel can come back whenever he wishes. He has taken much better care of you than I ever could. If he returns, I'm nothing but his servant."

"I-I don't know what to say. I would love to stay here, but I've already caused too many problems."

"I won't take no for an answer," Julian said with a dimpled smile. "Unless you want to go back."

There was no going back now. I thought it before, but I knew it now. Eden *was* my destiny. It would always draw me back.

"Alright. You talked me into it. Is there anything else I should know? My heart can't take any more suprises."

"Nope. What you see is what you get," Ava said.

What I actually got was my life back. The only real surprise was the phone call Julian personally and secretly placed to Gabriel, asking for him to return. Gabriel declined; he was taking a late semester course at the college. He promised to visit though, and Julian offered for him to come anytime. I took advantage of my newfound home and all the perks it offered. I immersed myself in reading from the library, and I asked to go on a delivery soon. Ava said she was waiting for something more exciting for me. She claimed that the last few were in and out deals, and she wanted me to enjoy myself. I didn't tell her that going anywhere at all was exciting to me. I had only visited two states, let alone a different country. She was being overprotective, and that was fine. I knew I'd get to go sooner or later, and I asked Ethan to talk to her.

Jade was once again the rain on my parade, but not in the sense that I would have thought. I was frankly, a little scared at her constant absence. She sank deeper into her instability, and Walker tried to intervene more than once. She hardly ever left her room, and on the rare occasion that she did, she literally growled at me when I passed her. Her appearance was the most curious thing of all.

Normally, even on her worst day, every hair on her head was in place. Her makeup, if she wore it, was usually picture perfect, complimenting her olive skin. Lately though, I wondered more than once how often she was showering. Her hair was greasy, and her celery-colored eyes bore deep, black circles underneath. I left well enough alone, and kept my mouth shut about the whole thing, even though I was sure everyone else had noticed too.

Julian never pressured me to reconnect with him on the same level as before, and I was relieved. We spent every waking minute together, except for the few times I went shopping or out to eat with someone from the house. I wanted to find myself, and that meant distancing myself romantically from both Gabriel and Julian. He did continue to visit the library with me though, and we spent the cooler nights in front of a roaring fire with one of the classics.

Gabriel called after I had been in Eden for a week or so, and told me he was going on a date with a girl from one of his classes. It stung at first, but I wanted so much for him to be happy. My heart pounded when he called after the date.

"So where did you go? What's her name again?"

I knew what her name was. Katie. Katie. Katie. I hated myself for knowing.

"I took Katie to the movies. We saw that new horror movie about a pandemic and zombies," Gabriel told me.

"Uh-huh." I tried to be nonchalant, but I walked downstairs into Gabriel's old room with my new cell phone I purchased for myself a few days before. I sat on his bed, thinking I would feel somehow closer to him. We had sent all of his things back to him a couple of days before, but I still felt *him* in the room.

He rattled on about the date some more, and finally I couldn't stand it.

"So how did it work out for you?" I asked.

He was quiet for a moment, and then he sighed. "I thought about you the whole time."

"Gabriel you know I don't want a relationship right now. I want to figure out who I am. You should have given her a fair chance. I've told you a million times not to wait around for me."

"I'm willing to wait an eternity to get the things I want the most. Anyway, she wasn't my type. She was too... Her hair was too short," he finished lamely.

"For real? Her hair was too short? You're making excuses."

"I have a test in the morning. I love you." He hung up the phone without waiting for my response.

I didn't want him to wait around on me. Julian either. I encouraged both of them to pursue other people. It hurt more to know that Gabriel was waiting around for me than it had to know he was out with someone else. I didn't want either of them to make any more sacrifices for me, but my wishes were as futile as if the roles were reversed. I would sacrifice anything for them, I had almost given my life to save Julian's.

I decided to take the opportunity to make my last amends. My debit card had been given back to me almost immediately upon my arrival, and I took it to an out of town bank on the way to my destination. I punched in my code, and the numbers had increased drastically from the original amount Gabriel and I had gotten so worked up about in Ellaville.

I withdrew a huge sum of money and went on blind faith I'd find my way to where I needed to go and see who I wanted to see.

Eventually, though, I did find it, and I walked into the gas station where I swindled the cashier's money by mentally commanding him to give it to me.

He looked up, and stared nervously.

"Do you remember me? You let me borrow some money a few months ago. I wanted to tell you that you really saved me that night, and I'm bringing it back to you with interest." I took his chubby hand and stuck the paper sack filled with bills inside his fist.

He blushed twelve shades of purple before he could muster up the courage to speak. "I don't know what to say. I never expected... Are you sure it's okay?" he asked nervously.

I laughed. "I'm sure. The money was made honestly. My aunt works for a very wealthy, um, entrepreneur." I smiled.

His hands shook nervously. "Anytime."

"Good luck to you." I waved as I left the store. All of my debts were paid, and the planets seemed to be aligned just perfectly for me.

The next night was Halloween, so we all piled up in Walker's new SUV (he traded his car for a truck exactly like Gabriel's) and went to Screwdriver. Ava wore a sexy pirate costume, and Sebastien and Savannah went as vampires. Walker came out in full pimp costume, complete with a top hat and cane, and he looked smokin' hot. Ethan wore all black, but he would never own up to a character. I wore a tiny white toga, and wound a band of ivy in my hair.

We had an amazing time, though this time drinking was not part of my revelry. I danced the night away, and slept until noon the next day.

My birthday neared closer and closer, and I considered going to Ellaville to celebrate the event. Instead, Julian called and invited Gabriel to come and stay until after Thanksgiving holidays. Gabriel was scheduled to arrive the weekend after my birthday, due to a final he couldn't miss. Millie was going to Biloxi, Mississippi to gamble with her friends for Thanksgiving, and Uncle Doug and Gabriel's dad were going on a fishing trip with a few friends from work.

I hugged Julian and thanked him for calling and inviting Gabriel. I was ecstatic he was coming, and even more so that Julian was turning over a new leaf by finally accepting my best friend. I stood on my tiptoes to kiss him on the cheek. It was the most physical contact we had shared since the night I fled from Eden with Gabriel.

Jade passed us in the hall, and her glare cut me to the bone.

She caught up with me a few days later by the dock. I wanted to take the boat out and learn how it worked. Ava went inside to get us a blanket to warm us from the biting autumn wind, and Jade found me alone.

"This isn't over. You won't have him this time," she warned.

"You've lost it Jade. Go inside and put your straightjacket back on." I wiggled my fingers at her. "Bye."

I wasn't scared. Nothing could ruin my good mood.

The colder days took on a festive feel. It was going to be the first holiday I celebrated in Eden besides Independence Day. Savannah decorated the house in festive jewel tones. Red berries peeked out from underneath forest green garland running along the main staircase. The chandeliers dripped turquoise and royal purple glass ornaments. Pheasant feather centerpieces complete with fresh deep red and burnt orange colored flowers decorated all the tables.

The eve of my birthday dawned cloudy and cold. It was perfect. We gathered into the den, and I decided how I wanted to celebrate. Gabriel was arriving two days from then, and we planned accordingly.

"So I have a chef whose making an authentic Japanese meal for lunch, and for dinner, you will be having your favorite- a seafood feast," Ava said.

"Yummy! When do I get my cake?" I asked, my mouth watering at the thought of all my favorite foods.

Julian laughed. "You can't have a cake until Gabriel gets here. He has forbidden you to blow out one candle until he's here to witness it."

Talk about a one-eighty, I thought. I was happy for the change. Everyone I loved (except for Millie and Doug) were going to be in one room, and all getting along.

Jade stumbled into the room. We all stared at her, but Julian was especially appalled. I really don't think he had actually *looked* at her up to that point.

"Julian, could I please refill my vial? I don't feel so well," she said. Her voice quavered, and the look in her eyes was half-crazed.

"Here," he handed her the key. "Help yourself." His lip curled in disgust.

We ignored the scene and continued to talk about plans for my party.

That night, I laid in bed thinking about how much my life had come full circle. I glanced at the new alarm clock I recently purchased. I hated not ever being able to tell what time it was. It was the strangest thing to live in a house with no way to know the hour besides an old watch I brought from Ellaville the first time. The clock read 12:30, and I was giddy at the thought of Gabriel's arrival in less than forty-eight hours.

I snuggled deep into the memory foam mattress, dreaming of a fondant birthday cake with thousands of candles.

I awoke to a billowing fog in my room. At first I thought it was the cloud cover that usually burned off early morning in the Florida sun, but that didn't make any sense. Why would my room be filled with early morning fog? Upon my groggy awakening, I rubbed my eyes with my fists, and recognized the prismatic haze from the Fountain. Normally when someone ingested it or poured it on a wound, the haze was light and airy. This was so thick you could have cut it with a knife. The figure it poured from was unrecognizable, it looked like a ghost. I began to panic. The effects of drinking that much of the water were unknown, but we all knew the more you consumed, the stronger the effect.

"Who's there?"

A sultry voice rose from the air.

"What's wrong, Arianna? You usually love meeting people in the middle of the night."

PHANTOM

My head began to throb, and I stood up involuntarily, and got out of bed.

"Jade? What are you doing?"

"Shut up. I didn't tell you to speak."

I tried to talk, but the words died in my throat. I couldn't talk, no matter how hard I tried. Any attempt to make a sound resulted in a stomach-clenching gag.

"This is what's going to happen," she said matter-of-factly. "You are going to die. Are you scared? I want to *hear* you beg." She said the last word as if it were as vile as I was. Her vibrant green eyes flashed with hatred.

The binding that held my voice silent suddenly broke loose.

I only had one chance. I screamed as loud as I could, but the sound only lasted a few seconds before I was silenced again. I knelt before her. Her dark figure towered over me, and her teeth gleamed in the darkness.

"If you try anything stupid, it will only seal your fate sooner. Are you ready to see your parents again? I want you to *beg*!" She railed.

"I am begging you. Please Jade, I am nothing compared to you. Please don't kill me." The words were not mine, and I cried. My head felt as if it would split. I would have welcomed death to soothe the pain of a zillion razorblades slicing through my thoughts.

Mind control. The water was potent in tiny doses, but she must have consumed enough to overpower the fact that, I too drank from the Fountain. Normally, the water made us immune to the effects that it caused if something like this was inflicted from another Keeper.

I remembered Ava telling me not so many months ago that Julian had tested the theory once. He and Sebastien had a battle of minds, and it was a draw. Neither could overpower the other, but when Julian took a second dose, he easily whipped Sebastien, and made him do a series of embarrassing antics.

I remembered something Madame Zoya mentioned, and Ethan expounded on. As long as Gabriel was close to me, I was protected. But he wasn't here. He was miles and miles away in Ellaville, tucked safely into his bed, and I was open and vulnerable to all the sick ways Jade envisioned to kill me. I tried to hard to fight back, but I failed.

Jade hummed to herself, and the soft noise dragged my mind back into the room to await my fate. I suddenly flew backwards and cracked my head on the marble floor. The sound my head made from hitting the floor sounded like a watermelon being split open. Jade stabbed her black stiletto into my stomach like I was an insect to be squashed. I dug my hands into my hair, and pulled out chunks of it by the roots. My face wore bloody trenches my own nails had dug.

"Not so pretty now, are we?" she cackled, and the torment went on and on.

Finally it stopped for a moment, and I believed the worst had passed until I walked toward the balcony door and turned the knob. I was terrified of what my body was making me do. I turned to look at Jade.

She grinned her sadistic grin, and I climbed onto the rail of the balcony. A fall from the height would kill me instantly, and I thought about the sweet moments I spent here in my dreams with Julian. My body swayed back and forth.

Suddenly, the contact broke. I was able to bend and safely grab hold of the bar I was standing on. The move enabled me to regain my balance. I heard a low mumbling outside my door, and the sound grew louder as it drew nearer.

"Nothing is wrong Gabriel, I'm telling you. She's asleep. I don't know why you're calling in the middle of the night, or why you would think she's not safe here. I'll check, but-"

Ava flung open the door to my room, and she seemed to move in slow motion. She was confused at first, and then understanding flickered across her face. She threw the phone down and tore off down the hall.

"Julian! Someone help!"

Jade shifted from one leg to the other. She was indecisive about whether to follow Ava or stay with me. Ava didn't get far once Jade was able to calm herself enough to gain control of us both. Ava reentered the room and fell face first on the floor. Her movements were robotic; Jade was our puppeteer.

"Ava. I've always liked you. You don't want to meet the same fate as your precious niece do you? You should have minded your own business. Gabriel will have to be taken care of now too, and I always held an attraction for him."

She seemed to stop wistfully when she thought of Gabriel, but not for long. "Oh well, back to the matter at hand."

I stood erect once again on the balcony, and held my arms out from my sides, ready to fly, ready to jump.

Ethan must have heard the commotion, since his room was right next to Ava's. He understood immediately, but he didn't try to run. He must have known she could overpower him, because he made no attempt at escaping.

"No, Arianna. Don't do this. You can break her hold. Gabriel is here with you." Ethan grabbed his abdomen.

The water was strong, but it wasn't powerful enough to control all three of us at once. Jade placed her fingertips on her temples to stabilize her thoughts, but the move was futile. I crouched down and held on. Jade finally lost her domination of Ava completely, and she made off to alert the house to what was happening. The more she tried to control Ethan and I simultaneously, the less she succeeded in having command over any of our actions.

A small army of sleepy Keepers of the Fountain of Youth assembled in my bedroom. Julian was the last to join, and when he entered I felt a twinge of relief.

The haze billowed around him, creating an even thicker cloud than the one enveloping Jade.

No one spoke. I stood on the thin rail, and teetered on the edge. The water I consumed when I saved Julian was the only thing that maintained my balance. I was Jade's only focus now The clash of the push and pull I felt from the conflicting commands Julian and Jade forced upon me was unbearable. I wanted so badly to give in to Jade. The pain seared like a hot iron brand upon every inch of my skin.

"Don't let her win, Arianna. Listen to Gabriel," Julian told me.

I tried to feel anything but pain, but all it did was hurt more. When I closed my eyes, I felt a thin, elastic surface between my mind and theirs. I pushed as hard as I could, and at first nothing happened. I pushed harder.

Gabriel's image flashed through my head, and a light burst through the darkness.

Gabriel. It was hard to envision him to begin with, but the more memories I invoked, the less pain I felt. Gabriel holding my hand through the drizzle of the saddest day of my life. Gabriel and I dancing at prom. Gabriel kissing me. Gabriel in his graduation gown. Gabriel nuzzling closer to me as we slept curled up to one another so many times.

The memories swept through me, and the pain lessened until it was an inferno that was slowly being extinguished; the embers glowed, but the fire was no more.

Jade was losing. She was as powerful as a human being could be, but she was no match for the bond that connected Gabriel and I.

Once I was able to crawl down from the balcony, my tempo increased tenfold, and I sprinted across the room to confront her.

I wanted to rip her limb from limb, but Walker and Sebastien held me back.

Julian grabbed her by her throat and held her high against my wall.

"I'm going to give you a head start Jade. Get out of my house. Now. I *will* hunt you down, and I will take every pleasure in snapping your tiny little neck."

He released his grip, and he inched her by the throat back down to the floor. Her eyes were wild, and she looked like a caged animal. She screeched and grabbed her neck as she ran from the house. I followed to see her flee down the stairs, and I watched from the foyer as she fell on the cobblestone driveway and left Eden on foot.

I fell to the floor and wept bitterly when she was out of sight. Ava hunched to comfort me, but the stress of a near death experience was too much for me. It was the second time I had almost died in a matter of a month, and I had myself a good, long, relieved cry before I could speak.

"How did you know what was happening?" I finally asked (through my sniffles) anyone who would answer.

"Gabriel c-called me when he heard the commotion. He said he knew something was wr-wrong. Y-you could have easily been killed." Ava was frenzied. Her eyes darted from me to Julian. Sheer terror lurked in her gaze.

"Not if Gabriel was here. I was so stupid." Julian rubbed his forehead. "I really did think she'd be safe with us. I thought I could protect her, regardless of what she shares with Gabriel."

"You saved me," I reminded Julian. My attempts at comfort were wasted on him. I knew he'd blame himself for everything, just as he'd always done.

"I have to go after her, and I will. But I'm going to wait until Gabriel is here to protect you." He took my face in his hands. "If staying near Gabriel means you living in Ellaville permanently, then so be it. I'll build you a castle there that dwarfs the size of Eden, but you have to promise me you won't ever be far from Gabriel again. I can't offer you the protection he gives you. I thought I was strong enough, but I'm not."

"You can't leave," I burst out.

Julian smiled and went upstairs. It had been a long night, but I didn't grasp just how long until I saw the sunrise creeping through the window. In the entire time I was at Eden, I never once got up early enough to watch the sun come up over the ocean. The only time I had seen it was in my dreams, with

Julian.

Ethan must have known what I was thinking, because he put his hand in the small of my back and led me to the water's edge. We sat together and watched the sun rise until it broke free of the horizon. It was freezing cold outside, and we shivered walking back to the mansion. The house was dead quiet inside, and Ethan kissed my cheek and went to bed himself.

"Let me know if you need anything," he said before he left me.

"I will," I assured him.

I went into my closet to grab something warm to wear, and when I went to leave the room, Julian was standing watch at my door. When I opened the heavy wooden door, I hit him with it in his forehead.

"It serves you right, you know. I don't need or want a bodyguard. I'll be fine." I stepped past him and went to the kitchen to make myself a mug of chamomile tea.

When I came back upstairs he was sleeping soundly in my bed and I nudged him.

"If you don't need a bodyguard, how about a bedmate?" he suggested. "I can't leave you alone, but I can't sleep on the floor, either." He barely finished the sentence before he was asleep again.

I ran my fingers through his dark brown locks, much the same way I did Gabriel's so many times before. Gabriel looked like an angel when he slept, but Julian looked like a tormented prince. It still hurt me to look at him sometimes. It was unfair for him to look the way he did. An Adonis at the least, I wished I shared an ounce of his magnificence. I curled into him, but only long enough to make sure he wouldn't wake.

I sat in the den and tried not to dwell on all the possible havoc Jade was wreaking on the general public. I couldn't help but to watch several news networks, looking for any signs that hinted toward Jade wrecking through some town or another proclaiming the secret our mythical home held.

I heard a roar of an engine in the driveway, and I froze. My heart seemed to stop beating. I was paralyzed for a few moments before I could move. A soft knock at the door made my heart beat faster. I didn't know what I was afraid of. Jade wouldn't have knocked, she would have torn the door down.

I cautiously stepped toward the door. Everyone else was surely still sleeping. Someone yanked on the door handle.

"Who's there?" I asked cautiously.

"Come on Arianna, it's me," an impatient voice prompted.

PURGATORY

I threw the door open at the sound of Gabriel's voice.

He spun me around. "Happy birthday, baby." He handed me a box. "Are you okay? I still can't get over the whole thing. Ava called to tell me what happened, and I came as fast as I could. Where is she?" he asked, referring to Jade.

"She's gone," I told him, and relayed the events of the night.

It was a long time before everyone was up and about. We sat in the den and speculated on what Jade's next move would be. One by one, everyone came down, and we all talked the ordeal to death. We were shocked she had taken it so far that she would try to kill me.

Julian came down after everyone else, and he was fully clothed in a pair of chalk white pants and a pale blue shirt that matched his eyes.

"I'm leaving," he announced.

We were all silent. Julian had not ventured more than a few hundred feet from the house in over a hundred years. Eden *was* his curse. He was imprisoned by the water that had allowed him to live so long. He wore his vial about his neck, and my heart broke at the sight of him. His vial was his albatross, and he wore it in the same manner as the mariner.

He walked over to me from where I lounged alone on a chaise lounge.

"I love you. I will never love anyone as much as I love you, but I have to go. I won't sleep until I am sure Jade will never bother you or any of the rest of us again. Your heart belongs to someone else, and you shouldn't ignore it.

You and Gabriel are the same person. You're connected to him in a way I can't be. I will come back one day, but until then, happy birthday. You have saved me in so many ways. Memento Mori."

He leaned me back and kissed me deeply. Gabriel leapt up and crossed the room in a matter of seconds. His fists were clenched by his sides, ready to throttle Julian.

"Calm down, Gabriel." He tossed something shiny into the air, and it landed in Gabriel's hands. "Go have yourself a drink."

Gabriel opened his hand to reveal the keys to the Fountain. It was Julian's last farewell. He left us, his curse, his fate, and walked out the door.

"No!" I cried, but I knew it was what needed to happen. Julian was finally free.

I pressed my nose to the window beside the main entrance.

"Does he even have a car?" I wondered aloud. *If he doesn't have a way to leave, he has to stay.* My thoughts were irrational to say the least.

"Not exactly," Ava replied.

A jet-black BMW motorcycle raced out of the driveway. I stared numbly until it was out of sight.

"Like you said, he's big on exits," Ethan laughed.

DECIDING

I spent my birthday with everyone from Eden, minus Jade and Julian. The event was a somber one. I shied away from any mention of it for the rest of the day. I cancelled all the events Julian had planned for me. It wasn't the same without him to enjoy all the hard work he put into making my day special.

I was sure he would come to his senses and return immediately, but I was wrong.

I missed him every day he was gone.

It wasn't long before Julian began to send postcards and packages from the places he went every few days. They were all addressed to me, but I always shared news from him with everyone in the house. I prayed he would be home by Thanksgiving, but he was absent from all of the festivities.

Barcelona, Paris, London, Madrid- his travels began in Europe and then moved into the Far East and back again. Each card came with a gift, but the gifts were worthless to me without Julian.

Gabriel and I traveled home to Ellaville for Christmas, but we brought Savannah and Sebastien with us. Ethan and Walker decided that family gatherings with grandmothers and uncles were not exactly their thing, but it was for the best, we couldn't leave the Fountain unattended anyway. Savannah cried her eyes out, and told us she had never had a Christmas dinner with a real family (besides her Eden family) in her life.

I learned a lot about her over the holidays. I was floored when she told us that she was completely blind before she drank the water. She was given up by her birth parents because of her disability, and spent most of her life with abusive foster families. She met Sebastien when she began attending a blind academy, and she was making her way across the street when she fell. Sebastien stopped to help her, and fell completely in love with her when he looked into her unseeing eyes.

His face was the first thing she ever saw. She said that she had no idea what beautiful was supposed to be, until she opened her eyes to him. Millie cried like a baby over pumpkin pie when she told us the story. It was the most romantic thing any of us had ever heard.

The day before we left, Uncle Doug gave me the best present I had ever gotten. He was on his way home from work, and he stopped by one of his friend's houses to drop off some firewood. The man's dog just had puppies, and he brought the runt home to me. It was a sickly little thing with dirty white fur. Doug told me the dog would be small, so I named him Viking. I figured a good strong name might make him a good strong dog, even if he was itty bitty. It was love at first sight.

We returned to Florida, and rang in the new year Eden style with a bash at Screwdriver. During the cold months, I longed to get away. Viking was the only bright spot, he was the most well-treated member of the family. Even Ava spoiled him to death despite the fact that Doug gave him to me. She bought him a designer collar, of course, and every chew toy known to man. He quickly became healthy, and I once caught Sebastien and Walker letting him lap up Fountain water out of a bowl.

One day, Ethan told Gabriel and I that he had reserved a special delivery to one of the original Keepers just for us. We went to Las Vegas, and met the handsome playboy known as Silas.

He showed us a great time. We played the slots, and I never won a dime. I loved the shows, but Gabriel was more interested in the buffets the hotels offered. Silas was so down to earth, and when we left we made him promise to come visit Eden soon.

I was glad to be home, and I felt refreshed, with a newer, more positive outlook.

Ethan and Gabriel became inseparable. They stayed up all hours of the night talking. I was happy to see their exchanges. I was the only friend of Gabriel's closer to him than Ethan.

As the days became warmer, Julian's absence was missed even more.

A package came early spring, and I tore into it, ignoring the diamond pendant he had bought for me in Europe. I tossed it to the side devouring any news from him. Viking sniffed the pendant cautiously. I pulled the envelope from the paper wrapping, and scanned his note for information.

My Dearest Arianna,

I hope this letter finds you safe and happy. I caught up with Jade outside Paris, and I can assure you, she will not bother us again. I have met up with some old friends in Germany, and I am taking an extended tour of Europe. You are in my every thought, and I will see you very soon. Emily sends her regards, as does Edgar. I love you more with every passing day. Memento Mori, my love.

Eternally yours,

Julian

I felt a newfound lightness to my step when I read his words. *I will see you very soon.*

At the window, waiting, is where I found myself too many times. I found happiness in Gabriel and all of the Keepers. Something felt like it was missing, and it was. The key component was gone. I felt as if I were in purgatory. Not heaven, and definitely not hell, just floating somewhere in between.

Gabriel and I shared my room, although the relationship remained purely platonic, as it had back home. Gabriel helped take over all of Julian's affairs. He said he felt like he owed it to him. He bought all the plane tickets and organized almost everything for the deliveries, and kept the Keepers organized. Sebastien helped by coordinating staff times with Henry over the phone.

Gabriel enrolled in the college Walker attended, and I was stunned by how well he juggled all of the responsibilities he took upon himself. He did a great job, and everything was always taken care of. Even though he completely submerged himself in Julian's lifestyle, he still refused to drink from the Fountain. He said as long as he knew he wouldn't be taken away from me, he had no reason to prolong his life. A sense of normalcy crept through all of us, but even so, Julian was missed.

As much as I loved Julian, I loved Gabriel. I was stuck, utterly and completely. I analyzed my situation from all angles, but I never could quite make up my mind. There was no guarantee they'd still be waiting on me, but it was a chance I took. For all I knew, Julian could have a different lover in every country, and I still tried to convince Gabriel to take out a girl from school. In my wildest dreams, though, I would live happily ever after with my true love, and it had to be one of them right? If I ever made a decision, and the one of them still wanted me, it would be final.

Late one night, I walked out to my balcony with Gabriel sleeping just a few feet away. Viking was snuggled up next to him, and I smiled at the pair. Gabriel had been so busy taking care of everything, he had barely slept. I was grateful to see him sleeping so peacefully, but at the same time I envied him. Every time I closed my eyes lately, I envisioned in my dreams a set of scales, in which Julian and Gabriel's lives hung in the balance, and I could only save one.

I was tired and overwhelmed. The amount of work I put into helping Gabriel lately was astronomical. I always felt the need to please everyone. I worshiped my family, and I worked so hard to make them all happy all the time.

I felt as though I rarely stopped to breathe, so I took the opportunity to take a deep breath of the night air. Stars shimmered overhead, and I had one of those dumbfounded moments when I stopped to take in how small I was in comparison to the vast, endless universe. The wind whipped around me, and everything hit me at once. I hadn't slept more than a few hours at a time in months, and I paced the balcony in the wee hours more often than not.

The harder I tried to empty my mind, there was one face that haunted my every thought. I felt as if the earth was spinning out of control for a moment before it all became clear. There was no contest. There never had been. As much as I loved one, I was completely in love with the other. Gabriel and Julian alike left their indelible mark on my heart, but one penetrated me through to my soul. Yes, there was one I couldn't let go of. One who was a part of me more than anything.

I wanted more than anything to be finally free of the question that everyone, including myself, wanted the answer to.

The dark angel or the archangel? I smiled to myself. I knew exactly what I wanted, and I knew exactly what I was going to have to do to get it.

www.ingramcontent.com/pod-product-compliance
Lightning Source LLC
Chambersburg PA
CBHW020333180626
46812CB00001B/185